M000281123

the fable of wren

by
Rue Sparks

RS

Content Warnings:

Chronic Illness
Death
Grief & Loss
PTSD & Anxiety Attacks
Terminal Illness

The shattered glass crunches under my stumbling footsteps.
I reach out trembling fingers to steady myself
on ash-covered walls, paint flaking under my fingertips.

In my mind's eye the room is a pristine, disfigured paradise,
built without blueprints and crooked in places,
a patchy perfection that spoke of love and determination.

Before me now, the eye of the hurricane,
the moment when everything broken hangs in denial,
frozen cries of disbelief hover in my throat, not yet thawed
enough to form.

Tomorrow, I will wonder, 'how will I survive the wreckage,'
and the world will be turned on its side
along with everything in it.

For now, my heart cracks in the very first moment
when the home we'd built for ourselves
became for 'me' instead of 'us.'

**For my wife,
and everyone who ever had to wonder
if tomorrow was worth living without 'them'.**

PROLOGUE

I RUN, ADRENALINE THICK like mud in my veins. My heart beats in my brain, a loud thump to accompany the pounding of my feet on the forest floor. I try not to think of what I've left behind in the woods and what might be happening. If I do, I won't be able to run anymore.

I'm close now. I can see the brick of buildings and concrete through the edge of the trees. The thought should give me a burst of strength, but the adrenaline drains from me like flour through a sieve.

No. I have to keep going. I push my exhausted limbs further, further, just a little further.

I come through the edge of the trees so suddenly that the change from leaf litter to grass trips me. My knees hit the edge of the grass, and the heels of my hands slap down hard onto cracked pavement. It stings and knocks the breath from me, but I don't have time for pain. I allow myself three breaths— one, two, three—then with a choked sob, I push myself up on shaky legs and run along the pavement, through the parking lot of Jay's Diner, towards the entryway.

I throw open the glass doors, and I am screaming for help before I can form a coherent thought. The shocked faces around me are a blur, the blood pounds in my ears, and I try to speak the words to get them to *move.*

"Wren." The words, soft and cajoling, like speaking to a child, grate on my nerves, but I clutch onto them like a lifeline. "What happened? What's wrong?" Hands carefully touch my arms and lead me forward, deeper into the cooled air of the building.

I choke out a sob, but that's wrong. There's still time. "In the woods," I say instead. "Please, help!"

The rest of the story overflows like a waterfall. The reaction is immediate, and the next few minutes become a blur of "Get the sheriff," "You'll be okay, Wren, don't worry," and "Please sit down, you're bleedin'." I'm led to a stool where someone puts a damp, cool towel around my neck to try to soothe my overheated body. I'm shaking as I clutch weakly at a glass of water.

I want to pass out, to let my bones relax into a chair and let my whole body recover down to its atoms. What I need is to know he's okay.

I give up on the water, set that and the towel on the counter, and pace like a wild animal. I watch for the sheriff and debate running back to find him myself. Hot tears streak silently through dirt down my cheeks that I can see in the glass doors. I ignore the alternately concerned or rubbernecking stares of the diner patrons as we wait, ashamed of them seeing my weakness but too tired to put up a front.

When the sheriff comes what feels like hours later, with the ambulance and a search and rescue crew, I think that they'll find him and he'll be alright. I breathe.

For just a moment, I think it's all going to be okay.

ONE

EAST OF THE MISSISSIPPI RIVER and south of the Mason-Dixon Line, the sleepy little town of Spastoke is one you'd be hard-pressed to find on a map. Half our roads are dirt or gravel, and we don't have the World's Largest anything to boast about. Our cell phone service doesn't make it a hundred feet past the roadways, let alone into the woods, and on the hottest days, the whole town's electricity goes out if we're not careful. People don't come to visit or to put down roots. People just don't come.

And yet, it's the only home I've ever known. The only one I probably will ever know.

But now, home is just a word. Will that ever change?

I scratch at the dark blue striped tie around my throat

and let out a muffled yell as I nearly strangle myself trying to loosen it. It's a choking weight, and I can't take the feel of it anymore. "If one more person tells me they're sorry for my loss, I'm gonna fly off the handle!"

Mrs. Delaney touches my arm, and I stop pulling at the tie so she can remove it. She tugs the silk knot apart with shaking but sure hands, a focused expression on her face. When she's done, she lays the tie in my hands. I throw it onto the gray-veined granite counter. My eyes feel like fire as I try to keep tears at bay.

"Now don't you cut a shine; you know they mean well, child," Mrs. Delaney says. "Just like when my Avery died. They don't know what else to say." She sighs and tangles her fingers into the gold charm bracelet on her wrist—a gift from her late husband. Her dark-brown face is grim, her mouth tight in disapproval, but she says, "Jeremy would understand." And I know she understands too.

We're in the restroom of the only funeral home in our little town. The room is clean and modern, with crisp white paint and a box of tissues in a light blue ceramic cover. In front of it is a small sign with a quote in a thin font: "Those we love don't go away, they walk beside us every day." I scoff at the senti-ment, and the bitterness leaves my throat raw.

Friends of my Uncle Jeremy, locals, a few distant family members—the few who still spoke to us enough to have heard the news of his death—all came to be supportive, as Mrs. Delaney said. All of them have invaded what should have been a private event for those of us who still gave a damn while he was alive. None of them will stay past dawn, and we all know it. I am an orphan at eighteen, and there is no uncle to save me this time.

Uncle Jeremy would call me ungrateful and tell me to give it a rest. I can practically hear the echo of his reprimand, but that sets off the waterworks, which only makes me angrier. The emotional whiplash is more than I can bear. I scrape at my face and rub my eyes until they feel red and blotchy. Mrs. Delaney moves her arms around me and pulls me against her shoulder.

I have held the tears at bay through the trek home from the hospital to the funeral arrangements. Days spent in a rush, holding the pain until this moment when it leaks out of me like a dam torn through. I cry like I haven't cried since I was young enough that Uncle Jeremy had to tell me bedtime stories to keep me in my bed all night, and that thought makes me cry too.

It feels like I spend hours letting out muffled wails into Mrs. Delaney's shoulder until a stray who didn't see us go into the restroom opens the door before they apologize and retreat. And then, the moment is gone. I lean away from Mrs. Delaney. I search the room for the tissue container, my sight blurry. She gives me a wan smile, exposing some of her missing teeth, but it's wide and as beautiful as poetry. She pulls tissue out of her purse and hands them to me without a word. I know I love Mrs. Delaney then. She never asks anything of me that I'm not willing to give.

"I'm glad you're here," I say finally. It doesn't feel like

enough. "You're the only one I even want here with me. Half these people never saw him anyhow. Not before."

She nods and pats my arm a few times. The quiver in her hand signals the beginning of one of her shaking fits. I want to take my words back, afraid she might stay until she knows I'm okay and put her own health in danger.

"I can handle this," I say. I know it's said and done—she won't be leaving me here alone—but I still give a token protest. "You're not feeling too well. None of them mean nuthin' to me. And Uncle Jeremy'd think this whole thing was a farce anyway."

She shakes her head as I knew she would and puts her hand onto my back. She starts leading me to the door.

"No chance in hell. You didn't give me a moment's rest when my Avery passed, and I'm grateful for it. I ain't gonna be given you none either." I open the door to the hall, ignoring any protests, and wave her through. With a deep breath, I follow, uncertain if I'm ready despite my words.

The room is half full of supposed mourners, all decked out in their Sunday best. Black and navy suits, some ties loose, others missing. Women in knee-length dresses and skirts, dark and dreary against flowers dotted along the sides of the room. The lilies were Mrs. Delaney's idea. Uncle Jeremy only knew enough about flowers to know which native ones were poisonous.

I search the crowd for any familiar faces and catch sight of Sean, Sheriff June, and Mr. Turney in the scattered groups under the low ceiling and fluorescent lights. Their faces are grim, their eyes like caged animals, and their mouths set in lines. There's a group congregating around the visitor's log, and I wonder who they could possibly be, if they even knew Uncle Jeremy as more than passing acquaintances.

It's like every little detail of the world gives me more reason to mourn.

I take Mrs. Delaney by the arm as gently as I can manage and lead her toward the middle of the room. There are several rows of folding chairs, brown metal with paisley patterned seats. "Please at least sit for now, yeah? It'll make me feel better if you let your legs rest a bit."

She nods, visibly grateful for the breather. She sits down slowly, and I give her a tight smile. It is all I can manage, but it will have to be enough. I squeeze her hand, and she squeezes back before I straighten and scan the crowd again.

I avoid the gazes of the mourners. I don't want to tackle that beast quite yet. At the front of the room, Uncle Jeremy lies in his casket. My heart stutters at the sight, him on display like a museum piece under bright spotlights, surrounded by flowers and some of his larger wood carvings. I haven't yet built up the courage to see him, but time is running out. It's now or never.

I push through the crowd, nodding to acknowledge more "I'm sorry for your loss" comments, biting my tongue. Each platitude is like a notch in my bones, and I wonder when they'll crack.

I exit the small crowd of mourners abruptly, and the air is knocked from my lungs at the suddenness of the sight of my uncle, dressed in his Sunday best, still as a wax statue in the glistening casket. I avoid looking at his face and let my eyes steer towards the wooden casket itself.

It's a beautiful, umber-stained oak, with finely detailed layers of molding along the top and hammered steel hardware along the arm and tip of the bar. On the foot of the casket, a carving of a finch is set into the top. The Trickster himself.

"Do you think he'd like it?" The voice comes from my right, and though it catches me off guard, I find my body too numb to startle.

It's Turney, my uncle's mentor, and best friend. He's older than Uncle Jeremy, in his seventies, soft-spoken and quaint. Since my uncle died, he's taken it on himself to make sure I have meals, company if I want it. He texts me terrible dad jokes and awkward emoji strings. There was one day where he sat at my kitchen table whittling while I lay on the couch staring at the ceiling.

But seeing him now, eyes sunken in dark circles in contrast to his moon-pale pallor and blotchy complexion, white hair looking thinner and more out of place than normal, I feel a camaraderie with him I've never felt before.

"I carved it myself," he says, gesturing with a nod towards the bird carved at the end. "Arthur did the rest, but I thought it'd be appropriate. Well, it wouldn't be right if anyone but a Citizen carved it, would it?"

He lets the question hang, and I'm suddenly hit that he's looking for my approval.

"Of course." I try for a smile. "Citizens need to look out for each other."

"We will, you know." His voice is surer now, and he takes out a handkerchief and dabs at his eyes. "Take care of you. You're one of us, Wren—a Citizen. Family. One of the best. He trained you well. I knew when Jeremy took you in, you'd go far; we could all see it. You've done him proud."

The words seem to send him deeper into his sorrow; he becomes quiet and looks towards my uncle's face. I glance, then look away quickly. He wouldn't want me to see him that way. He'd want me to remember him how he was.

Instead, I look to the left at a set of tables that showcase Uncle Jeremy's carvings, including a few of his larger ones. He was a master carver, working with anything from a small knife to a chainsaw. My fingers hover over a swallow mid-flight. I remember when he'd carved it, sitting at the kitchen table as we talked about our day.

"Have you thought about your future, Wren?" Turney asks, gently placing a hand on my arm. "The future of the shop?"

I draw my hand back immediately, from the bird and Turney. I wrap my arms around myself as I feel a shiver run up my back. "I haven't."

"How is your carving coming? Are you-"

"I haven't," I say. "Carved anythin'. Not since…"

And with that, it's like I'm in the room in the hospital, surrounded by the smell of antiseptic and the un-realness behind my eyes closing in.

"I have to go," I whisper, cognizant of the light-headed

feeling that is filling my skull like a well. "I...I need air."

I turn around and walk toward the back of the room where the preacher is organizing his things, shaking hands with the funeral director. My mind is far away. My feet are moving, but I don't feel the ground beneath them. Each step is a trial of faith that the ground will catch me.

I brush past people, arms, shoulders, and hands, but I don't feel them. I'm swimming through debris in a flood, the air like water pushing through my fingers and pulling them apart. When did my body become so numb? Words are being said, and I nod at them, not registering any of them. They're honeyed, but I can still taste the bitterness. I have to get to the door, so what does it matter what they say?

The room begins to sway—or is that my body?—the air thin, sparse. My lungs won't fill with oxygen; there's not enough in the room for one person let alone a whole crowd.

A whole crowd of people, here for Uncle Jeremy.

Only they're not here for Jeremy.

Mrs. Delaney says they're here for me.

I can't breathe...

Then, I'm falling.

TWO

THE ROOM IS FAMILIAR, though it looks different now. My childhood bedroom—posters of Pokémon and Hot Wheels taped onto the walls, action figures and Barbies piled into a toy box too full to shut.

Uncle Jeremy sits on the plush chair next to the bed. He's the same as I last saw him. His hair is close-cropped, salt and pepper. His skin is the angry red of a new sunburn, and he's as unshaven as the day he died. He joked he'd need the 'extra protection' for the frigid air the cold spell had brought us. He's in his camouflage, shades of tan and brown tucked over a white t-shirt. His boots are muddied, covered in flecks of grass and bits of leaves. The debris crumbles onto the floor when he moves, but I say nothing about the carpet.

He's not really here. I know in my heart that he's gone, that he's dead. Whatever he is now—a memory, a ghost, I don't know—this moment is too fragile to question it. There will be no talk of regrets, of what could have been. They would spoil the gift I'm being given.

Even though Uncle Jeremy looks like he did the morning of the day he died, I am not the person I was that day. My arms are the same light beige with the spattering of freckles, but I'm young, early elementary school age, my feet barely halfway down the bed. In my mind's eye, I remember a school photo of a younger me: pale, barely-there eyebrows over straw covered hair in wisps, cut short and falling at awkward angles over my chocolate brown eyes. Some things haven't changed.

I'm under the covers, leaning back against a pile of pillows. I look at the ceiling with the glow-in-the-dark plastic stars that we took down years ago. I'd declared them too childish but didn't throw them away. Instead, I tucked them in a box of memories.

Out of the corner of my eye, I see Uncle Jeremy move. He's beaming, the corners of his eyes creased, wrinkles on either side of his mouth.

"Uncle Jeremy?" My voice is small, full of wonder and fear.

"Let me tell you a story, Wren." The familiar timbre is like a balm. There's a choking sensation in my throat, pinpricks at my eyes. "You're not so old you can't have a bedtime story. This is more than a fairy tale; this is truth. The truth about the world around ya, the world you'll inherit when I'm gone.

It's a cruel world, Wren, but there are lights if you look hard enough."

He opens a book, one I hadn't realized he'd been holding. It's the size of a children's picture book, but when I lean over to peek, he pulls it towards him with a wink and a smile.

"Now, now. Don't spoil the surprise," he says, and I settle back to let him continue.

"No fair," I say. The whine in my voice is forced, but I know he'd expect a token protest. His smile in return is sympathetic, like he understands this is a farce and what we both want to do is hold each other close for the time we have left. But we can sense it; in this dream, there are roles we are to play.

"Come on now, Wren. I'll show you when you're ready. Now, let's start at the beginning." He clears his throat and taps the first page. "Not so long ago, there was a Little Bird, like you. They were a wildfire—passionate, energetic, brash, and brave, especially for one so small. And just like you, they weren't a boy or a girl; they were both and neither. Even before they had words to say so, they knew. They lived in a small yellow house on the edge of town with their parents. The three of 'em were happy together."

He turns the page and leans back in the cushions of the chair. His voice rises and falls in pitch, in volume. He had been a fantastic storyteller, and I feel a pinch in my throat.

"But one day, their parents didn't come home. Somethin' bad happened, and they went to Heaven, leaving Little Bird alone. They were sad, because they loved their parents, and they were angry because what happened wasn't fair."

I cover my mouth with my hand, not wanting to give away my hiccupped sob. Why would he bring this up?

"Little Bird was taken to their uncle, where they would live from then on. At first, Little Bird didn't like their uncle. They got angry all the time, isolated themselves from everyone, and got in fights at school. Little Bird's uncle wasn't sure what to do, but then he had an idea."

He leans forward, chest covering the pages of the book, holding his hand up to his mouth, whispering as if it's a secret meant for only me. "You see, Uncle had a special talent, one that set him apart from the rest. One that he shared with few other people in their small town. He was a Citizen."

I inhale slowly, remembering when I was first told about the Citizens, the wonder I felt that I could become something, be part of something. Unbidden, an impish grin wavers onto my face at the same time my eyes water. A soft, sutured happiness blossoming in my chest.

"What's a Citizen, you ask?" His voice gets louder, filling the room with his gentle tenor. It thrums like magic, and I'm basking in it. "Only the most loyal, the most brave, the smartest in Spastoke can be Citizens. And to be one, ya have to do one thing: find the Trickster."

He leans back now, propping the book back up in his lap, a mischievous smile wide on his face. As he speaks, he turns the page, gesticulating as if he is telling an epic tale.

"The Trickster is more than a bird. They're like a ghost, a spirit, a gift of the gods. They don't disappear through the trees; they are the trees."

Eyes closed, I mouth the words I know practically by heart. Their imprint on my soul is a brand.

"Only Citizens have seen the yellow spots flickering down its back, like gold spilled onto it when some blacksmith was making a king's crown. Ain't no one gonna pretend they seen one when they haven't either. The first time someone sees those stars down its back, it changes them. We see it in each other's eyes."

I open my eyes to see him, Uncle Jeremy, through the sight of a child again, so small and young, looking up at him literally and emotionally. I want to linger in this moment.

"Uncle knew that Little Bird was destined to become a Citizen. So one day, he brought Little Bird to the woods. They searched and searched, and finally, Uncle told Little Bird the secret to findin' the Trickster: don't look down."

"Don't look down," I echo, the phrase a mantra I'd uttered with soggy boots, on cold spring mornings and sweaty summer evenings, all the memories a miasma rolling into one pinprick of a feeling. When Uncle Jeremy said it, it meant something else: *love*.

"No Citizen would tell anyone outside their family the rule. Don't look down. And that's when Little Bird saw him: the Trickster. That was when Little Bird became a Citizen. That's when Little Bird and Uncle became family."

He closes the book, and I feel a panic rise in my throat. Our time is coming to a close.

"Little Bird, I know you're hurtin'. You've hurt before. Remember, there are wonders and terrors out there you can't

yet imagine, and people out there you don't yet know are
family."

He stands up, sets the closed book down on the chair
behind him, and places his hand on my shoulder. I lean into it,
not wanting this dream to end.

"Now you rest up, Wren. You get scared, you just say,
'Uncle Jeremy, I need a hug,' and I'll chase those beasties away."
His soft smile is as crooked as ever, and I want to burn it into
my memory. "I'll always be here when you wake up."

I know in my heart it's a lie.

THREE

MY PANIC ATTACK—hyperventilation leading to fainting, the doctor said—doesn't pass without repercussions. It's two weeks before Sheriff June allows me back at the records office. Time drags in an endless slog, each sunrise a disappointment and each sunset met with resignation. I spend my nights wishing on stars for things that can never come true.

The dream haunts me. I remember Uncle Jeremy's face when I close my eyes, his face so real I could reach out and touch it. I ache to see him again, but the dream is timid and flighty. I wonder that it felt so real, and whether the realism makes things better or worse. I want to talk to Turney, but the many texts I've sent him have gone unread, leaving me with a mix of worry and anger.

On my first day back at the office, my mouth is dry, and my eyes are caked in sleep crust. But I'm grateful to be out of the house. I normally spend the afternoons on weekdays and mornings on the weekend helping out Mrs. Delaney at the records office in the Spastoke Town Hall. Mrs. Delaney is spry for her age but with enough lifting, she gets worn out. I've been doing it since I did an internship my junior year of high school when I fell in love with it. I'm relieved to be back.

The work is hard after being gone so long. I'm not used to the physicality, but mostly, every piece of that room holds a memory. By the time the day is done, I'm emotionally drained.

I'm hanging around the front desk of the town hall, about to say my 'goodbyes' to the other staff and volunteers, when Sheriff June trudges through the glass doors. There's a dour look on her dark tan face, curled hair tousled out of her normal ponytail. I glance back at Sean sitting at the front desk, and he raises a single eyebrow—he'd noticed it too. The sheriff without her coffee in hand is rare and never a good sign.

I debate asking Sean where the sheriff has been, but the sight of her quietly closing her office door without sparing a glance at either of us seals that possibility. Whatever happened, it was bad.

I say a quick "See ya" to Sean as he starts pointedly focusing on some clearly already finished paperwork and I'm out the door.

The second the glass door hits the perfect angle, I am hit with a wave of heat and humidity. The town hall is one of the few places where A/C is a guarantee, but outside those walls, we're all at the mercy of the soupy air that turns to sludge in your lungs, thick enough to choke. It makes most people reconsider living here and pushes those with no choice but to stay to stick indoors where at least a fan and shade will shelter them from some of it.

When it gets real bad, Sean pulls out the bingo cards for the adults and they put a water sprinkler on the town hall's lawn for the kids. A flyer goes up on the bulletin board for everyone to keep their electricity to a minimum to conserve energy so we can keep the town hall as cool as possible and prevent any power outages. The entire town hunkers down in the center; we cook giant communal meals, and we wait out the heatwave.

I'm thinking about Mary, the line cook from the diner, and the vegetarian baked beans she makes especially for me, when I spy an Eastern Starling, clacking and rattling its beak between a stuttered warble, clearly trying to attract a mate and failing miserably. It brings a smile to my face—something that feels unnatural since the funeral.

I pull out my watching notebook and find a shaded spot under one of the few trees next to the town hall. It's spring, and though this isn't a prime birding spot, it seems like the birds have found me today. I immediately spot two titmice and a grackle and mark them down.

I'm trying to determine whether the grackle is a male or female and whether I should get my binoculars when I'm startled by a voice.

"Holy shit, how is it so hot?"

I turn my head toward the glass doors to the town hall, where I see someone with short, tightly-curled black hair and dark brown skin. He's wearing silver-rimmed aviator glasses and rolling up the sleeves of his t-shirt before he wipes the back of his hand over his brow.

I don't recognize him, which can only mean one thing. *Outsider. City Boy.*

"Ever heard of global warmin'?" I quip, closing my notebook and getting ready to leave. The outsider's arrival has immediately soured my mood, and all I want to do now is head home.

He flushes but doesn't take the hint. He holds out his hand towards me as if I care who he is.

"I'm Jethro! I just moved here. New intern, supposed to meet everyone today. Do you work here?"

I wrinkle my nose at my suspicions being confirmed. He's clearly far from home. He has a thick Midwestern accent. Maybe from Chicago?

"I'm Wren." I cross my arms, ignoring his hand, and he lowers it slowly. "Last I knew, I was the only intern. What department you here for?"

I'm about to see how much I can put the fear of God in him, but I'm distracted by the sound of compacting gravel. Our single ambulance is pulling into the drive. There are no sirens, and the lights aren't flashing, so I calm my beating heart. I see Ned through the window as he pulls by us, thick sunglasses low on his face. He turns the vehicle toward the entrance near the back of the sheriff's department.

The sight is odd enough that I gravitate towards it without

thinking. I know Ned and also know he's got a mouth connected directly to his ears. You couldn't keep gossip away from him to save his life. If anyone knows what it is with the sheriff, it'll be him.

"Sean's at the front desk, can't miss him," I call back to the City Boy, not looking at him as I walk away. "Catch you later."

There are telltale signs of footsteps behind me, and I inwardly curse, debating whether I can slip by the outsider and still get to Ned before he leaves. I head towards the vehicle, pace steady and body rigid, brokering no argument. Whatever is going on, I have to know.

The footfalls continue behind me, but I ignore them. Ahead, Ned leans back to tug on something in the ambulance. If I can catch him as he moves towards the building with whatever he is carrying I can get a few pieces of information from him while we walk.

I am ten yards away when I stop dead in my tracks. Ned is pulling a gurney out of the ambulance, and the wheels dislodge and hit the ground with a loud thunk before they squeak to a halt on the concrete.

The gurney isn't empty. On it, inside a vinyl body bag, is a human shape.

My breath hitches, and I feel my heart pound in my fingertips and up my arms. My feet are welded to the broken remains of the parking lot.

The morgue for the hospital is in the basement of a different building. The only reason to bring a body to the morgue in the sheriff's department is for open cases.

Movement in my periphery makes me turn toward Jethro, still stunned.

"Hey, you all right?" he asks. I shake my head, dazed.

At that moment, Ned notices us standing like a spotted deer in the parking lot. His face is grim and tinged green.

"Oh, Wren," he says softly, sputtering out the words. "Hey, I'm sorry about all this. I know he was your friend and all."

I shake my head at him, still in a daze, but my heart drops in my chest. "What you mean, Ned? Who you talkin' about?"

He bites his lip and wipes his arm at sweat on his forehead, avoiding my gaze. "Aw, shit. You don't... I'll catch you later, Wren. I gotta... well, I just gotta go." He walks backward and pulls the gurney slowly toward the doorway. The wheels continue their high-pitched screeching, interrupted by thuds from the little holes along the way. The sounds echo in my ears. A whining joins it, and I try to blink it away.

I become aware of Jethro gently touching my shoulder. My breath comes in quick, sharp intakes, and the world tilts. My vision swims as Ned pushes the button for the handicap entrance and disappears into the shadows of the building, the gurney behind him.

"I'm fine," I mumble vaguely. "Leave me alone."

Jethro grabs my arm, and I resist for a moment before I let him move me towards the edge of the pavement, where I slowly lower myself onto the curb. The colors and shapes around me swirl in a miasma, waves in my field of vision. My fingers grab the edges of my shorts, grasping the light fabric hard, and I scratch my hand through it with my fingernails.

I close my eyes, willing the strangeness and unreality to go away. To bring me back down into my body. I become aware of a voice talking in a calm monotone. I focus on it and let my breaths seep into a smooth, unfettered rhythm.

I force myself to let go of my shorts, run my fingers along the rough concrete, and focus on the feeling of the ridges along my fingertips. I breathe in deep as I open my eyes again and count the tree trunks along the parking lot to bring myself back to the present—just like my social worker told me to.

When I am nearly back into myself, I realize it is Jethro talking. He's sat right down in the dirt and dried grass next to me, sprawled back as he continues on with a story I didn't hear the beginning of.

"...and you know, she was right. Next thing we know, Jon's back on his feet, going to these meetups on being an entrepreneur and how to market yourself and all that. He's been working as a waiter at this restaurant in downtown Philly while he saves up, trying to get a food truck someday. He's doing alright. Says he's not looking to date right now, which is fair."

He pauses and locks eyes with me, his face in a crooked smile.

"You back with me?" he asks. "Seemed like you got a scare there."

I bristle. I'm angry at myself for showing weakness to an outsider. I'm angry at him for bearing witness to it. But I can't, won't tell him that.

"I'm fine," I say through clenched teeth. "Got caught off guard is all."

He frowns, and I bristle at the sympathy that's clear as day on his face. "I'm sorry. I got a cousin who gets that way. He tells me it helps to have someone talk to get him grounded back in reality, you know? Thought it might help." Jethro looks over his shoulder towards the door Ned disappeared through, curiosity plain on his face. He squints his eyes in a thin line behind the metal frames. "What was that about anyway?"

I stand up slowly, cautious of my unsteadiness. Once I'm well and rooted, I wipe down the back of my shorts and swipe away the loose gravel and grass. I'm sure my shorts are covered in dirt stains, but I have bigger fish to fry.

"Ned's the driver of our town's only ambulance," I say. "And this is the entrance to the sheriff's morgue. If he brought a body here, it means there's a criminal case."

Jethro's eyes widen, and he jumps to his feet. "You serious?" He stares at the ambulance as if someone else will come out of it. I consider trying to get in, but I'm not sure when Ned will come back, and it'd be tough explaining any snooping.

As much as the sight left me shaken, fingers tingling like ants trying to crawl out of my skin, I know I have to find out what's going on. If what Ned said is true, whoever was on that gurney is someone I know, someone I care about. I have to know.

Uncle Jeremy said that was my fatal flaw—curious as a cat, and always going around my ass to get to my elbow.

I walk toward the front door to the town hall. I don't bother to look back to see if City Boy is following. I can hear his skittish footfalls on my heels, clearly not a hunter or tracker with the racket he's making.

"Where you going?" he asks.

I pause before the entryway, thankful for the shade from the edge of the roof after being in the sun while having a panic attack. "I'm gonna see what's goin' on. Somethin's gone wrong, and I wanna know what."

Jethro scratches at his chin and looks at the door. "Will they tell you anything? Doesn't seem like our business."

I huff, cross my arms in front of my chest, and lean on one foot with my hips at a tilt. "Who says anythin' about 'our'? And I'm not leaving till I see what the fuss is about." I wipe at the sweat that has beaded at my brow, now cooling in the shade. "They may not want to share, but once I get sight of a bone, I ain't letting it go. I don't care if they want me to know or not."

Jethro shifts his weight from foot to foot and digs the toes of his sneakers into the sweltering concrete. He avoids my gaze and talks straight to the pavement. "I could help, you know. I'm curious too. You don't have to do it alone."

I drop my arms to my sides. "I'm always alone," I scoff. "I don't need anyone's help; I get by just fine. Don't follow me."

Conversation over, I pull the door open by the metal handle. The sudden onslaught of A/C cools my sweat near instantaneously. I shiver.

It will be a trick to get the information I need. I'm like a long-tailed cat in a roomful of rocking chairs. But something is wrong in my town.

I won't take no for an answer.

—

When Sean sees me walking towards his desk, he ducks his head and pretends to type when he's probably scrolling Facebook. The idea of him hiding behind the monitor is laughable. He towers over the computer screen, form lanky with a thick head of red hair. His face ashen-white and mottled in freckles, in stark contrast to my vague suntan from being outdoors. He can no better hide behind that computer than he could a sheet of paper.

I can't blame him. I've already said my goodbyes, so my reappearance means I needed or wanted something. Sean and I usually get along pretty well, but he also knows me and knows I tend to put my nose where it doesn't belong. He's called me "mini June" to get my goat, knowing that while Sheriff June and I are amicable, our mutual curiosity and controlling natures clash at the best of times.

So he's going to do anything he can to avoid my questions. But I won't let him. I figure the direct approach is as good a technique as any to start.

"Sean, what's going on with the gurney? And the sheriff— she looked like she seen a ghost."

Sean doesn't move his gaze from his computer, but I see him pause in his supposed typing before he gives up the pretense. He starts back on his scrolling, and I lean over the computer to see what's on his screen. I was wrong; he's on Twitter this time.

"Didn't know you're on Twitter." I try for nonchalance, a distraction.

Sean pulls the computer back so I can't see over it any-more. "Yes, I've started using Twitter. No, even if I knew what was goin' on, I can't tell ya. You wanna complain, you gotta talk to the sheriff."

"All right, all right, Mr. Cranky Pants," I say. He rolls his eyes but I can see from him biting his lip to hold back a smile that he doesn't take me seriously. *Simmer down, Wren, or you'll get nowhere.* His tone means no argument. I sigh and run my hands through my bangs in exasperation. My hands are tied, so I try to stall. "When's she coming back? Her door's closed."

He looks up at me this time, his nearly gray eyes suspicious and eyebrow raised as he tries to read me. "She's in there now, but she's busy. You wanna see her, you gotta wait. There." He points at one of the cheap plastic chairs outside Sheriff June's door. "You sit there, and you don't move until she's out. Or until you give up. Your choice."

"You're no fun," I huff, and push his shoulder playfully before leaving him be, thinking that at least waiting will give me time to come up with a plan. I sit down in the black chair with the ratty cloth seat, and it whines in protest.

I'm leaning my head back onto the gray walls of the office when I see Jethro come in through the town hall door. He looks around, moves this way and that, and looks closely to read posters and signs along the wall. *The hell he think he's doing?*

I ignore him and think about how I can possibly get the most tight-lipped citizen of Spastoke to spill the beans. The chances seem slim. If I show my hand too early, Sheriff June will simply close her door and not answer any questions. Sean might let details slip, but at this point, he's proclaimed he doesn't have any. I have no choice but to wait and keep my eyes open for an opportunity.

I see movement to my side and spot Jethro as he looks with curiosity at the old cannon we have situated in the middle of the entryway. The only such relic left in the town, it is bordered on all sides by a rope to keep visitors from touching it. Jethro is reading the plaque that explains its history in the Civil War.

It's at that point Pat comes down the hall. I hold my breath but try to not seem like I'm snooping so Sean won't catch on. Pat is our town's coroner and part-time detective. She's short and stocky, brown curly hair cropped short framing a round olive face. She's wearing a brown blazer over a starched white shirt. She is no-nonsense and straight to the point, a former Navy Hospital Corpsman who was elected in a landslide for the position. She has to have information on what's going on, but where Sean is hesitant, Pat will be downright aggressive about not passing on anything. She has a manila folder in her hand that she sets on Sean's desk.

Sean pauses scrolling, and his face pales as Pat nods at him, a stony expression. Whatever is going on, it ain't good.

"The sheriff in?" Pat nods towards her office door and ignores me.

"She's in but meeting with the mayor right now." Sean grabs the folder and moves it closer to himself. He eyes me warily, and I try to show no emotion. If the mayor is involved, this is big. If I strain my hearing, I can hear their muffled voices.

"Well, you get this to her as soon as possible. I'm gonna finish up, but this is my initial report. We gotta work fast if we're gonna get on his trail." She pats it with her hand twice before she looks toward Sheriff June's door. Her gaze pauses on me before she turns away.

Sean pulls the folder closer to himself, nearly over his computer. His face is pale, eyes downcast. "Yeah, I'll get it to her soon as she opens her door."

Pat nods, looks at me one last time with a face as blank as concrete, then turns back down the hallway.

I need to get my hands on that folder. It's got to be about the person on the gurney. I'm sure of it. But I have absolutely no idea how I can get a hold of it with Sean protecting it like a mother hen.

I'm debating my options when a few minutes later, I see my chance.

"Hello." The interjection catches me off guard. It's Jethro. He makes his way towards Sean, an expression of shyness and uncertainty on his face. "My name's Jethro. I just moved here, and I'm going to be interning at this office with Mrs. Delaney. I was wondering if you could help me with something."

Interning? With Mrs. Delaney? Oh, hell no. We haven't had an intern in the records office since I started, and I'll be damned if some outsider will ruin what we have going. I'm about to jump up and tell him so, but something makes me pause.

Sean turns off his monitor and sends Jethro a toothy smile. His entire posture changes, his shoulders back and chin tilted up in attention. Interesting.

"Oh, yes, I remember Mrs. Delaney mentioning you! Nice to see a new face 'round here. I'm Sean. What can I help you with?" His voice is honeyed, dripping with barely disguised interest.

"I wondered if you could show me around a bit? I don't want to get turned around, and I would love to help out in whatever capacity I can. Maybe you can introduce me to the other workers?"

Sean's face lights up like a firefly before it dims slightly as he glances down at the folder. *Come on, go for it.* This is my chance. *I guess city boys are good for something.*

Finally, Sean holds up one finger to Jethro. "Give me one second, and I'd love to! If ya hold tight, let me get things settled here, and I'll take ya 'round to meet everyone. I'm sure they'll love ya." His grin is sugary sweet, and I want to roll my eyes.

Jethro backs away and starts looking around, and Sean waves to me vigorously behind the monitor where Jethro can't see. I walk over, raising my eyebrow at him, but he gives me a desperate look behind a hand and points to the folder.

"Listen, Wren, this guy is cute. Do not mess this up for me. If the sheriff opens the door, give her this." He points to the folder. "If ya want to be here long term, we gotta be able to trust ya. This is a test. It's very important, okay? She needs it immediately. Door, open, folder. You can handle that, right?"

I shutter my expression, nodding carefully before retreating back to my seat, inwardly crowing at my luck.

Sean stands up and moves around the desk towards Jethro.

He leans entirely too close, smirk wide and eyes glowing.

"Thank you for waitin'. Ya know, it'll be great to have someone around here that's got a new perspective on everythin'. Everyone here is so determined to do things as they've always done it. I'm sure we'd all love the help."

He's laying it on entirely too thick, and I gag in my mind. But Sean waves his hand down the hall and leads Jethro towards the other offices and away from the desk with the folder on it.

Just as Jethro moves out of my view, he turns to me and winks once.

Well. City Boy's got guts.

When they're out of view, their footsteps echoing right before they open the door to Accounts, I leap to my feet. I have minutes, *seconds*, before either Sean or the sheriff appears again. I find the folder, held together by a paper clip.

I remove the paper clip, flip past a few pages of introduction and legalese before I get to the form that's titled "Autopsy Report." I search for a name.

The autopsy report identifies the victim, and I feel my gut drop.

It's Turney.

I reach a shaky hand behind me, grabbing for Sean's seat, and barely manage to sit before my feet give out. Something shatters in my lungs, and I pull in a sob before it leaves my mouth, covering it with my hand just in case. I can't let on that I know. I take in deep lungfuls of air, trying to remember what my social worker said. The tears threaten to fall almost immediately.

Turney was a Citizen, Uncle Jeremy's best friend, and he was becoming more to me—a mentor, a grandfather, whatever you could call it. And now he's gone, too.

I breathe through my mouth, eyes closed, trying to get my bearings enough to look through the report.

The initial few pages are all demographic information, so I breeze through until I get to a section detailing where his body was found.

Margaret found him while on a hike, and she alerted the sheriff immediately. I read through the details; his body had started to decompose in the heavy humidity we've had, so they are still running through the full autopsy. I try not to gag as I read the details, most of the terms unfamiliar, but words like "bloated" and "putrefaction" jump out and leave my stomach roiling. Poor Margaret.

I look up to check that the hallway is clear before reading on. The next section is an initial assessment of the body's condition—multiple ragged lacerations suggest an assault at the minimum.

My breath catches at the words. He was a sweet older man, no enemies to speak of. And he was a very methodical hiker, moving slowly and purposefully past every tree and fallen branch with a sense of respect and caution. He wouldn't make stupid mistakes, and he wouldn't be easy to sneak up on. But why would anyone want to hurt him?

By the time I set the folder back down, replace the paper clip, and lay it as close as I can to where Sean left it, I've made up my mind, even as I'm biting my lip near through to hold back tears.

I'm going to catch Turney's killer.
No one messes with my Citizens.
No one messes with my family.

FOUR

I SIT BACK DOWN OUTSIDE Sheriff June's office and wait for Jethro and Sean to get back. I avoid Jethro's gaze when they round the corner, not wanting to imply any connection between us to Sean lest he figure out what I'd done. I wait ten minutes after Jethro leaves before calling out that I'd check with Sheriff June tomorrow.

When I leave the cool air of the community center building behind, I'm surprised to see Jethro sitting out on the concrete curb around the corner from the glass doors. He has his shirt off, and I try not to snort and alert him to my presence. He clearly isn't used to the humidity, his shoulders, chest, and face wet with sweat, and as I watch, he wipes at his face with his shirt as he squints up at the sky.

I shouldn't be surprised, of course—he helped me back there, so he must think I owe him something. Outsiders were like that. The thought irritates me. I didn't ask for his help... though without it I may not have gotten the information I needed. My shoulders tense and I grind my teeth, jaw clenching reflexively, preparing myself for an argument.

When he sees me, he jumps to his feet and fumbles with his t-shirt while avoiding my gaze. He gets one arm in but struggles with the other one. He starts to say something that I don't catch with his shirt covering half his face.

I wait until he's well and fully dressed before I wrinkle my nose at him. "Ya look like you took a dip in the river. You keep downwind of me, all right?"

He pulls at his shirt, trying to keep it from sticking to his skin I suppose. His discomfort is clear, and I wonder about his lack of confidence. Sometimes the excitement is palpable in his face, his eyes open wide and smile infectious. Right now, he avoids my gaze, fingers twitching.

I sigh, knowing I'm partially to blame for that. I've been harsh.

I consider what to say for a moment and look toward the line of trees leading up to the road. The air is still thick as soup, and the late afternoon sun bakes the concrete and yellowed grass. It won't let up for hours yet, but it's still too late in the day to try to catch Turney's trail. That'll make ducking away from Jethro easier.

Best to bite the bullet and get on with it.

"Thanks for your help there. I wouldn't have gotten

anythin' if it weren't for you." It comes out terse to my ears, but I hope he misses it. He smiles, a slight upturn of the sides of his mouth, but it's something.

"No problem." His voice is softer, gentle even. "I'm glad I could help. Figured Sean didn't know me so well, probably didn't think we got along."

Get along is a bit of an overstatement, but I don't say that. I'm trying to be nice, after all.

"Did you find anything useful in the folder? I assume that's what you looked at."

I nod but wonder if it's wise to share what I learned. He's shown me he can be stealthy, and although he has a kind soul, I don't yet know how well he can keep a secret. But I can think of no other way to finish this conversation without sounding ungrateful, so I give in.

"I was right; there's been a murder. Mr. Turney. He's one of our older hikers."

I hear Jethro's breath catch, and his eyes widen. "Seriously? That's horrible! Why would anyone do that to an old man?"

I shake my head, wondering the same thing. "No idea. He was sweet, never did anyone any harm. He is..." I pause to catch my breath, holding back tears. "He was a friend. I don't know what the murderer was thinkin'."

He frowns and scratches at his arm where I can see a red, irritated bite. So he's been introduced to our friendly mosquito population. I would have laughed were we not discussing something so heavy. If my heart weren't cracked and threatening to shatter.

"I'm sorry for your loss, Wren," he says finally.

That phrase again. I stiffen, stuff my hands into my short pockets, and grit my teeth. I take a few deep breaths, trying to calm myself, but the words fall from my lips anyway.

"You're *sorry for my loss*?" I say through clenched teeth. "That's the best you got? Seriously? My friend was murdered, and the best ya got is you're sorry he's gone? No. Not good enough."

I rush forward, shouldering him aside as I pass, determined to go to my car and go home where I can get my pack ready for tomorrow's trek. I'm running through a list of supplies in my head and opening my car door when I hear quick footsteps rush up from behind me. When I turn, Jethro is at the hood of my car, a hurt look on his face.

"Hey, what did I do? I don't understand. I thought that's what you needed to hear. Tell me what's wrong."

I slam the car door shut and lean on one arm on the car, other hand on my hip. "What's wrong? What's wrong is my friend is dead, murdered, and someone's to blame. I don't care how sorry ya are, any of you. Not for Turney, not for Uncle Jeremy. You're not the ones coming home to an empty house, missing their voice, the way they knew the right things to say, or not to say, or, or—" I slam my hands against the top of the car. I lean forward and touch my forehead against the cool metal to cool my rage and heartbreak.

I try to catch my breath, short gasps coming quickly and turning into hiccups that choke the air from me. I focus on inhaling deeply, trying to get ahead of the panic attack. I feel his presence hovering nearby, and though I'm thankful that he doesn't come any closer, his being so close rankles me. And yet in some ways, him being so near means I have to force myself back into control. I won't be caught out in front of him again.

After a few minutes of breathing, I straighten and turn towards him, shoulders back and chin forward.

"I'm going to find Turney's killer."

Jethro's eyebrows raise high, his glasses falling down his nose. "You're what? That's crazy, Wren."

I let out a huff and fiddle with the keys in my pocket, refusing to show my nervousness. "I'm the best tracker we have. The sheriff may be good at her job, but she's still new here. Only been sheriff for a few years. She doesn't have the connections in the town and knowledge of these woods that I do. I don't know I can fully trust her. I knew Turney and the Citizens better than any of them. And I—"

I pause as my breath catches, but I won't show weakness. Not again.

"I won't just sit by again."

Jethro is shaking his head and crosses his arms, looking down at the pavement to avoid my gaze. "I can't let you go into danger like that."

"You don't have a say," I respond, grit in my tone. "Why do you care, anyway? You're not my friend." I open my car door, leaning in to sit down and get settled.

"Wren," he starts.

I want to ignore him, slam the door shut and not look back. The old Wren would have. But there's a voice echoing in my ears. *There are people out there you don't yet know are family.*

"We could be. Friends, that is," he calls out.

I shut the door and back out of the space. I pretend not to watch Jethro out of the corner of my eye in the windshield and then the rear-view mirror, voices echoing in my mind that I can't seem to block out.

—

When I make it into Town Hall the next day the mood is dour, but there's no announcement yet about Turney's murder. It's likely his family is being informed before they let anyone else know. I wave to Sean, but by the haunted look in his eyes and the unenthusiastic wave he sends back, he knows too.

Mrs. Delaney, however, is her normal chipper self, which is a relief. We spend the morning filing paperwork, then the afternoon doing whatever chores she sees fit. I'm moving giant, coffee-stained, musty books from the shelves to the counter for one reason or another—who knows with Mrs. Delaney—when Jethro peeks around the door.

Mrs. Delaney sees him first and calls out to him. "Ah, yes! Jethro was it? Come over, child. I need to move 'round more books." She waves him over, her wide smile and missing tooth making her seem all the more approachable.

I drop the books I'm holding hard on the desk. Jethro winces when dust kicks up, but he closes the door behind him and stands there awkwardly, timid as a fawn. He peers at me under shaggy eyebrows. His thin smile and slightly hunched

shoulders show he isn't sure what to make of me after yesterday; my unblinking glare probably has something to do with
that.

I jump when Mrs. Delaney whacks my shoulder, unim-
pressed by my posturing. "Now you stop that," she says in a
clipped tone, "You know I wouldn't let just anybody in here."
She rubs a small circle onto my abused shoulder. I try to stand
my ground, but her chuckle shows I've failed miserably.

Jethro looks overjoyed that Mrs. Delaney includes him
as 'not just anybody,' and he seems to come alive. A broad,
white-toothed smile replaces his skittish one. She opens up the
small hatch in the counter that divides the sitting area from the
shelves.

"Hi, Mrs. Delaney!" He squeezes quickly through the
opening, probably afraid I'll shut it on him. "I got a little
turned around in the halls, but I found it. I'm so excited you're
letting me help out like this. I need to do an internship for my
degree, and I figure even though it's not technically a library,
working with an older filing system and learning how to digitize records will help me-"

I had started to tune him out, but then my brain processes
his words. "You're not changin' any of these records," I bark
like a coyote defending her pups. "They been written by hand
since the town was built, and we don't need anyone coming
through and changing that."

I push my shoulders back, sticking out my chin like I'd
seen Uncle Jeremy do when he caught someone trespassing in
our woods while he didn't have his gun on him. He'd say that

how you hold yourself tells more than any weapon.

The memory stings, but I push it down.

Jethro doesn't seem to be intimidated, because he carries on over my protests. "But there's such great technology available now! We can scan the whole library, and there's software that will change it into plain text you can input into the computer. You can automate a search instead of doing it book by book. It saves space, supplies, and is more environmentally friendly."

I roll my eyes at him. I've heard the same argument before, from the mayor and even the sheriff. I've held my ground so far, and no new kid is going to make a dent in my resolve.

"Computers get hacked. Files get lost or corrupted. Electronic signatures get forged. It ain't worth the risk."

His mouth thins, his brow furrowing to the top of his glasses. He pulls his shoulders back, and his chin rises in rebellion. "Not if it's secured, and everything would be stored in a cloud. Things get forged on paper as easy as computers, but computer files don't burn or get water damage." He gestures at the long wall of shelves filled with files. "Besides, you wanna dig through all this for a single misplaced piece of paper, or would you rather do a file search that takes seconds?"

I grit my jaw and try not to grind my teeth. I am already tired and beaten down after yesterday, and now a fire I can't quell is burning in my chest, all because he doesn't know when to back away. But as the feelings war within me, exhaustion wins out.

He seems to sense my weakness and continues on his spiel.

"With computer files, you can send records instantaneously throughout departments, to different cities if needed. You can go back through ancestry and-"

Mrs. Delaney has been quiet until now, nodding vigorously as we spoke—as much as she can with her tremble from her Parkinson's—but now she touches Jethro lightly on the shoulder to cut him off.

"That's wonderful dear." She nods meaningfully and pauses before she moves on. "But for now, the mayor just wants us to start puttin' new records in the computers they bought us."

Jethro deflates a bit but nevertheless nods at her. "Right. Sorry, I got excited there. I get it. It's not my business to be making changes like that right away."

Mrs. Delaney pats his shoulder, and I can tell she's already become fond of him. "It's alright, child. Now, Wren, don't be rude. This young man is Wayland's grandson. You know him, lives at the end of Oak Ridge Drive? He asked me if I'd take his grandson on as an intern. Now, introduce yourself. Proper." She points to Jethro as if there's anyone else in the room.

I cross my arms, but out of respect for Mrs. Delaney, I do what she says, not wanting to let on that we've already met. "I'm Wren. My pronouns are they and them. Ya know what that means, being a city boy, right?"

He holds out his hand, catching on quick, but I frown when I realize I'll have to take his this time. "I'm Jethro. Nice to meet you, Wren."

I quickly grab his hand and give it an unnecessarily tight squeeze. He lets out a high-pitched squeak before I quickly let it go.

"Wren!" Mrs. Delaney exclaims, but Jethro laughs.

"It's okay. They have a stronger grip than I expected, that's all. Where's this computer you talked about, Mrs. Delaney?"

He moves along with Mrs. Delaney, still as eager as a puppy as she brings him over to the pale gray paperweight Mayor Jones purchased a while back. It has done nothing but gather dust up until now since Mrs. Delaney isn't tech-savvy and I don't approve of digitizing anything.

Jethro hesitates when he sees it—it's probably not up to his standards. He pulls back the squeaky office chair with the one bad wheel and gingerly takes a seat. He presses the power button on the tower, then the monitor. Mrs. Delaney crowds near him, and I can practically see the discomfort oozing from him. He's acting less like an eager puppy and more like a tired veteran gone to battle.

I shake my head, unwilling to get too involved. If the mayor wants new records digitized, there's nothing I can do about it, but I don't plan to make it any easier on him.

I decide to browse through some of the old town records while I wait for them and pick up a random dusty tome off the shelf. I wipe it down with my palm before I set it on the counter. The dates show it's nearly a century old, and I feel like I'm touching something sacred when I peel the cover back from the pages.

When I first started looking at the old records, it was

difficult to read the scrawling script. With practice, it has become easier but not easy. Even the words themselves seem foreign, strange turns of phrase and odd spellings.

And yet, when I read the records, I feel the warmth of home. This is our legacy, our history, the grandparents of my grandparents. They're where we come from, and I'll be damned if it's lost.

"Wren?"

I look up, searching the room for who called my name, and spot Sean peeking through the doorway. His ivory skin looks paler than normal against his spattered freckles, and my gut drops.

"The sheriff wants to see you," he says. We lock eyes, and I realize Sean knows that I know. No need to pretend to be confused as to why the sheriff would want to see me. I nod at him, and he closes the door with a barely audible click.

"Wren, what's all that about? You get into some sort of trouble?" Mrs. Delaney asks from where she's still working with Jethro on the computer. I close the tome I'd been looking through and shake my head.

"It's nuthin' to worry about, Mrs. Delaney. Can you put this away for me? I better not make Sheriff June wait."

She beams, and it's a comfort, the white of her albeit fewer teeth against her warm brown skin a contrast, and the sight is like a warm blanket. "Of course, child. It'll give me a chance to show Jethro our filing system. Go on now. Best be getting to her office."

I start to leave but pause and turn around, a plan forming

in my head. "Mrs. Delaney, I think I'll head home early after this. It's nuthin' bad, just think I need air."

Her brow creases in worry, and I can see shakes betraying her emotion, but there's no avoiding it. "Of course, hun. Are you sure there's nuthin' wrong?"

I grab for the door handle so my back is to her, knowing I can't lie to her face. "Nuthin', Mrs. Delaney. Have a good day. I'll see you tomorrow."

The deception tastes like ashes.

—

My knock on the sheriff's door is light, but the "come in" is near instantaneous.

Even though Sheriff June has been sheriff for the past three years, her office feels nearly as sparse as her first day when she introduced herself to me and the others. The only paraphernalia lining the walls are miscellaneous notices from Town Hall, a few photos in frames on her desk facing away from me, and a carved stone bear that must have come from her tribe.

Sheriff June herself looks exhausted where she sits, rubbing her hands across the cool umber skin of her wrinkled forehead. Her black hair has wisps coming out of the low ponytail, and her olive brown sheriff's hat sits on the table next to her. On her desk is a paper clipped folder, looking worse for the wear from repeated readings.

She looks up to me, her hand hooding her eyes, and I see the purple circles beneath them and the haunted look before she schools her features.

"Wren," she says, and waves a hand at the chair across from her. "Take a seat."

I dutifully sit down, too tired and struck by the sight of the exhausted sheriff to be the first to strike.

"I wish I had ya comin' in here under better circumstances," she says. "Let me get straight to the point. I know you're still reeling from the death of your uncle, and I don't wanna put any more on ya. But I thought you should hear it from me."

She pauses, then folds her arms on the table before taking a deep breath.

"Adrian Turney passed away. We're still investigating what happened, but we're doin' everything we can to figure out what happened."

She watches my face, and even though I knew, I find that I don't have to pretend. Hearing it out loud, said by Sheriff June, right at this moment, the pain is so acute, I can't hold back a sharp intake of breath, and I can feel the expression on my face morph to one of pure pain.

"What do you mean he's dead?" I say. "And what the hell you mean you're investigating what happened? How do you not know how he died? Where was he?"

She leans back in her chair, hands folded on the desk. "I can't share that information with you Wren, not with an open case. We're gonna figure it out, but it'll take us time. Be patient."

She folds her arms over her chest, and from the apologetic

look on her face, I have a feeling she's gearing up to say something else I'm not going to like.

"I know it's a lot to ask, Wren, but I need a favor. I hear
you're involved with the Citizens—so was Adrian. I hope you'll
be my go-between with them. They need to be told one of
their own has died, and his granddaughter, Leigh, has refused.
If you don't want them hearin' through the grapevine, they
need to hear it from you, and soon."

I don't have to fake the tears that sting the edges of my
eyes, threatening to overcome me. I hadn't thought that far
ahead, to telling the others another one of our own had fallen.
That one of our greatest had met his end in the place he
should have been the safest.

"I'll do it," I say in a whisper. "I'll call a meeting tonight."

She nods and grabs her hat from the table before settling
it back on her head. "Good. I gotta get going, Wren, but if the
Citizens need anythin', you get in touch with Sean, and we'll
see what we can do. We don't want any trouble."

The insinuation rankles, and I grit my teeth. Of course
she'd think that. "We're never a problem."

She stands up and brushes her hands over her shirt to
smooth out the wrinkles before taking her jacket off the back
of her seat. "Good. Then we're done here."

I stand up fast enough that the chair screeches behind me as
it's pushed back, and Sheriff June jumps. I'm ashamed, but tears
drip down my face, in pain, in frustration, in hurt. I hadn't known
that Sheriff June had taken the rumors and cold looks towards
the Citizens seriously, but the fact that she did pisses me off.

I turn towards the door and kick the chair back into place as I go. I hear the sheriff call back "Wren!" after me in annoyance, but I'm out the door of her office and the town hall before they can hear my sobs.

—

"See you at 8 then" I text Molly before I shut down my phone to conserve battery, then stick it in a waterproof pouch and zip it. I stuff it in a side pocket of my pack and snap it closed, double checking it's safe before I check the rest of the pockets to make sure I have everything I need.

I'm at the trunk of my car in the town hall parking lot, on the other side from the records office so Mrs. Delaney and Jethro can't see me through the windows. After I got out of town hall, I calmed down in my car before I texted Molly, the Citizens' president, that we needed to have an emergency meeting. She'd been confused but had taken my urgent proclamation in stride, coordinating the other Citizens, knowing I wasn't the most patient communicator at the best of times, let alone after a family death. We were due to have the meeting tonight.

In the meantime, I had a trail to catch. I'd planned on trying to catch Turney's trail after my shift at the records office but getting out early gave me the perfect opportunity to spend more time dedicated to the task. It was still cutting it close, but if I waited until the weekend, the trail might be gone. There was a chance it already was.

I finish my task of checking I have everything I need, and

satisfied with my supplies, shut the trunk with a bang.

I jump when I realize Jethro is standing at the side of my car, watching me with a curious expression.

"What the hell you doin'?!" I snap. "You scared the shit out of me."

"Where are you going?" he asks.

I cross my arms and glare at him. "Why you answerin' my question with another question?"

He crosses his arms and leans against the car, attempting to copy my stance. "Why are you answering my question of answering your questions with a question...wait. Why are you questioning—" He rubs his face with his hands and lets out a huff of exasperation. "Damnit, Wren, I'm coming with you, okay?"

I stare at him.

"You are not coming with me."

He stands up straight and takes a step towards me. "Yes, I am. I won't let you do this alone."

I take a step towards him, and even though we're about the same height, he winces back.

"Why you wanna follow me?" I ask. "Why you wanna talk to me at all anyway?"

He hesitates. "A distraction?" he says, though it comes out more as a question.

I raise an eyebrow at him. "You really expect me to believe you'll go after a killer for a distraction?"

He rubs a hand over the side of his neck and looks away. "Well, no..."

He drops his arm and looks down at the pavement.

"I know this sounds stupid, and you can laugh...but when I was walking up to Town Hall, I was thinking about how I'm here in the middle of nowhere, I don't know anyone, and my only grandfather is dying, and I needed something, someone, to get through. And there you were, right when I looked up, standing there outside in the sun like you belonged."

He looks up at me, a sheepish expression on his face, one that softens his features.

"You're kind of an ass, but you're also kind of cool, too. You're loyal and stand up for what you believe. I think that's awesome."

I let out a rushed exhale. From anyone else, it would sound bogus, but he's shown he is nothing if not an earnestly good human being who wants to help.

I can't get the dream of Uncle Jeremy out of my head. *There are people out there you don't yet know are family.*

"Fine," I finally say. "Get in the car. It's not far, but we don't have time to walk."

His face lights up, and I'm mad at myself that it makes my heart jump.

FIVE

"WHEN DID YOU KNOW YOU WERE...YOU KNOW."
I can barely hear Jethro over the nearby river crashing from
rock to rock, and it takes me a moment to register his question.

"Know I was what?" I use my walking stick to press down
on the pile of wet leaves and undergrowth in front of me,
making sure it is solid ground underneath.

We decided to start our search east of the river, traveling
along it so we could orient ourselves to the area more easily.
The report had said Turney's body had been dumped in or near
a body of water off the riverside, so it's as good a place as any.

The sun is at its peak, beating down on our skin and
sending me into a sticky sweat. We stay away from the stone
outcroppings along the river edge, not wanting to risk a dip in

its rocky current. There's something of a path along the river's edge where the grass doesn't grow quite as thick, the sharper grass keeping towards the water's edge.

He stays silent, and I wonder at me finally being able to shut him up for a moment's rest. Jethro was horrified when, fifteen minutes into our walk, his phone became completely useless. This deep into the woods in such a small town, there was no cell service to be had. We were well and truly alone, and it was like he was assuaging his fear with mindless talk. His constant chatting scared off the majority of wildlife, so I've seen barely half of what I normally see on my hikes alone. I miss the sound of warblers and chickadees, and it sets my teeth on edge.

The area is damp after recent rain, and the water that the bushes have collected on their leaves keep falling onto me as I push through when the trail thins. I pull the collar of my shirt tighter around my neck when a trickle of warm water sprinkles from the leaves and goes down the back.

After a few more minutes of miserable hiking, Jethro starts to lag, getting stuck in low vines with thorns that cling to his jeans. *At least he's wearing jeans—can't say he's having a great time hiking in those sneakers.*

"Know you were...you know, you?" His voice is closer now, but the words aren't any clearer.

"When did I know I was me? You ain't makin' any sense." I stop and turn to him, annoyed.

Jethro stops and leans against the trunk of a tree covered in greenery. He swipes his arm over his sweat-covered face.

"When did you know you weren't a girl?"

I shake my head. This is a conversation I've been dreading. "When did you know you were a man?"

"I've always known. I've never really thought otherwise." Jethro shifts, frowning and itching subconsciously at his arm.

"Well, there's your answer." I push off from the tree and start moving again. "Oh, and by the way, you're leaning on poison ivy."

I smirk when I hear rustling and swearing. My pace is slow, easy enough for City Boy to catch up. My eyes scan the undergrowth for any clues. Years of hunting for berries and mushrooms give me experience and a keen eye—if there is something to be found, I will find it.

Our several days of rain isn't helping. All the leaf litter is still damp from the downpour and humidity. There are puddles but no prints. I spot plenty of signs of wildlife—prints from a bobcat, scat from rabbits, and eggs and a molting from an unidentifiable snake species. I keep that information in the back of my mind to investigate later.

After a while of scanning the forest floor to no effect, I squat down and turn my head sideways, looking for signs of a man hiking through.

The change of view makes all the difference. The disturbance in the leaves is so subtle even I have trouble seeing the pattern. But now that I've seen it, it's plain as day. I move so the sun is behind me to see the shadows from leaves turned on their sides, and If I look closely, patches where the leaf litter has been moved completely back. I see areas where branches and even a log has been moved, exposing wetter areas in the undergrowth, clear signs of physical disturbance—something big moving through without any care. *Would be odd to be Turney, he's meticulous.*

Jethro shuffles to a stop behind me, and I grab his arm. With the other hand, I point at the broken branches and trampled leaves. "There. We look this way."

Jethro squints at the area. "I don't see anything."

I smack his shoulder lightly and smirk. "And that's why I'm the ones' gotta be lookin'. There's a trail. Somethin's been by here."

He leans forward, still squinting. "Can you tell what it was?"

I hold a hand up, signing for him to stay put. I inch forward to the side of the disturbed leaf litter, making sure to preserve the integrity of the trail. I move slowly, leaning forward and turning my head this way and that to get the right angle.

The path moves into the tree line where the shadows dapple the ground like patchwork. There's an area headed through the trees where the thick grass is pushed into the mud, like something large walked through it. I take a few steps forward and see pushed back branches and bent up leaves. A clear sign of someone who wasn't in any hurry to mask their steps.

"C'mon," I say as I carefully enter the tree line. "Trail leads this way. Don't step on the trail, though. Walk alongside it."

Barely inside the tree line, I spot white out of the corner of my eye. Expecting more snake molting, I'm surprised to see a damp, wrinkled piece of what looks like faded notebook paper. I bend forward to pick it up, careful to not let it crumble and fall apart in my hands. Jethro comes close to me, leaning over my shoulder, but I push him back with my elbow, uncomfortable with his staring and proximity.

"What is it?" he asks, trying to see from his vantage point.

The paper is jagged on its edge, seemingly roughly torn out of a notebook. On it is...gibberish.

"It's nonsense. 'The trees are falling, gotta get it out, it's too wet I'm drowning, what happened to bird'? I don't get it."

Jethro leans from foot to foot, looking up at the trees and squinting his eyes in the sun. "Poetry?"

I shrug, debating dropping the paper back on the ground. "No idea."

He leans forward again, eyes narrowing to read the splotchy handwriting. "Do you think it was Turney?"

I consider his words. Could it have been? The bird part is logical, but what about falling trees? And getting what out?

"It's worth holding onto, I guess." I drop my pack on the ground from my shoulder, handing Jethro the paper. I dig through my bag, pulling out a paper towel and a small, zippered bag of pretzels. I dump the pretzels on the ground, figuring the birds could get a meal out of it, then wrap the paper in paper towel. When it's laid flat, I carefully slide the paper into the Ziplock and put it between the pages of my notebook.

Jethro's eyebrows are raised as I sling my bag back onto my shoulder. "Smart."

I shrug. "You don't get anywhere in these woods without common sense."

At that, we continue our trek past the edge of the woods. The sounds of the river become more muffled within the canopy, the creaking of tree limbs and the swish of leaves in the wind taking its place. As we go, I become more sure it's a man-made trail based on the height of the displacement of branches, the gait of the leaf litter disturbance, and the occasional mud stain on the trees along the path. When I see two muddy footprints my theory is confirmed. The further we follow it, however, the less convinced I am it's Turney's. The path is erratic, branches broken at shoulder height as if the person weren't overly concerned with keeping the landscape undisturbed. Turney would never be so careless.

We're a couple of hundred yards into the tree line when I realize exactly where the path is headed.

"There's a deer blind up here," I call back to Jethro. "Uncle Jeremy and I used it for watchin', but lots of hunters come by for deer and the like."

The blind comes into view, rotting wood holding up a small shelter. When I get near, I smell the mustiness of wood rot, though the structure is still sound enough for use. It's nothing fancy, handmade long ago by some forgotten soul, but it's become a communal spot. It isn't uncommon to come out with the intent to use it and end up having an impromptu party when others had the same idea.

The trail is clear here. Almost too clear. He must have been dragging his leg, long streaks pushing mud back along with clear footprints. But it's not mud.

"The hell..." I let the thought free but don't have an answer.

Mixed in with the mud is what looks like blood.

The trail ends at the ladder to the blind, dried muddy footprints mixed with dark copper staining the weathered wood of the ladder, and I can see where he must have slipped on one rung. The trail starts back up again a few feet away. The hiker must have taken shelter in the blind, then moved on.

"Holy shit, is that what I think it is?" Jethro has come up behind me, and he's staring at the ladder in horror.

"Only one way to find out," I say. I drop my pack and walking stick near a tree and dig inside. I pull out my small spray bottle of hydrogen peroxide I keep for small injuries and walk over to the ladder.

"What are you doing?" Jethro asks, leaning over my shoulder.

I hold a finger up to him, asking for silence. I pick a small spot of thick dried blood and spray it until it's wet.

It bubbles.

"What does that mean??"

"That was hydrogen peroxide," I say. "So yeah, that there's blood. Which means we found Turney's trail."

I hand Jethro the spray bottle, ignoring his protests as I climb the ladder, careful to avoid the muddied, bloody footprint on the rungs. I gently push open the cracked door to the cramped space. The smell is stronger on the inside, the sourness of decay with a strange metal tinge that catches me off guard. It's dark, the light from the openings on either side shuttered by tarps barely making a dent between the roof-covered space and the dark from the forest canopy. But there is clearly something inside.

I move back into the doorway and step down the ladder. Jethro has caught up and is inspecting the blind. I wonder idly if he's ever seen one before.

"You use it for huntin'. You stay inside and the critters can't see or smell you. Easier to hunt or watch."

He wrinkles his nose. "I know that. It doesn't seem safe, though, does it?"

I roll my eyes and look around the ground for a suitable stick. I find one, small enough to fit in my palm but sturdy enough not to break right off.

"What're you doing?"

I don't answer his question, but head back up the ladder and push the door open again. Inside, I kneel down using the twig I'd found to poke at what is left in the blind.

There are wrappers from gauze, a large bandage, an empty canteen, and another piece of folded paper. When I open it, I find more gibberish. It's dry, so I put it in my pocket for safe-keeping. I'm now certain it was Mr. Turney who'd been writing the notes. He must have been injured and used the blind as shelter to tend to his wounds. Had he been shot or stabbed? Was he being pursued? All I can tell from the remains of his stop was an injury. And why would he waste time on poetry if he was bleeding out?

I straighten, frowning. We knew where he'd been, but we don't know why. Something isn't right, and I can't for the life of me figure out what it is.

I turn back, ready to leave the blind when I see it.

The initials "AT" written in blood along the wall in shaky letters.

AT, for Adrian Turney.

The panic wells up before I'm able to think. My breathing turns shallow, and in my mind, I'm screaming at myself. I'd seen plenty of blood in my time—I hunt, I've been injured, seen others injured. My head is a volley of self-reprimands and panicked flashes of memory. Of running, gurneys and *please don't let us be too late*. My vision starts to seep into darkness.

"Wren?" I hear Jethro as if through water, the sound tilting and waving into existence, but I can't respond. My mouth is too busy gulping in thin bits of oxygen, trying to keep me awake even in my fear. Even when my mind fights to turn itself off.

There's a hand on my shoulder, pulling me to sit down at the edge of the ladder. I know I can't move down it as I am now, but it's okay because there's an arm under my knees lifting me up, then down, back onto my feet. I'm in a fog; I can't breathe; everything is too bright and too loud.

Once I'm back on solid ground, he leads me a few yards away, my breath coming in gasps now. He pulls me down onto the trunk of a fallen tree, facing me toward him. His face is blurry, his eyes like coals. My struggling brain wonders when they'd been lit on fire.

"Tell me five things you can see," Jethro's voice echoes while I float behind my skull, held in some strange limbo between my body and my memories.

I manage a noise that is intended to be a question, but my

mouth doesn't quite understand the syllables.

"Can you name five things you see, Wren? Can you do that for me? Five random things, whatever catches your eye."

I try to tilt my head towards him, but it feels like more than my body can manage. I feel weak, a clenching in my chest.

My eyes catch green.

"Leaves." The murmur comes out so quiet, it's stolen by the wind. "They're green. And brown. The leaves."

I can feel Jethro squeeze my hand, though it's far away. I don't remember him taking my hand in the first place.

"Good, good. What else do you see?"

I blink my eyes, forcing them to focus away from the swirling dots of color my vision has become. I choose a spot in the distance.

"The trees. A dragonfly. The river. And…and a dead tree."

"You're doing great Wren. How about four things you can hear? Can you do that?"

It feels like I'm clawing through mud, like I've missed my step. I've misjudged the swamp and sank into its depths and am slowly pulling myself out. Jethro is grabbing my hand in more ways than one.

"I hear the river. Chickadees. Your voice. The wind and the rustlin' of leaves." I inhale deep, unsure when I'd started breathing so tightly in my chest. I feel the tension siphon out of me.

His hand tugs at mine, and I manage to curl my fingers around his. He squeezes back.

"You're doing great Wren. Just a few more. What are three things you feel?"

I close my eyes, and the darkness welcomes me like folded arms around my back. Like Uncle Jeremy when I'd had a nightmare as a child. My chest constricts.

"Hey, hey Wren. It's okay." Distantly I feel him lean into me, hand resting on my shoulder, arm behind my neck. He rubs my shoulder gently. "Can you tell three things you can feel right now? With your hands, what are you touching?"

I try to stop the sob in my throat, but as it chokes out, I lose my tenuous hold. After the first one leaves me, the rest grapple in my chest, aching to be let out, and they do so in waves.

Jethro holds me in a side-hug, my head tucked onto his shoulder, and I lean my tear-drenched face into him. I try to speak, try to tell him. To tell him what I feel now and what I can never feel again.

I feel Jethro's arm around me. I feel my nails digging into my knees. I feel my feet crunched tight in my boots.

But in my mind, in my memory, I feel the rough flannel of Uncle Jeremy's shirt clenched in my hands as he lies on the drenched leaves and moss of the forest floor. I feel how my pain has been like a tick gone into my chest, poisoning my blood and making it run hot and thick. And then I refuse to feel anything.

Eventually, the sobs became dull whimpers chased with sniffing to clear my nose. Everything feels muffled, my mouth over-full with spit. My head pounds to my heartbeat. I turn my face to the side, rub the wetness off on the arms of my t-shirt, and pull away from Jethro.

He's been mostly silent, though I may have not heard what he's been saying. He lets go of my shoulder but grabs my hand back to squeeze it. "How are you feeling, Wren?"

I'm thankful he doesn't ask the details of my fit, but I can practically see him trying to hold back his questions.

"I feel like I've been run down by Nina's Hummer and then dragged down Foster Road by a chain." I pull my hand away and wipe my hands on my shorts. "Just ask. I know you're itchin' to. You look like some pup holding back from table scraps."

His smile is soft, and I wonder at the sudden gentleness in his normally grating voice. "I won't ask until you're ready. I'm glad you're more aware; I was worried, you know. But I get it. You can keep your secret unless you're ready to talk."

I stand up, trying to wipe off the dirt and crinkled leaves clinging to my jeans. The back is soaked, but it'll dry soon enough.

Jethro takes the cue and stands, not trying to salvage his jeans. He squints back towards where we've come, to the broken-down deer blind.

I don't look back. I don't need to shatter again.

"I figure we keep movin' up the river. We get in another hour before we turn back."

Jethro bites at his lip, looks me up and down. "You sure you're good to keep going?"

"I'm fine." It's easier to be upset than it is to be embarrassed.

I search for my walking stick, finding it leaned against a

fallen log with my pack and Jethro's stick. I grab the pack and
fling my arm through the strap. I pick up my walking stick and
follow the river at a brisk pace before Jethro manages to grab
his own stick.

I keep walking, pushing brush and tree branches out of
the way, not waiting to see if he is following me. There's a
wildfire in my gut and thorns in my chest. I hold onto it like
I'm hanging by my fingertips off a cliff.

I can hear Jethro struggle to keep up, his sharp swears breaking up the noise of him pushing through leaves and branches.
The sound is more and more distant, then stops entirely.

I pause and wait for it to continue, but there's quiet except
for the rush of the river and the occasional crow.

I turn back to steal a glance, but I can't see him. The afternoon sun shines at an angle on the facets of the rocks scattered around and in the river. The trees cover the water's edge,
branches hovering over the water.

The river is an open cut in the landscape. Like a wound
that keeps flowing open, never able to heal. It feeds the trees,
the brambles. In turn, they give way to wildlife. The same deer,
foxes, and rabbits that feed the town. But for that to happen,
the wound can never close.

I hear Jethro swear, then he pushes back through the
foliage, carefully peeling back the layers of leaves and branches
between us.

Some wounds can't stay open.

—

We've been following Turney's trail for over an hour when I feel the first drops. The river has thinned into a stream, pockets of water creating small ponds along its edges—a sure indication we're getting close to one of the side bodies of water Turney was found near. Though I've noticed the clouds slowly cover the sun as it starts to set, I've been hoping it would hold out long enough for us to make it to the end of the trail and back home again.

Now they're dark and looming, the light fading, the sharp scent of water thick in the air. The whole landscape is taking on an eerie blue hue, one that would get worse as the rain did. I curse to myself and pull my shirt as far up my neck as it will go.

"I think it's about to rain," Jethro states as if I hadn't felt the same wetness.

"Yeah, no shit," I bark in response. I pull him into the cover of the trees, away from the river. Cat tails and thick, sharp grass litter the landscape, areas where it's pushed down a clear indicator of Turney's trail. But I know how quickly the rain can turn from a drizzle to a downpour around here this time of year, and anything downhill will be flooded by water fast. We have to abandon our mission.

"Change of plans. We're headin' back." I take one last look at Turney's trail, the bushes bent back at awkward angles where he'd pushed his way through. He'd been traipsing through like a bull in a China shop, none of the usual finesse I'd expect of a Citizen.

His trail had been going in circles, each repetition slightly different on his trek. But the overall pattern was clear: he'd had no idea where he was going. From someone who knew the woods as if guided by a road map, it had to mean something. If he was injured, he should have been heading towards town. Was he being followed? But then why not go in a zig-zag towards town?

I also knew from my time hunting with Jeremy that the more wreckage left in an animal's wake, the more injured and close to death. Turney's trail had been wide enough for a horse to go through. There had also been more and more frequent spots of blood along the trail. Based on the amount of blood and the closeness of his steps, we had to be close, but I wasn't going to risk Jethro's life or mine on it.

"It's just a little drip. We can keep going. I thought you wanted to get to where he'd been killed." He sounds annoyed, confused. He holds his hands palms down over his forehead, probably trying to keep his glasses as dry as he can.

"You're new here, so you ain't seen what the rain is like. This time of year, you don't know when it's gonna get worse. The humidity ain't for nothing. We've had bad rains the past few weeks, and it ain't gettin' any better."

He's walking at a slow pace, and I sigh. I grab his forearm, ignoring his yelp as I pull him along. I have a general idea of where we are, which way is home, and I don't want to be stuck out here longer than I have to be. "Best to get back as soon as we can. Just in case. Besides, the trail's gonna be swept away by the rain."

"But we didn't learn much about what's going on. We could go a bit further." He's dragging his feet now, digging in

his heels against my pulling. I roll my eyes even though I know
he can't see it with my face turned.

"You wanna get caught in a flood, you go for it. But I ain't
gonna die out of curiosity."

I let him go and don't turn back as I head through the
forest at a steady clip. I know once I get far enough ahead that
he'll quicken his pace. He isn't an idiot. He has to know being
out here alone will be a death sentence for him.

The forest engulfs me in an eerie darkness as I head
through the thick of the trees, the canopy taking the edges
off the falling raindrops and giving me respite. Sure enough,
it's not past a minute when he yells up to me, and I hear the
crunching of leaves as he runs up to my side.

"If we're done looking, can I ask you something?"

I feel a shiver that has nothing to do with the rain. I knew
he'd ask. I couldn't be so lucky as to get by with having a panic
attack and not get questioned on it.

But I owe him. He handled it without tearing me down,
and as much as I hate to admit it, I've developed a soft spot for
the chatterbox.

"You can ask." I let it hang for a while, my gaze on my feet
as we walk through the now soaked leaf litter. The debris and
mud sticks to my boots and my ankles, and despite the heat
and humidity in the air, I feel a chill. "But I got the right to not
answer."

"Fair enough. Does that happen often? The panic attack,
that is? I'm only asking 'cause I have a cousin—we were close
as kids. Well, he had attacks like that too, ya know? So I wonder

what you want me to do if it happens again."

I understand the questioning considering he looks determined to tag along on this hair-brained sleuthing, but it
scratches at old wounds.

"I don't need you to save me. I got a social worker, Mrs.
Delaney, the Citizens, the Trickster. I'm fine." I emphasize the
point with an increased clip, and he's quiet for a while as he
tries to keep up.

As we walk in silence, I notice that sure enough, water is
pooling in the gullies and trenches around us. I focus on keeping us uphill as much as possible, not wanting to risk going
through any part of the water.

"I don't want to save you." The response is quiet, near
covered by the rain.

I snort. Of course he doesn't; he doesn't know me. "Why's
that? Don't think I'm worth it?"

"I don't think you need to be saved. You know that, right,
Wren?"

I roll my shoulders, uncomfortable, the rain pelting our
backs and causing an ache in my muscles.

"I know that." I don't know if I believe it.

"Well, then good. I don't want to do the wrong thing is all.
Think about it, yeah?"

I refuse to express it, but the words soothe the burn of the
question. No one has ever asked me that before. "Fine."

As we walk through the mud, carefully now, he tells me
about his father and his grandfather who they'd come to take
care of in his old age. How he wants to finish his degree in

library sciences, get a job at one of the big libraries that have technology centers.

His voice is impassioned, excited by everything he's working towards. When he talks, it's like his whole body is lit aflame, his shoulders no longer hunched and his hands in flight as he gestures along with every moment. I know I'm in trouble then—it will be impossible to step away now. Because if there's one thing I've admired, it's people who come alive by telling stories.

I also hear the love for his father and his grandfather, enough that he's putting his own goals on hold. I think of my Uncle Jeremy then, and the envy stings.

The scent of petrichor and standing water rises with the humidity, and though the canopy delays much of the rain falling on us, when it does, it falls in thick drops that run down my arms, neck, and legs in rivulets. Our trek slows as the mud clings to our feet, sucking us in, but we can't stop to rest even as my calves burn. The sky is dark, the clouds shuttering out the remainder of the sunlight, and I know we're fighting a losing battle with the remains of the day. Yet somehow, the tenor of his voice and the exuberance he relays his stories with makes the time pass quickly.

"Oh, I have one more question."

It catches me off guard, but I grit my teeth.

"Fine," I say, wanting to get it over with.

"Who's the Trickster?"

SIX

I EXPLAIN THE STORY of the Trickster and Citizens to Jethro as we walk and I am overwhelmed with prying questions as we drive back. We make it to town hall before the Citizen meeting by the skin of our teeth. The air is cool by then, the rain steaming off the asphalt. The parking lot has a mish-mash of cars, SUVs, and trucks of the Citizens, waiting for my arrival, a lone light on the door to the community center building. It flickers like a giant firefly in the night, a reminder of so many cool spring nights spent in communion with the other birders of the town. It's my north star tonight, yet it fills me with a cold trepidation.

As Jethro drives away, presumably back to his family for the night, my mind reels with the enormity of the task ahead of me. The community center banquet hall is in one of the small side buildings connected to town hall, the trim and roof tiles peeling back paint. The center is used by clubs for meetings and parties. It's sheer luck that it wasn't being used tonight, so Molly had been able to get the key from Sean before town hall had closed.

The fading light reflects a bluish hue along the sidewalk, the twilight the perfect hiding spot for my sense of dread and the creases on my frowning face. This was the last place I wanted to be, and yet the only people who had any chance of understanding the severity of the situation were cornered in this room, waiting for the news I had to relay.

As I open the creaking door, I nearly run into Nathaniel as he opens it inward from the other side. He jumps, setting a hand on his chest before taking in my appearance with a raised eyebrow.

"Wren! I was about to step outside to call ya and check in. Are you ready for whatever this is about?" Nathaniel is our secretary and one of the more detail-oriented people in the group. He runs a tan hand through his close-cropped, black mustache and beard around a sour smile.

Nathaniel is one of the few people that Uncle Jeremy never quite connected with. Not necessarily because of anything he had done but because they were so different in personality and presentation that they rubbed each other the wrong way. And yet, it was Nathaniel who had guided me through some of the more complicated aspects of Uncle Jeremy's death, from sending off death certificates to approving the costs of the burial. When I'd run into issues paying for the funeral costs, he'd been the first to step up with solutions.

It makes me wonder how much the world had lost that people Uncle Jeremy didn't spend much time with were so affected and moved by his passing.

"Sorry it took so long," I say, and he moves back to let me in through the door. It opens to a beige hallway with thin, gray dappled carpeting disturbed by the occasional stain. As we walk towards the main open section of the building, I take in the sight of chairs being pushed into a circle, the Citizens, my people, a disparate conglomerate of individuals all brought together for one purpose.

It feels right, for all that it hurts.

There's a light pat on my shoulder, and I try not to wince, not usually fond of being touched. I let it go this once with the knowledge there are sure to be more in my near future.

Molly comes up to me, a soft but questioning grin on her tan face. She's Nathaniel's twin sister and his complete opposite in many ways. Her dark hair is in curls along her cheeks, her wardrobe of purple scrubs making it clear to me she's come straight from her work at the lone doctor's office in town. She is compassion incarnate, the type of person you want to spread your worries out before like a painting on canvas.

She touches my arm, lighter than Nathaniel, barely a brush before pulling back to clasp her hands in front of herself. "Wren, hun, everyone is here like you requested. Is this somethin' about Jeremy? Whatever can we do for you, you know we're here."

I glance towards the rest of the Citizens, milling about but clearly watching me while trying to seem innocent in doing so. Gazes turn away when I meet eyes, and though I know it's well intentioned, I feel caught out and raw.

"It's not, actually," I say, turning back to Molly. "Not exactly. It's a request from the sheriff, that I speak with everyone."

There's a sharp inhale and a frown from Molly, a shared look between her and Nathaniel. Distrust, confusion. She twists her fingers in a light chain around her neck, a small charm of a swallow hanging from it.

"Surely there's nothing anyone here has done to warrant that kind of attention." It's Nathaniel that finally speaks up. "They're always lookin' to blame us for things, the town is. I had thought the sheriff wouldn't take those rumors seriously."

I shrug, knowing the feeling, the wariness the rest of the town sometimes expressed about us whenever we met in groups. It had never made sense to me, yet it persisted.

"It's nuthin' we've done…" I pause, stuffing my hands in my pockets and avoiding both of their gazes. "I'm sorry, I'd really like to say this once."

Molly touches my arm again and squeezes, nodding in understanding. Appeasement. "Of course, Wren. Let's get everyone situated."

There is a call for everyone to sit, and then we're all in a circle, Molly asking for quiet, everyone's eyes watching me as I sit awkwardly, half in half out of my chair as she runs through miscellaneous housekeeping things before Tom speaks. The attention makes me squirm in my chair, the news clinging desperately to my tongue, aching to get out but fearful of its own finality. *There's no going back.*

"Get to the point, Molly. Why are we here? Meetin's not till next week, and I got work at daybreak."

There's a tension in the room, though Tom was saying what everyone else was thinking. I straighten, trying to decide the best way to break the news, but there's a catch in my throat every time I try to say the words. It's a suffocating clenching that robs my breath from me, and the room begins to spin. The lights flicker around me in slow waves, and I blink away the haze. There are words being exchanged, Molly talking to Tom, Nathaniel trying to talk over them both, the room in disarray, our carefully crafted and trimmed group falling into disorder.

"Turney is dead," I finally say, though it's mostly lost in the noise of the room. But Carrie next to me inhales, then shouts for quiet. The room feels cold and oppressive, the air from the A/C blowing down my back and sending my hairs to stand on end along my neck and shoulders.

"Wren," a voice says—Molly?—and then a hand is holding mine between theirs. "Wren, what did you say?"

"It's Turney." It comes out as a rattling croak. "He's gone. They found him in the woods. He's gone. He's dead."

The hands drop mine, and the room exhales all at once. There's silence, and I wish for the oppressive sounds of life from before. A flag has been dropped between before and now, and I already desperately miss the before, when none of this was real.

"Are they sure?" It's Nathaniel, a whisper, a plead for uncertainty. "We saw him the other day; he seemed well enough. Could they be wrong?"

I find myself shaking my head minutely, staring straight ahead at the ratty hiking boots of the person sitting at the other end of the room from me. Like those twisted laces and threadbare leather have the answers to the universe, like they could change the course of the past if I study them enough.

The quiet is oppressive, but what is there to say? Two of us lost in such a short period of time, two of our pillars lost to the woods that we venerated. What can you say about a god that's forsaken you but bear it with horrified awe?

Molly is the one to break the silence. "If the sheriff believes it's Adrian, I have no doubt in my mind that it's true," she whispers, hands wringing in her lap, gaze on her fingers.

"What do we do?" It's Carrie this time, and I hear the wetness in her voice.

"What we do best," Nathaniel says, sitting up straight in his chair and holding a hand on Molly's shoulder. "We take care of our own."

There's a part of me that knows it's not that simple, but I cling to the words like a lifeline.

—

By the time I open the screened-in porch of Uncle Jeremy's house—now mine—it's night, the stars bright lights hung between the trees. It's dropped nearly fifteen degrees since we first went into the woods. I'm cold, wet, and tired. Pinpricks travel up my fingers, my legs numb.

I wish I could say it had been worth it, but I'm not so sure. We made progress, but not enough. There is plenty of snooping left to do in the woods, trail gone or not. Surely there has to be something more to be found if the deer blind means anything.

The meeting with the Citizens was short after my announcement, talk of a candlelight vigil and fundraiser for Turney's granddaughter, Leigh, proposed but no progress made in the dead of the night. It was too new, too soon, and I hoped things would seem clearer in the light of day.

I grab the handful of mail out of the black drop box along the side of the house then flick on the yellowed porch lights that attract small gnats and mosquitoes buzzing between the bulbs. I fumble with the keys and purposely don't look at the half-carved statuettes standing like silent guardians next to the old lawn chair. Uncle Jeremy had set them on the porch for the days he wanted to carve in the sunlight. There's still wood shavings and his carving set sitting on the glass side table, ready to be picked up again by someone who is never coming back. A monument to the stillness my life had become.

Moving through the door, I calm the ache with whispered curses, letting my anger be my stalwart partner against the tide of grief.

The house is a minefield, each photo a ticking bomb ready to burst before my eyes with memories I'd rather not relive, so I settle at the table and decide to tackle the mundane task of going through the mail. The steady stream of bereavement cards has trickled down now, and the mail with Uncle Jeremy's name on it has begun to wane.

Instead, there are bills now in my own name for my own home. As I stutter through opening envelopes and browse through statements, I feel my fingers itch to scratch at my arms and bite my lip. It feels wrong to be responsible for electricity, water, and waste management at my age, and there's a numbing stress that eats into my stomach lining as I go through the costs. It's too much. With no income coming in without Uncle Jeremy's steady stream of clients and projects, I've already been forced to sell off personal items, but it's going to get to the point soon where I have no other choice. I have to go into the workshop and decide what I'm going to do with Uncle Jeremy's business.

The shed behind the house is larger than most, more of a restructured garage than anything else. It was Uncle Jeremy's workshop, the place where he created his masterpieces, and I've managed to avoid it until this point. But if I'm to continue his business, I need to know where we stand, what projects I can realistically complete, and how I am going to move forward with my life.

I push the bills into a pile, dropping the envelopes in the blue recycling bin next to the fridge with a thwap. *It's now or never.* I consider getting a jacket but take that as the avoidance it is and exit the kitchen through the back door onto the deck. A few steps down, and I'm walking to the dark building that feels twice it's normal height before me, arms crossed around me, the nip of the cold air sending a shiver down my spine.

I click on the light switch from the outside and see the dark illuminate through the window in the door. The ventilation unit comes to life, the sound loud in the night. With a calming breath, I push the door handle that opens the side door into the workshop, my breath caught in my throat.

It's as we'd left it the night before he died. The sawhorse with planks of wood we'd set there to get off my workspace for a new project, sawdust littering the floor from our late night working together, his half-finished five-foot carving of a bear, the face just coming to life, teeth bared in a roar.

I stuff my hands into my pockets and tiptoe around the sawdust I can't bear to disturb, aiming for the desk to the side where Uncle Jeremy had kept all the notes on his orders. The pile is haphazard, papers crumpled and dusty and in no particular order, but if I'm to have any hope of making something of my uncle's business, they're my golden ticket.

Browsing through them, my heart sinks at the level of expertise needed for the majority of the projects. Uncle Jeremy taught me a lot, but he was at a different level entirely. If Adrian Turney were here, I'd be able to manage with his guidance—he'd been my father's mentor after all. But with both men gone, it feels like an impossible task.

I gather up the papers and hold them to my chest, tears gathering at the corners of my eyes, but I refuse to cry. I choke back the wetness cloying my mouth and walk to the door, letting my eyes sweep in the sight of the room one last time before closing the door and turning off the light.

SEVEN

WHEN I ENTER THE RECORDS ROOM DOOR, I realize Jethro is already there. He and Mrs. Delaney are looking intently at something on the computer. I feel the beginnings of annoyance, fairly certain of what they're doing.

I debate letting the door slam shut, but not with Mrs. Delaney there. I lift the hatch, setting my bag in a cubby under the countertop. Mrs. Delaney notices me and waves her hand at me. "Come here, child. See what young Jet was able to do."

My shoulders tighten in an instant. My heart quickens, but I don't say a word, not wanting to assume anything.

I shouldn't have bothered holding back. On the screen is an image of a page from one of the more recent book logs, the date showing it's from the early 1970s. The page is slightly yellowed, every little scratch and pit in the paper visible. There are red and blue boxes, thin stripes of each color, overlaying the page.

"What are you doin'?" I ask but I know.

"We're digitizing records." Jethro's voice is filled with thinly veiled caution, and he's not meeting my gaze. "Trying to, at least. I got the scanner up and working, but the algorithm is having an issue with the handwriting. It'll get better the more pages we scan."

It feels like a betrayal after our day in the woods, to come here and go behind my back to do the very thing I'd warned him off of doing. It felt like we'd built camaraderie if nothing else. It stings to be wrong, but I bottle it up, the energy a miasma in my gut. I grit my teeth, but I know there's nothing I can do or say that won't sound childish, complacent in how things have always been. I want to say that it's not the technology I fear but what we stand to lose, but I don't have the words to explain. So I stay silent.

I do, however, turn away without a response and move to where there's a pile of records ready to sort. I immerse myself in the process, trying not to spare a thought for what's happening across the room. I let the folders slap onto the countertop as I sort them, looking for a way to let out the caged energy at my fingertips.

My fit doesn't go unnoticed. I see Mrs. Delaney come towards me, grabbing one of the folders before I can cause more of a ruckus. "Wren, don't be like that." The words are meant to soothe, but I won't be calmed.

"We talked about this. I thought he was puttin' in new records, not digitizing old ones." I try to keep my voice from sounding like a whine, but I'm not sure how much I succeed by the look on Mrs. Delaney's face.

"Child, you needn't be so protective. Just because somethin's been done one way doesn't mean it needs to be. The way it's written down won't change the stories it holds. Give our young man a chance."

I sigh, gripping the countertop with white knuckles. "Fine," I say through gritted teeth. "He can try."

She smiles, the kind of smile that says she knows I'm humoring her but won't comment on it. "Good. Now that you're here, though, Sheriff June said she wanted to talk to ya both when I came in this mornin'."

I freeze in my sorting, and I can feel the blood draining from my face. That can't be good.

"I do wonder what it could be about. You didn't get up to any mischief yesterday, did you, Wren? I can't imagine what she'd need to talk to Jet about." She shakes her head and shrugs. "Anywho, you two pop over to her office, then come back when you're done."

I set the folder I've been looking through down, avoiding Jethro's gaze as I lift up the hatch. I wait for him when Mrs. Delaney gives me a look, holding the countertop up for him to ease through.

Jethro is acting cautious, more so than should be expected considering our disagreement. I don't have time to consider it though—the sheriff is not patient.

We get through the door and a few feet down the hallway before Jethro grabs my arm, pulling me to the side. "Wren, we have a problem."

I look at where he's holding my arm, and he lets go as if burned. "Why do I get the feeling you know what Sheriff June wants to talk to us about?"

He looks guiltily down at his feet, putting his hands into his pant pockets. "Well, it's about yesterday. I think my dad may have called the sheriff and told her what happened."

The story is so absurd, it takes a moment for my mind to catch up, but when it does, I go from calm to white-hot in seconds.

"What? Why would you tell your dad that we were secretly investigating a murder?!"

He leans back, and I realize I'm in his face now. I pull back a bit but not all the way.

"I don't know. He asked me about my day, and I was so nervous, and he kept asking questions! It kind of all just came out."

I throw up my arms and roll my eyes. "It just came out?! Why would it just come out?"

He rubs at his face, and I see the misery in his expression. "I don't know. I'm on edge with everything going on with my grandpa. I'm so frantic all the time and he took me by surprise. I'm sorry!"

The mention of his grandfather sobers me, and I feel the calm like a wave. The reminder of why Jethro is in this city is like a stone in my gut, and I'm filled with a sense of empathy.

I know what it's like to feel on the edge of a knife at all times, and I can't blame him for his grief.

I consider our options. Denial is out of the question. Sheriff June can smell a lie like a bloodhound on a fox's trail. We could apologize, say we'd made a mistake and that we would stop the investigation, but Sheriff June knows me better than that.

"Okay," I say as if reassuring myself. "Okay. So, Sheriff June knows. We can't play innocent. All we can do is downplay it."

He nods, but I can see the anxiety in his posture, the way he avoids my gaze. This is not going to go well.

"Let's get this over with. " I turn away from him, heading towards the sheriff's office.

He grabs my arm again, and I pull it back automatically. He looks hurt, but I don't have time to tiptoe around his feelings.

"I'm sorry, Wren. I really am."

I nod, because I know he's sorry. It's clear on his face.

"Come on. Let's face the music."

—

Sheriff June is a monolith, an unbending part of the community, in the eyes of all the townsfolk. Sitting in her sparse, organized office, my hands clasping the scratched pine of her chairs, I feel the full weight of her stare like concrete blocks on my shoulders.

We done wrong. I know it, Jethro knows it now, Sheriff

June surely knows it if her expression is anything to go by. If Uncle Jeremy were still alive, he'd be laughing his ass off at my situation. "You get what you give, Wren," he'd have said. "You look for trouble, you'll get trouble."

Sheriff June isn't laughing.

Or talking, for that matter.

I've not been on the receiving end of the sheriff's wrath often and never to this extent. I'm not sure if her silence is an interrogation technique or if she is simply that angry. The whirring of the ceiling fan holds at the forefront of my hearing, occasional grunts and paper shuffling from Sean in the next room over the only respite. I keep my eyes trained on the posters behind Sheriff June, determined not to be the first to speak. There is a grayscale poster for the Fourth of July potluck, an electricity conservation notice from a month back, and a list of names and phone numbers for easy access. I study every word, pixelated clip art, and amateur photo like I'm in a museum.

Jethro cracks first.

"I'm sorry my dad called you, Sheriff June," he starts, wringing his hands in his lap and hunching forward in shame. "He was overreacting. I was sharing my day, and I didn't mean for it to become an issue."

Sheriff June's chair creaks as she leans back, her arms straight in front of her and holding onto the desk. I can tell from the corner of my eyes that she has her gaze trained on my face.

"That isn't the issue, Jethro. Your father called me out of

concern. As he should have." The chair lets out a high-pitched squeal as she leans forward in it, folding her arms on the top of the desk over the small stacks of paper littering the desktop. "The problem is, you two weren't supposed to be lookin' for anythin'. It ain't your job, and you, Wren, put you both in danger in your foolhardy attempt at playin' detective."

She taps her fingers on the desktop idly. I see her gaze turn to Jethro and let out a relieved breath. I allow myself to turn toward her face. Her jaw is tight, eye blazing. Not good.

"I know you're new here, Jet, so I get you ain't got no idea how things are run around here. But you ain't off the hook. Whatever made you think pursuing an open case was a good idea? Y'all are civilians. You ain't trained for this, and I won't have you putting yourself in danger and messin' with our crime scene."

She turns to me then, and I feel goosebumps rise at her stony stare. I scratch at the arms of the chair, thinking no wonder it looks like a cat's gone at it with a stare like that.

"Lord willing and if the creek don't rise, we'll have this solved and put behind us within a few weeks. But I don't want y'all interferin' anymore? Y'all are going to stay put in town, no runnin' over hell's half acre trying to do my job."

I lean forward, summoning all the courage in my gut to stare back without my voice quivering.

"You know I'm the best tracker we got. I've seen more of the Trickster than anyone else in town. I know those woods; I know how to find anythin' in them. If we got any chance of catchin' who killed Mr. Turney, ya gotta let me help."

Sheriff June leans forward over the desk, and I lean back

reflexively. Her eyes just about shoot flames. "What exactly did you get into?"

I keep my mouth shut, knowing I've shown my hand too soon. I turn away first.

"Figurin' this out won't bring him back, Wren. Either Turney or your uncle."

I take a sharp breath and turn to face her directly. I can feel a bone-deep chill travel down my spine, and I know my face has gone pale. I can feel Jethro's stare, but I don't stop looking straight at Sheriff June. I won't give her the relief.

"I know that." My tone is sharp, clipped. I don't care. She's gone too far, and I'm gonna let her know it.

Sheriff June leans back in her chair again, and it groans at the abuse. This time, her expression is gentler, apologetic. "I know you wanna help, Wren, but this is a case for the police. It's too dangerous for civilians to be lookin' around."

I raise my chin, looking down my nose at her in defiance —unwilling to back down. My teeth clench. "I'm not a civilian. I'm a Citizen."

She sighs and leans forward again; the sound grates at my ears. She rubs her palms over her face, wiping at sweat and grime. "In the eyes of the law, they're the same thing."

"We won't go outside looking for trouble." I nearly jump, having forgotten that Jethro is still here. I glare at him, betrayed at his words.

"Good," Sheriff June says, brokering no more argument. "Keep your heads down, don't make no more trouble. And Wren, you hand over those notes, now."

"They're in my bag," I say through clenched teeth, and she nods.

"Good. Then you get them and bring them back to me as soon as possible." She stands, stretching her back before gathering a few papers in her hands. I glare at them—at her hands, the papers, the desk, everything. There's a fire in my chest, and I want to quicken it.

I'm furious at Sheriff June and don't want to be coddled, treated like a child. I am acting childish, I know, but I can't force myself to care. There's a rock in my throat, and I hate it.

Jethro's shoulders droop at my apparent anger. He lets out a huff and starts heading towards the door. After a moment I slam my hands onto the scratched-up arms of the chair and push myself up. I follow his lead.

"Wren." It's Sheriff June, and I pause with my back to her. "This is for your own good."

I don't respond, shaking my head as I grab for the door handle. I throw it open before stomping through, not waiting for Jethro to follow.

—

I go directly to the records room, my safe space. My safe space that has been taken over by some upstart city boy. An upstart city boy that I had been growing fond of, but now my feelings are all muddled in my chest. He may not have intended a betrayal, but it's what it feels like.

Out of respect for Mrs. Delaney, I don't fling open the door or let it slam shut.

I shouldn't have worried, though. She isn't there. I open the door back up and see a note on yellow, green-lined paper that says Mrs. Delaney went home, that she isn't feeling well. I spare a moment to be concerned before it gives way to renewed anger as Jethro rounds the corner.

I glare at him and would lock the door if it weren't public property. I want to be alone, and I'm beyond caring if my actions appear juvenile. I'm swimming in my frustration, a noxious gas that leaves me lightheaded and warm.

As it is, I decide to simply ignore him completely until he leaves.

I move towards the counter, lift the hatch to the back, and walk through. I don't wait for him, just set it back down behind me.

"Look, before you say anything, I have a plan."

I don't look up. I pick one of the unsorted piles on the counter of current records and begin sorting the folders by type.

"Why are you so angry all the time? I'm trying to help, you know."

I do know that. But I don't want his type of help. The type of help that paints me as some weak-willed, out of control bystander. I don't need a hero; I don't need this. I struggle to keep it in.

"What plan do you have exactly?" I don't stop sorting, determined to feign indifference but I feel a niggling of curiosity.

"I said we wouldn't get into any trouble *outside*. But you said the trail would be gone now, so there's no point in going outside anyway."

I pause in my sorting, caught off guard. The folder hovers between two stacks, and I look up at him, eyebrow raised. "And?"

"And whoever did the murder would need a motive, right? Most of the time, the motive is money or personal. The exact sort of thing you would find evidence of in a records office."

I drop the folder between the piles. I look at him, making my face as unreadable as possible to see how much I can make him squirm. From the concrete stare he's sending my way, I wonder if he's got more backbone than I originally thought. *Maybe he's more than endless chatter.*

If I think about it, I have to admit his plan makes sense. It will convince Sheriff June that we're following orders. He hadn't outright lied to the sheriff, something I don't think either of us could have managed. It had been a lie of omission, and it worked.

I feel something akin to pride for him, but I squash it down reflexively. Then I consider it. Yes, he made a mistake but he's doing his damnedest to make up for it. The least I can do is let him.

"Alright," I draw the word out, a challenge. "Then where exactly do ya suggest we look first?"

His face relaxes back into the sweet, innocent beaming I've started to associate with him. Excited, even. He moves towards the opening of the counter, pulls up the hatch, then replaces it after he's come through. He moves to my side, tapping the folder I'd been sorting.

"These are all recent, right? There could be a clue in here on a motive. Like, what if Turney owed someone money or there's a will where someone's got something to gain? Or if there are any arrest records for anyone around him. Anything to connect him to someone who'd want him dead."

I consider it, rubbing the side of my cheek with my hands to mask my smile. "You know that's slam up illegal, yeah? We'd be violating so many privacy laws, I bet."

It's his turn to snort. "We're volunteers here. I'm sure you see this kind of paperwork all the time. There's nothing here you're not supposed to be able to look through. What's the harm? You know this town best; you know who's who. I bet you can find a key in here somewhere quick."

I fight the upturning of my lips, cheeky. "Flattery now, huh? Trying to butter me up?" And like that, the tension is gone like a morning fog.

I push half the folders towards him, ruining my piles, but I don't care. We'll sort them later. I move another stack towards us, pulling up two of the creaky wooden chairs. "I'll bring those notes to the sheriff, then when I come back, we'll start. If anyone comes in, we're sorting, got it?"

He nods, and opens the first folder. "You know, this would be so much easier if we digitized everything."

I glare at him.

"Absolutely. Not."

EIGHT

WE'RE IN MY ROOM AGAIN, and the memory of the last
time I was here resurfaces slowly. The same posters and knickknacks are arranged around me, a time capsule into my adoles-
cence and a harsh reminder of when things were simpler. My
uncle sits in the plush chair looking as he did the day he died,
typical Uncle Jeremy smirk on his face like he had no worries
in life—or death.

There are nuanced differences. *A Beginners Guide to Birdwatching* on my side table. A gold-tipped wing feather tied to a
string hanging from a nail near the light switch. Drawings of
birds taped to the wall by the desk. Signs of a young watcher, a
Citizen in training.

I'm in my summer pajamas, shorts cut from a pair of old

sweatpants and an oversized t-shirt. Instead of the thick bed-spread, I'm left with thin sky-blue sheets, somewhat threadbare but with no holes yet. But my feet still hit the bed halfway down, so I know it can't have been more than a few months from when I was here last.

When I turn to Uncle Jeremy, he's waiting patiently, a twinkle in his eye and the same book in his hands. His smile turns soft- the one he reserved for me.

"I know you're frustrated, Little Bird," he says, like I'd appeared in the middle of a conversation I vaguely remember. "Every Citizen has times when the Trickster gives 'em the runaround. You're not the first and you won't be the last. The thing to remember in watchin', and in life, is you can't always do it alone. Let me tell you a story of a time when a little bird had to learn to ask for help."

He cracks open the book, flipping back and forth through the pages as if looking for a particular section. He licks his thumb and turns through a few pages—a habit I'd scorned when he used it on my books as a child—before he settles the book in his lap, looking down at it for a moment before he turns to me with mischief.

"Well, this one should do it. It was a dreary day, clouds thick that blocked out any lick of sunshine. But you insisted this would be the day you would see him. And so, we made the trek into the green and yellow thick of the woods. You refused to let me carry anythin' for you, and your binoculars hung heavy 'round your neck. But you're a stubborn one, Little Bird, and I knew you had to learn this lesson on your own."

He turns the page, tapping one section of it as he beams.

"You wanted to carry your own pack, which you said you had to pack on your own, and by the time we were an hour in, you were near in tears. You'd brought too much and carried it too long. We settled down near a thicket on a dead tree trunk to take a rest soon enough, despite your protests."

He turns the page again, this time leaning forward, not seeming to read from the book as he speaks, eyes staring straight into mine.

"That's when you heard it for the first time. The trill. You didn't know what it was at first, but you turned to me in wonder. You couldn't have known, but that was the watcher in you. It's there; it's in your blood."

He lifts his arm towards the far corner of the room as if seeing a set of trees that weren't there.

"And there he was, southeast of where we was sitting. Your very first Trickster, not ten yards away. I whispered to you, tried to tell you where he was, but if I'm not mistaken, you shushed me and said you had to find him on your own. That you were big enough you didn't need my help."

He chuckles then, shaking his head, eyes filled with mirth and crinkled at the edges.

"You're a spitfire. Always have been. No, you didn't want my help. So, there you were. Tired. Dirty. Sweat through the armpits of your t-shirt. Face starting to burn—you wouldn't let me help put on your sunscreen. Hair a rat's nest from the hat. You were near tears as you turned this way and that in the middle of the woods, tryin' to find where the sound was coming from, first with your eyes and then with your binoculars when that didn't work."

His chuckle fades, and he closes the book with barely a sound. He looks at me with sadness and resignation in his eyes, brow furrowed and forehead creased.

"Sometimes the thing we need more than what we search for is the help to find it. To ask for the aid we need. Pride is the enemy of good. Remember that day? I took you in my arms, pulled the leaves out of your hair, taught you how to share where a bird is by time, like the hands of a clock. And you saw the Trickster for the first time. Help is there for the ones who ask."

He leans forward and pats my hand.

"All you have to do is ask."

NINE

THE DREAM REVERBERATES through my ear like a metronome, but I steel myself against its call. I won't be assuaged by
its siren's song, not with so much at stake.

For the next two days, we pour over each folder, each
paper, each line, with no success. My patience is razor-thin, and
I have taken to picking up random books off the back records
and reading through the sprawling script to calm myself. I'm
like a toddler carrying a favorite teddy or blanket; the familiar
loops and ink splotches soothe me.

"I'm through the last pile." Jethro has been determined to
finish the papers in front of us today, working steadfastly while
I tried to calm my nerves. I have to admire how dedicated he
is to our research. He is methodical and detail-oriented, taking

organized notes of anything he thinks might be relevant.

But so far, any hint of a lead has fizzled out. There has been one bankruptcy, two minor thefts, and a whole lot of noise complaints but nothing connected to Turney.

"I guess we could make our way through the older records. Maybe from the past six months?" I look at the large row of records dated from this year and bite my lip. The volume feels intimidating, insurmountable.

Jethro follows my gaze and walks over to the shelf. He runs his fingers along the edges of the folders. Looking over to me, he sends me a cheeky grin. "You know what I'm going to say."

I sigh. "I'm startin' to get your point." The admission wins me a light laugh. "I'll think about it, all right? I don't think we should jump on the digital train just because we can. What about tradition?"

He shrugs. "I don't get it if I'm honest. What keeps you coming back to all these old books? Don't get me wrong—I love books, I love knowledge. But I also like accessibility, technology, ease of use." He waves his hand in the direction of the way back shelves. "How can you find anything in these stacks? It would be better to digitize and store these properly. They should be preserved, kept safe."

I feel resistance bubbling but spending several days poring over paperwork with Jethro has built up my respect for him. He isn't an outsider, not really. He doesn't deserve my ire. I push it down and take a deep breath.

"Some of the important records we got in the library were

preserved and scanned. But that was done a long time ago when the money was there. There used to be a fracking company around here, so the town got a little money that way. But they got chased out, so we ain't got the funds no more. And anyway, what's the point in havin' our history if we can't see it, can't feel it? Here, look at this."

I go to a random shelf, way in the back where our oldest records are kept. I pull down a tattered, yellowed volume. Its dusty pages fragile, I hold it like a child, careful of the edges and cradling it.

I bring it over to the counter and Jethro follows. I set down the tome on the counter after wiping it down for any dust. Its cover is a dark brown pliable leather, no inscription on the front. I pull it open, the pages a deep yellow, brittle. I pick a random page, right in the middle, and open it so both of us can see.

"Look. It says it's from 1892. It's all handwritten, every single record. And some of the people who worked in this office—well, maybe not this office but wherever it was—they wrote down what the weather was like, who was doing what, everythin'."

I lightly trace the edge of the pages, not wanting to get the oil from my fingers on the pages proper. When I see an interesting section, I point at the swooping text, careful not to touch it. "Look, here's all handwritten accounts about death rates that year. Scribbled verse too."

Jethro pushes up his glasses and leans forward, squinting to read it. After a moment, he shakes his head and rubs the back of his neck. "I can't read that. Can you?"

"I can read some of it; the rest is all worn away. 'If Trick-sters fly from sprig to bough, trilling notes of fear. Their duet is a warning cry, The Reapers soon draw near.'" I point to a particular section that's underlined. "See that? Death records from something called The Reaper. No idea what that is, though."

"The Trickster? Really? That nonsense goes all the way back that far?"

"It's not nonsense." I gently close the book, laying it flat on the counter. I lightly draw my fingers along the side of the binding. "I wanted to know about our history. So yeah, I taught myself how to read it."

He bumps his shoulder against mine, and I look up at him startled. I must look angry because he pulls back suddenly. He recovers quickly though, leaning against the counter next to me.

"That's impressive, you know. We have algorithms that can read a lot of text, but the more decorated, the harder it is for the computers. Some stuff has to be transcribed by hand. I bet you could do that; you'd be good at it."

I bite my lip and tap my fingers on the counter, staring off at the opposite wall. I debate my words before deciding that he might understand. "It's stories I like," I say. "All sorts of them. These records are our past, the tales passed down from records keeper to records keeper. How can I not love them?"

I walk back into the stacks and locate a book I'd purposely left not-quite flush against the others so I could find it easily.

It's a brown hardback, crumpled along the edges, but it still holds as I place it on the table.

"See this? A Citizens record from way back. Names, dates, and apparently this particular records keeper was a bit of an artist because there are drawings in the margins. Birds mostly, of course."

Moving towards the bookshelves, I look on another shelf for a book I know is hiding there. I spot the light tan spine and pull it out, bring it back to the table, and set it next to the others. After flipping through a little bit, I find the page I was looking for.

"See here?" I point to a line of text set in a table, the black ink more legible than the earlier records. "This is from when my grandma died from complications from a snake bite. My Uncle Jeremy don't talk about her much, but there's records of her marriage, her birth certificate, land ownership, everythin'. I can connect with her even though I never met her."

I look back at him, and he's got an expression on his face I can't quite read. I take heart that it's not confusion, at least.

"You know," he says, then pauses. He folds his arms and leans his back against the counter. "I guess I can understand. It's why I love the library sciences. Yeah, we disagree on the vehicle which the stories should take, but I think we agree on their value, their importance. We will only ever repeat the past if we don't learn from it."

I let out a hum, lean my elbows forward onto the counter and stare off again. "I think it's more complicated than that."

"How so?" he asks, and there's no anger in his tone, only curiosity.

"Well, the victors tell the stories. And that goes for secondary and tertiary sources. People re-write history all the time for their own gains. Everyone hides the truth for their shame. Even primary sources are biased. I don't think we can ever know the godly truth, and so we relearn from the same tragedies over and over."

I brush the hair out of my eyes and turn my head to face him. He's smiling the softest smile I've ever seen on his face, crooked on one side, eyes filled with mirth.

"We have a scholar," he says and chuckles. "Can I be honest and say I never would have guessed that about you?"

I let out an honest to goodness growl and slap him lightly on the arm. We both freeze for a moment, me in embarrassment and him stricken. After a moment, he lets out a nervous laugh, which turns into a real laugh when I smile back at him, shaking my head.

"You gotta stop saying shit like that. You dun know anythin' at all about me, City Boy. This is the start."

He sobers a bit after a moment, and he leans on the counter, avoiding my gaze. "I do have one question, actually. Seems how we're talking about the history of the town and all that. Anything in these books explain why everyone's so wary of the Citizens?"

I frown, closing the books and piling them together to put them back where they belong. I tap the topmost one for a moment, trying to gather my thoughts.

"I don't rightly know, to be honest. It's always been that way. I don't know if people are afraid of what they don't know, but we don't do anythin' bad. I don't understand it myself. The Trickster is a challenge, not a god. You'd think we were worshiping it for all they go on about us."

I straighten, stretching my arms in front of me. "Time to get back to work, I think."

He follows my lead, stretches to his full height, then lets out a groan. "My eyes are going to go cross-eyed if I look at any more noise complaints."

I smirk without pity. "You'll live."

—

I'm stacking the folders we've already been through into a neat pile by date when Jethro's phone rings. It's a tinny, 8-bit song I don't recognize, probably from a video game. I watch from the corner of my eye as he frowns and declines the call. It's the third such call in the past hour, and I can't kick my curiosity. He seems to be progressively more frustrated with the caller if how tightly he's clutching his pen and how he curls over the page is any indication.

I have a few options. I could leave it alone, which is what I'd normally do. I've never been much for friends. As a kid, I was the pariah, keeping to myself, and unsurprisingly, the other kids let me. I was too brash and critical for anything else. But there was something about his hunched shoulders and how he was biting his lip that made my chest constrict. It was an unfamiliar feeling, and I didn't like it.

"Who was that?" I finally ask. I try to sound uninterested, but I realize belatedly it sounds more accusing than anything. Too late to take it back.

He scrunches up his nose and mouth. He looks uncomfortable at my question, but he answers anyway. "My dad. We're having an argument, so he's being extra controlling."

It's not what I expected, and apparently, I don't keep the feeling from making its way into my expression going by his snort. He laughs for a moment, but a little of the tension seeps from him so I count it a win.

"What's the argument about? Not that it's any of my business," I add quickly. I'm not a gossip like Sean.

He shrugs, and the mirth in his expression turns sour. "It's about my grandpa. I told you he's why we're here, to take care of him. We're arguing about his wishes."

I scrunch my brow, frowning. "What does that mean? His wishes about what?"

Jethro stretches his arms back behind him, and I can hear the crack from where I sit. I wonder that he's still indulging my curiosity, and the feeling it gives me is foreign. Warm, vulnerable. I don't know if I like it.

When he's done stretching, he turns in his seat towards me and leans one arm onto the counter. "His wishes for when he dies. My family is Catholic, so my dad is adamant that my grandfather be buried in the cemetery. But my grandfather wants to be cremated. He doesn't want us to deal with the cost and to feel like we have to come back to visit his grave. He wants to have his ashes spread in the woods here and that be that. I think we should honor what he wants, but Dad disagrees. He's trying to buy a plot."

I can feel the blood drain my face as Jethro talks, my gaze focused on his lips as they move but it blurs at the edges. I know I should respond, *but it's too soon.*

"Wren?" I hear him ask, and it brings me out of the waters I was drowning in, just enough. "Wren, you okay?"

I close my eyes and inhale a deep breath, then breathe out slowly. Jethro is quiet, probably sensing I need a moment, and I'm grateful for his instincts. When I open my eyes, his face is filled with concern.

"Wren," he repeats, "you still with me?"

"Yeah," I respond, though my voice feels far away and like it echoes in the small room. "Yeah, I'm fine. Pulled back that time."

Jethro rubs at his face and covers his eyes, shaking his head the whole time. "God, I'm so sorry. I shouldn't have dropped that on you like that. You barely know me, and that was a lot. Ugh, I'm such a dunce."

I let out a soft laugh, but I don't think he hears me. His embarrassment and concern are endearing as much as I hate to admit it. I lean forward in my chair and poke his hands where they're still covering his face. He peeks through a few of his fingers, and I give him a sly smile.

"Don't think you can scare me away with that. You just caught me off guard."

He drops his hands to his knees with a slap, sighing. "Still.

That was a lot to dump on you."

I shrug. "Normally I wouldn't care. Only…" I pause, not sure how to proceed.

But Jethro surprises me. "Your uncle?"

My brow furrows in surprise, afraid he'd been listening to gossip.

"The sheriff mentioned him is all," he continues, hands raised in defense. "She said that finding the killer wouldn't bring him back. Was he…murdered?"

I shake my head, look down at my hands, and pick at my fingers as I debate how to answer. I'd never been asked. News spreads like wildfire in this town. I'd not had to explain to a single soul what had happened, and I found the prospect daunting. I'm unsure how to proceed, but when I think about it, I'm surprised that I *want* to tell him, to talk about it. I find the words falling from my lips without thinking them through.

"He died," I say, but my words come in stilted waves, stuttering and frail where they'd normally be brass and fire. "It was an accident. Or it was no one's fault. We were in the woods…he didn't make it. That was a few weeks ago. So when you started talkin' bout cremation…well. I had to make that decision on my own. I had him buried. I live here, so it made sense. I can visit him. But you don't, so." I shrug, hoping he understands what I mean through my incoherent babble.

I jump when I feel his fingertips touch mine. It's a gentle swipe before they drop back, but it stops me from picking my fingers to bleeding. When I look up at him, he has a gentle look on his face, amber brown eyes filled with compassion, and I feel a crack in my armor.

"You can talk to me," he says, his voice is a near whisper. "I'll listen."

The moment is precious and far too intimate, and it strikes fear like a stinging pain in my veins. I turn my gaze away, folding my arms and tucking my hands to my sides where he can't reach them, trying to forget the phantom touch when for a moment, I didn't feel so alone.

"I'll remember that," I say anyway. "Thank you."

I clear my throat and look up at the analog clock hanging on the wall, an excuse to break the moment. "It's getting late. We should probably put this all back in case Mrs. Delaney is in tomorrow. Don't want her to know we been snoopin'."

I hear the creak of the chair as he gets up and avoid looking at him as I pick up folders to put away. I'm shoving them into their proper place on the shelf when I find my bravery and hardheadedness again and make a decision. I force myself to look over while he's texting someone—probably his dad— and force my voice to a normal volume.

"Want to grab somethin' to eat before you head home?"

——

The diner is filled with the typical sounds of muffled chatter, the sharp clang of plates and silverware, and the low drawl of Johnny Cash over the crinkly speakers.

Walking through the antique wood doorway of the diner

feels like a rite of passage, like I'm bringing in an outsider to the fold of something sacred. I wonder if the lanky City Boy understands the significance, but he's been somewhat unaware of the gravity and meaning of these things in the past, so I let it go without comment.

Lisa comes up to us wearing the maroon shirt and name tag of the diner's staff, wispy ash-colored hair in somewhat disarray—probably from the dinnertime rush. "Just the two of ya, hun?" she asks in a clipped tone, and I don't miss her gaze lingering on Jethro. Everyone knows everyone in this town, which means everyone knows when someone doesn't belong.

And everyone is in everyone else's business.

"This is Jethro. He's helpin' out Mrs. Delaney while his family's in town," I explain, hoping to give context for an outsider being on her turf. "Thought I'd show him the best place to get a decent meal." My grin is crooked, and Lisa eyes me with doubt.

"Whatever, hun. There's a booth down here in the corner." She turns away, eyeing Jethro one more time before leading us to the back corner of the room.

The booth is lined with red vinyl, the wood scratched and the laminate peeling in places. It has never bothered me, but as Jethro carefully takes his seat, I have a brief moment of embarrassment. I squash it, reminding myself I don't care what Jethro thinks. The food will be worth it, after all.

Once we've sat, Lisa hands us laminated menus and turns away, walking to another table. The silence after her departure lingers, and I busy myself looking at the menu I know by heart.

Not much has changed in it my whole life.

I suddenly have a memory as my eyes slide over the kid's menu. Me, sitting in this exact seat, barely tall enough to see over the edge of the booth, hair cropped short and falling into my dark brown eyes. My Uncle Jeremy on the other side, smiling with his yellowed, crooked teeth and goatee, asking me if I had the appetite for the big girl menu this time. My adamance that I wanted to order off the big *person* menu, not the big girl menu. His frown, then a soft look in his eyes, a look of understanding.

He knew before I did the road I'd tread, and he loved me no differently for it.

I feel the choke before I hear it but can't pull it back. My eyes sting, and I lower my head, hoping my hair will cover my eyes. They were harder now than in my memory but the same brightness.

"You okay?" Jethro asks, and there's concern in his tone. I clear my throat and straighten my back. I look him square in the eye, then nod my head in the direction behind him.

"Seems now you're here," I say, keeping my voice clear and strong, "I should tell you about the people you're likely to meet, yeah?"

He turns around to look behind him, spying several groups of people in the diner behind us, all distracted by their own conversations. Except for one that steals glances our way occasionally. It's three men, heads all shaved, several with dark tattoos along their neck, and two women, one with brunette hair pulled back in a high ponytail, the other with light blonde hair falling loose. They all give off an air of unapproachability at best.

"Them," I say as he turns back, knowing he's seen them. "Stay away from them. Bigots the lot of 'em. Give them a wide berth—I do. Sheriff June doesn't tolerate bullshit in this town, so they probably won't do nuthin', but best not to let them try anythin' anyhow."

He nods, lips tight. "That's what I was afraid of when Dad said we'd be moving down here a while. 'Everyone's afraid of outsiders, so don't give them a reason to question you,' is what he said. But I noticed once we got into the highways down here, Dad didn't like to stop anywhere, even for gas. It freaked me out to be honest. I wondered what we were walking into."

I nod at that. "Most people are like that. You got your grandpa here, so you'll get somewhat of a pass, but those guys...they give me trouble. Freak of nature, he-she, all that crap they go on about. Fortunately, they're all talk. Can't say the same about all the towns 'round here, so be careful where you go drivin' around. But Sheriff June doesn't let that stuff go past talk."

He picks at the edge of the menu, avoiding my eyes. "Anyone else I should worry about?"

I lean back, turn my head up for a moment in thought. "They're the worst. There are a couple others that are mean but will do you no harm besides a stray word here and there. Tom and Eddie are braggity and they're here a lot. Tom especially is a liar; his dogs won't come when he calls 'em. Don't listen to a word he says."

I shrug, tapping the menu with my hand idly. "Other than that, keep your wits about you. People here won't trust ya, I'll tell you that, but they won't do you any harm if you keep to yourself and don't cause trouble."

His smile is rueful, hurt in his eyes. "Just like you don't?"

The guilt is a pinch in my stomach, and I turn my eyes away to look back down at the menu. "I'm startin' to." The words seem weak, but I won't lie.

He nods though, satisfied with my honesty. We're silent while he looks down at the menu, and I watch as his eyes move back and forth, scanning it. Up close, I can see dark freckles along his cheeks, hidden by his oversized glasses. His eyes are dark but not all black, a chestnut brown that looks darker if not in direct light, which he's in now. It's the first good, close-up look I've had at him.

I startle when I see his eyes locked on me now, and I force myself not to turn away. "Decide what you want?" I ask.

He doesn't answer. He sets down his menu with barely a sound, continuing to look straight into my eyes.

"Why are you helping me?" he asks. "Why take me to dinner, tell me who to watch out for? Don't you hate outsiders?"

Anger builds but I push it down. He isn't wrong. In all honesty, I'm questioning my own actions. But he's done nothing but try to help. He deserves to know.

"I'm helping you because you're helping us," I say, knowing how it sounds. "But it's more than that," I continue quickly. "You probably noticed this town isn't exactly rich, yeah?"

He frowns, turns his gaze away out of guilt. "I had... noticed, yeah."

I shrug, used to it. Unsurprised. "It wasn't always this way, apparently. Most towns around here don't like outsiders, but we used to be dependent on 'em for income. Used to be we had tourists come through, and the town thrived for a while. Not rich, rich, but we managed. Then the fracking started and the tourists left, but at least the gas company paid the bills. When that stopped too, there was nothing left to keep us afloat. Least that's what Uncle Jeremy and Mrs. Delaney would say—that was way before my time."

I lean back, picking at the hangnails on my fingers as I talk to avoid his gaze. "When outsiders stopped coming, people stopped trustin'. That's what Uncle Jeremy said. Hell, he was young when it started going south even. But when all you have is each other, everyone else seems like a threat. A threat to everything we got left to cling to. We help our own, but everyone else? They abandoned us. Why should we go out of our way for them?"

When I catch his gaze again, he's deep in thought, head tilted as he considers. "So it's us versus them sort of?"

I shrug and drum my fingers on the table. "Not exactly. We don't wanna fight with anyone. We just wanna be left alone. You're not asking for nuthin', though. So what's there for us to lose?"

Lisa approaches, bringing our conversation to a halt. As Jethro stutters through his order, I watch him, considering. About what Uncle Jeremy said about the outsiders, how the town clung to every bit to survive, why it all went down…and I'm filled with questions. Ones that seemingly have no answers.

—

No one speaks as we hand out candles and cardboard circles to catch the wax. It's like we are all working as one unit, everyone hushed and lethargic. Like any sudden movement will break a spell. Clouds dissuade the moon from shining down on us, leaving us whispering to each other in complete darkness as we work. I wonder at how appropriate it is that even the moon doesn't want to be witness to the procession. None of us wanted to be here, but we cling to the promise of catharsis with desperate hearts.

We huddle in a group in front of the Town Center sign, carved long ago by Adrian Turney himself. Flowers litter the grass in front of it, a vinyl sign with his name, a photo, and 'RIP' caught between two wooden dowels in the ground. The darkness feels oppressive, our lit candles the only things keeping the shadows at bay.

Even breathing breaks the silence, the sound loud to my own ears. There are hunched, quivering shoulders and hugs being exchanged, catches of light on tears as people mingle, dauntless against the tide of grief that threatens to overwhelm us.

Our community is shaken, but we won't be overcome.

Molly and Nathaniel inch towards the front of the sign, and Nathaniel sets down a large bouquet in front of it before they both turn toward us. Molly raises her voice, and it cuts the shadows like a knife.

"We're here tonight to honor Adrian Turney, a Citizen, one of our own, a wonderful father, grandfather, and a light in this town." There's a pause, and Nathaniel wraps an arm around her. "Adrian was a fixture that was always willin' to help, always there with a smile, and always one to lend an ear if ya needed it."

As Molly speaks, I spy a figure towards the back, not holding a candle and near covered in shadow. It's Leigh, Turney's granddaughter, holding her arms with her hands. She stares at the vinyl sign, unblinking.

I'm not necessarily surprised to see her—the vigil was planned by the Citizens, but anyone in town was of course invited, especially family of Turney. I wonder at her holding herself so far away from us, and I try not to grumble out loud about letting her fear of the Citizens burden her against taking the comfort we offered. *We're not just doing this for Turney.*

Molly finishes her speech and invites others to stand up and say some words. Carrie talks about how Turney had helped her when her second child was born pre-maturely five years ago, taking her to the doctor's office a town over—back when Turney was able to drive that far. Tom mumbles through a half-assed speech, crocodile tears we all know as him and Turney never got along.

When the crowd of people wanting to speak thins, I feel a compulsion, but it wars with my nature. I glance back and see Leigh is gone, and though I feel guilt at the thought that her not being here to witness my fumbling gives me the strength to stand in front of the sign.

There's silence as everyone watches me. It occurs to me that though I can name everyone in the town, where they live, and who they're related to, I haven't spoken one on one with many of them. *How out of character it must seem for me to speak.* But then I think of Adrian, the empty workshop, the research left to us to do in the office to find the killer, and it gives me a burst of courage.

"My Uncle Jeremy and Adrian Turney were like peas in a pod," I start but stumble. I shove my hands in my pockets and look down at the grass to avoid the stares of the other Citizens. "Losing both of 'em like this...I don't know what I'll do with myself. It's like ya don't know the people that are holding you up until they're gone, and then you're stuck swimming in a river against the current and there ain't anybody to pull ya from it."

I sigh and shake my head. *This isn't about me.* "Some people you can forget. Heaven knows we all know each other more than we'd like. But people leave, and you forget them after a while. It becomes 'you remember so and so' for a while, but eventually, they're only a memory."

I sniff, the sound loud in the night, trying to keep myself together. Suddenly, I'm aware of the wall of sound around us—the crickets, two owls calling to each other in the night, the rustling of leaves. *They would have loved that.*

"You won't forget Uncle Jeremy and Adrian Turney. They're a part of this town, no matter how long they're gone. They built us up with their actions and their words, and no amount of time will change that. This town owes them a lot, and the best I guess we can do is keep building it up. Build each other up. Like they would."

"That's all I have to say, I guess." I kick at a few stones and shrug, gaze straying to the edge of the woods, to where Turney drew his last breath. "I won't forget either of 'em. I can't."

Molly comes up and touches my arm, gives me a soft smile, and I take my cue to fall back to the crowd. I try to disappear into the night, and the shadows embrace me in their darkness. Out of the corner of my eye, I spot Leigh again, walking towards the Town Center and her car, shoulders hunched and shaking.

I know she won't forget them either, and it brings me the first comfort I've known in a long time.

TEN

A CALL TO MRS. DELANEY to check on her puts my mind at ease the next morning. Too many goodbyes, too many questions, and I need to know the one person I have left standing as a monument in my life is all right. She reassures me that it's nothing out of the ordinary, just a flare up, and though there's an ache in my chest that there's no way to ever know for sure, I have to trust she knows her own body.

I'm determined to make headway as I walk through the door to the records office. When I enter through the hatch in the counter, I see that Jethro has beaten me here and is staring at the computer. He barely raises his head in greeting, and I wonder what has him so fixated.

"What're you doing?" I ask. My voice has an

unintended edge to it. I don't know what I'll do if he says he's digitizing more records.

He looks up at me briefly, taps the mouse a few times, then turns the creaky chair so he's facing me.

"There's something you should look at," he starts, then pauses. "I wasn't going to say anything, but I realized that the records system here actually is the same as the sheriff's department. It was probably to save money to keep it all in one system rather than build it separately, I think, because the records are supposed to be protected. I can't access everything, but some of it is un-encrypted."

I raise my eyebrows and lean closer to see the screen, but Jethro blocks my view with his hands. "We had a graduate student a while ago from the town come back and volunteer to get the town hall's file system up to date," I say, "but I know Sean is always complaining they took short-cuts." I try to peek through his fingers. "Why didn't you say so earlier?"

"Because it's super illegal! What we're doing already toes the line, but there's no question of legality with this. They're not public records, and some of them are encrypted. I can get past it…but should I?"

I lean back in surprise, looking at him with appraisal. "You mean you can hack it? Where you learn that?"

He rubs his neck, avoiding my gaze. "You learn how to hack to prevent others from hacking you. It just so happens I'm good at it."

I lean back from the computer, from him, and consider

his words. "You said you weren't going to say nuthin'. What changed your mind?"

He sighs a harsh breath. He runs his hand through his dark curled hair. "The diner, yesterday. You were giving me a lot of trust and, well, I should trust you back. We don't have to do this, but I couldn't keep it from you either. It might help us, but we have to be certain it's the right thing to do."

I nod, understanding his initial hesitance and respecting his trust. Jet is right—if we hack into the sheriff's records, there's no denying the lengths we'll go to find the killer. There'll be no halfway about it anymore; we'll be in it completely, and there may be consequences.

Our choices are limited. Anything in the sheriff records are things that Sheriff June already knows. The only thing we could gain from the knowledge is if that related to something Sheriff June knew and we didn't.

"The full autopsy report," I say. "We'll look for that. I saw her initial assessment. There might be something more in the blood tests or somethin' else that was missed at first. But that's all we'll look at unless we find something important. I've already seen the initial report, so it ain't much more than we've already done."

He bites his lip, eyes turned away, and I know he's thinking through my words, debating their merit. He's methodical, so if there's any weakness to my logic, I know he'll discover it, and I find I respect him all the more for his careful considerations.

"Yeah, that's true," he says finally. "It's very specific,

something you've already seen, and probably isn't too much of a hack to begin with."

"How long will it take?" I ask.

He taps his finger to his chin a few times, eyes focused on the screen. "Probably an hour." He moves the mouse around, eyes completely focused on the screen. "I'll have to get out my laptop; this system isn't powerful enough to do what I need to do, and I need programs from it."

He stands up from the chair, stretching his arms over his head, head tilting back. "Maybe you can get sorting done while I work on this? Sean brought a few more files back. Don't want you to be bored, and we probably shouldn't look like we were slacking anyway."

The delegation itches at being bossed around by him, but I let it go. He picks up his bag, pulling a sleek silver laptop from it along with a thin white power cord. I turn away, realizing that while I want the results, the idea of hacking into the sheriff office's records system sets goosebumps up my arms. It's a violation of trust I didn't think I'd ever consider.

I set myself to work sorting through the pile of folders Sean must have brought by before I got here. It's not huge and not going to take me very long, but it's better than sitting on my hands as I set my newest—and really, only—friend to breaking the law.

—

"Hey, Wren, I got something."

I drop the files I'd been working on, and I'm across the room before I can consciously tell my legs to move.

"You get in?" I ask, and I lean over his shoulder, one hand against the countertop to his right.

"I got the autopsy report. It's a scan, but we should be able to read it." He pulls up a file onto the screen, the words 'Final Autopsy' printed in dark, muted green on the top, the rest typed in a different font. I see Turney's full name, date of birth, and estimated time of death. All standard information, though the time of death is a range rather than a specific date. Not unexpected.

"Can you scroll down?" I ask. He moves the cursor down, scrolling through more of the document.

The majority of the autopsy is undecipherable to me, measurements and weights of different organs and tissues. It's long, the words blurring together into blocks of text in front of my eyes.

"Can you understand any of this?" Jethro asks, and I shake my head. There are a few things that pop out at me but nothing relevant.

"Sharp force injury, incised wound on the gastrocnemius, posteroanterior... Oh, wait—here," Jethro says, pausing towards the end of the document. "There's a findings summary. If there's anything important, it would be there."

I look where he's pointing at the screen, trying to understand the medical terminology.

"Hypertension? That's high blood pressure, right? Somethin' about damage to the heart, too." I turn to Jethro, who's biting his lips as he studies the paragraph.

"You know what I'm not seeing though?" he says, then pauses for a moment. He moves up the document, then back down. "I see note of the wounds, but it doesn't seem to be the cause of death."

"That don't make any sense." I shove his hand off the mouse, scrolling through the document to try to understand the jargon. There are notes about a large knife wound along his leg, several knife wounds on his hands, but it doesn't seem to have been large enough to be the cause of death or sustained enough to bleed out. Just like Jethro said, the cause of death is listed as heart failure.

"So this wasn't murder? I don't understand," Jethro says, leaning back in the chair and letting his head fall onto the back of it. He's staring at the ceiling with a pensive look on his face.

I shake my head and cross my arms. "But someone still attacked him. Maybe they were going after him, chasin' him, but his heart killed him first."

Jethro shrugs, head still focused on the ceiling. He's quiet like I've never seen him be before.

I nudge his shoulder with my hand. "Hey. Come on. We can still figure this out."

He shakes his head and rubs his hands over his face before looking up at me, head still tilted back. "I don't know, Wren. This is complicated. I don't think we should be getting involved in this any more than we have. I don't think it's as cut and dry as we thought. I can't understand most of what was in that document and what I do understand leaves me with more questions than answers."

I throw my hands up in the air. "Come on, Jethro. We've come this far. We gotta see this through. Someone attacked Turney, and we can't let 'em get away."

He points at a line in the text. "Wren, look. A long wound in the lower leg. What kind of murderer slices someone in the calf? For shits and giggles? And how, even? How would someone have reached his calf but not his throat? He could have tripped on something that sliced him up and he bled out and that's it. No murder, no foul play."

Jethro leans forward in the chair, setting his elbows on his knees and looking me in the eye. "Plus, Sheriff June has already seen all this. She knows more than we do, done this longer than we have, has the experience to figure it out. Maybe we should give it a rest."

I feel a tightness in my chest, and I know I'm losing him. I can't explain why this is so important; I don't know myself. Or I don't want to admit it. Turney was Uncle Jeremy's mentor—could have been *my* mentor—and I feel robbed of the chance, of the future I should have been given.

"Let's take a break, yeah? We'll figure out what to do tomorrow." I turn away, moving toward where I'd dropped the papers and shuffling them into some semblance of order.

"Wren," he says, then sighs. I'm turned away from him, but I can hear the squeak of the chair as he gets up and a few footsteps as he comes to my side.

He sets his hand on top of mine where I'm fiddling with the corners of the papers. My first instinct is to pull away, but I push the reflex down. I need him on my side.

I turn towards him, look him dead in the eyes, and speak with conviction I don't feel.

"Let's sleep on it," I say. "We'll figure out what to do tomorrow. I need time, Jet."

I can tell by the way his face softens that it's the nickname that gets him. I feel a churning in my stomach. I can't let it go, and it's turning my insides.

"Alright. We'll talk tomorrow. It's time to call it a day anyway." He lets me go, walks to his laptop, and puts it away.

I watch him with a dying determination.

—

After everything I've been through the last month, getting groceries seems like such a mundane task that I nearly skip it and resign myself to eating expired ramen. Instead, I find myself at the small grocer on the way back from Town Hall.

The run-down, yellowed mural of vegetables along the outside wall of the shop would probably deter any newcomers to town, but I know Sophie's is the best and near only place to get good produce outside the farmer's market. It was also the only place I can realistically afford with a dwindling savings account.

The bell chimes to announce my entrance, and I warily scan the aisles, not wanting to talk to anyone after the day's events. I grab a cart and wheel it towards the produce section, an off-white set of peeling refrigeration units that hum steadily.

Slow country plays over the speakers, the sound scratchy from the old audio unit.

The shop may be run down, but Sophie runs a tight ship. Everything is clean, albeit needing to be replaced. I browse through the tomatoes, bright red and plump, picking out a few before moving onto the cucumbers.

"Wren, hun? That you?"

I turn to see Molly, sans Nathaniel, pushing a cart with a squeaky wheel towards me as she rounds the corner of the international food aisle. She's grinning, none of the wariness the other townspeople got when they saw me. I have a reputation for being unapproachable, and that suits me fine. Molly, however, seems impervious to it. *She's too nice for her own good.*

"I'm so glad to see ya here. I was going to try to contact you. You know how the town is; we heard you been asking around about odd jobs, and I thought I'd give ya a call."

Odd jobs? I haven't asked anything of the sort, but it doesn't take long for me to figure out who could have dropped the hint. *Mrs. Delaney, that scheming old grandma. Always trying to take care of me.*

"Well, I hadn't thought about it, but I can't really say no," I pause, "If you have somethin', that is."

Her expression twists into pity, and I grind my teeth at the implication. *I'm not poor. I'm having some trouble, that's all. I don't need your sympathy.*

"What you have in mind?" I ask instead, though it burns.

She beams wider at that, and I can see excitement in her stance. "Well, I know your Uncle Jeremy taught you all sorts of carpentry, and we're going to be re-doing the deck at Nathaniel's. I thought you'd be perfect for the job!"

My heart drops. "I'm sorry, Molly. I'm great at whittlin' and carvin', but I don't know if I can build a whole deck There's a lot of engineering that goes into it, and ain't that kind of woodworker."

She pats my arm, and I clench my jaw at the assumed familiarity. *What is it with everyone thinking because I'm grieving, they can touch me?*

"Of course I wouldn't ask you to do it all on your own, hun. Nathaniel is hiring Oscar to manage. You'd be doing mostly labor, and he'd teach you construction. Isn't that wonderful? I know you have woodworkin' skills, but I thought it'd be good for you to learn more so you can do a variety of work. Kind of like a mentorship."

For a moment, I stare at her, and the silence becomes awkward before I gather myself.

"That would be great, actually." My voice is uncharacteristically quiet, consumed by my gratitude. I hadn't thought of expanding my abilities when it came to woodworking, but if I was able to handle construction on top of carving that opened up a lot of possibilities for jobs around town. *Maybe I'm not as alone as I thought.*

"Well, you're a Citizen, Wren. We look out for each other, always." Her expression turns sad and wistful. "Adrian Turney believed that, and I know he would have mentored you himself if he could have. The least we can do as a community is make sure the people he loved are taken care of."

The people he loved... I feel a bunching in my throat, so I nod my thanks.

We exchange idle chatter, and while it normally would grate, for once I feel comfortable and thankful for the inanity. We walk down the aisles, her carelessly adding things to her cart and me more carefully choosing the cheapest and most logical options.

When we get to the register, I check out first, and before I can protest, Molly pays for my groceries with a cheerful grin and a wink. "Just this once, let me help, Wren."

I should feel hurt from the charity, but my chest feels warm.

It's when I'm loading the groceries into the back of my car that a plan begins to form. One that I know Jethro would never approve of, but there's no going back. I think of Uncle Jeremy, and Adrian Turney, and the problem I've in front of me.

Turney never turned his back on a problem. He would have done something.

I can't let it go.

ELEVEN

THE FENCE IS AN EASY HURDLE TO PASS. I know from the lack of barking on my initial walk around his yard that Turney's dog is no longer here. The fence is more decoration than anything, a waist-height faded white picket that could use a whitewash. I grab one of the sturdiest panels and carefully vault over it.

This is stupid, and I know it. But there's something we're missing in this whole mystery, and my gut tells me that Turney's home is the next best place to look. Jethro will be furious when—if—I tell him, but there's something niggling at me from the autopsy report. I have to see this through.

I keep my eyes on either side of the house as I walk towards the front steps. They're cracked but not crumbling, a weathered gnome with a red hat sitting to the right of the door. Surely it couldn't be that easy?

It isn't, of course. I pick up the gnome and there's nothing but a few ants that escape their hiding place. I search around but there are no more obvious stones or places to hide a key.

I open the screen door, wince as it squeaks, but the air around me is devoid of any noise except for crickets. I try the door handle, hoping to get lucky, but even though it moves slightly as I push, the lock catches.

I let out a huff and look around, hoping for inspiration to strike. I eye a window to my right, but it's high enough that I won't be able to reach it without a ladder or stool.

I step back and close the screen door with another squeak. Moving down the steps, I follow the sloped yard up, hoping the added height on this side of the house would allow for a window nearer my reach. Turning the corner, I spy a lone window at the top of where I would be able to crawl in.

This side of the house is in full darkness, and I give my eyes time to adjust. When the window looks less like a black maw and more like a wooden windowsill with a screen, I push the screen up, then test the window itself. Fortunately, it gives, moving up in stutters but up all the same.

When it's as open as it will go, I pull myself up, cognizant of the area in front of me and hoping I'm not coming in right above the sink.

There's nothing in front of me, so I shimmy my body through, land hands first, and pull my legs all the way in. When I'm back on my feet I look around. I'm in a hallway, and though it's dark in this room, there's a fluorescent light over the kitchen sink towards my right.

I'm three feet into the kitchen when it hits me that this isn't my brightest moment.

I've never actually stepped foot in Turney's home—apparently, he was a bit of a hoarder. There are papers stacked high on every shelf, table, and parts of the floor. My idea of 'quick in, quick out' flies out the window as I eye the room with a sinking feeling.

I pick up a few papers here and there, hoping to luck out and find a recent notice or letter to indicate a motive or any indication that he had enemies. Instead, everything is out of order, dates ranging from six months past to several years. Old newspaper clippings from the home and garden section, old bills marked 'paid' with a red pen, letters from his granddaughter.

I look carefully through the latter but nothing sticks out. Jethro and I had seen the paperwork to dismiss Turney's debts in the records office, mostly medical. There was no life insurance or money to be made off his death, which in my mind means that a murderer in the family is unlikely. And though I'd not seen them interact that often, from the sounds of his granddaughter Leigh's letter as I read through it, there is nothing but love left in that family.

The number of papers are insurmountable in the time I have, so I give up looking, deciding if there is something to be found, it will have to be something recent. All the papers in this room are yellowed and musty. If there's a clue to be found in them, I won't be the one to find it.

I walk further into the kitchen, noticing the half-cleaned counter and that there are no dishes anywhere along the sink—and no dishwasher. Someone has been by to clean up. I hold my breath and pull open the fridge, but it's empty except for a few cans of beer and an old ketchup bottle. *It must have been emptied already.*

I close the fridge, looking around for signs of any places that are undisturbed. Or rather, more likely disturbed by Turney than his family cleaning up after him. The kitchen is a dead end, so I go through the doorway, past an old velvet painting of a cat and a photograph of someone I don't recognize.

The living room is a museum to wood. Tan wood paneling along the walls, an antique wooden cuckoo clock hanging above a cherry wood desk, carved wood birds, cats, and deer situated on dark wood shelves. The room feels dark, ancient. A mod podge of disparate tones and textures.

The sub-floor creaks under my feet as I cross the hunter green carpet, the smell of dust and mildew strong in the air. I scan every surface for something to pop out. There's a brown, worn corduroy armchair in the corner opposite the TV on a dark brown TV stand. A light tan side table covered in papers and pill bottles sits next to it, overflowing with papers that are then scattered onto the ground.

I shuffle through the pile, the papers whiter and crisper than the papers I've seen in other areas of the house. Mail, much of it unopened. I check the return addresses—most of them are from a hospital a town over. They're likely bills from the signs of the different colored papers I can spy inside the envelopes. One green, two pink. Past due notices. These ones specify the orthopedic center. I vaguely remember that Turney had hip replacement surgery a while back. Was he not able to make the payments?

I notice one that specifies the oncology center, the letter a bright white and the only one of its kind. Possibly a recent diagnosis then? When I turn the envelope over, I see it's been opened, meaning it won't be noticed if I take a look at its contents. A breach of privacy, sure, but I moved far past that the moment I crawled through the window.

I carefully peel back the opening and pull out the letter. It's several pages, but I know the bulk of it will be in the first few paragraphs.

I knew somehow what it would show, but my heart sinks confirmation. It aches with a maelstrom of emotion—sadness, bitterness, confusion, betrayal.

A new diagnosis. Spinal Glioblastoma Multiforme. I don't entirely recognize the context, but I know enough to understand it's lethality. I read on, noticing the breakdown of approved treatments, treatments that would not save but put off the inevitable.

He hadn't told me. He hadn't told Uncle Jeremy, as far as I knew. It felt like a betrayal for all it wasn't our business. Would he ever have told me?

But something else stirs in the back of my mind. A memory.

Everyone knew everyone else's business in this town. And

though I didn't run in the same circles as Leigh, words had a life of their own. I remember second-hand gossip that she'd been run ragged trying to keep up with Turney's needs. I'd been furious at her at the time, but with Uncle Jeremy dying soon after, I hadn't thought much of it.

With a sinking feeling, I replace the envelope and look towards the top tier of the side table, covered in orange prescription bottles, organized into two sections.

With care, I look at each- vitamins, pain medication, and one empty. I look at the label, noting the date- a little over a month ago. There's a post-it note next to it with the words 'refill' and a date—a week ago. The prescribing doctor is local, so probably his general practitioner. The medication is Warfarin. I wrack my brain to remember its purpose. Blood thinner? For heart disease, high blood pressure? If so, he shouldn't have been without it.

The sinking feeling goes deeper, and I start looking around the room, then the kitchen for another bottle of the pills, but I find nothing. I go back to the living room, frantic now and not wanting the thoughts that are barraging my head. I look through the rest of the papers on the side, but there's nothing from his general practitioner.

In a last-ditch effort, I walk into the bathroom and find nothing there.

In the bedroom, I stop short. The room is a wreck, and I can tell from the pattern of clothes strewn about and bed-clothes torn from the bed that it's not from Turney. Someone has been in here, looking for something. There are piles of papers gone through scattered on the floor, boxes dumped out of the closet. Someone was looking for something. But did they find it?

I do a slow sweep of the room, but I know that if there's something to be found, it's probably long gone. What I do know is what I don't find— another bottle of Warfarin. Which means Turney had been without for the last few days of his life. The significance of that niggles at me. There had been something on Turney's autopsy about hypertension and clotting. Could they be related?

My mind is reeling, heartbeat throbbing in my chest, when I hear the slam of a car door. I pause, hearing voices. Rushing to a side window, I carefully peel back the curtain and spy figures headed up the walkway.

I retreat to the bedroom and close the door gently. The only way out is through the window, and I try to peek at the ground below to see how far of a drop it would be. *Can I make it?*

Who could be here at this time of night? Was it the sheriff? Leigh? Turney's killer come back to raid the place? But clearly someone had been through this room. What could be left to find?

I hear the jingling of keys at the doorway, and the knob to the front door turns. There's no way to talk myself out of this situation, which leaves me one option.

I push at the bottom of the window, and it jumps up in stutters—stuck. *Of course.*

There are voices in the entryway now, and I push at the

window as carefully as I can to avoid making any noise, but a loud squeak as it opens causes the vague fumbling and voices a few rooms over to stop.

I know I've been found out, and now my only choice is speed. I push up the screen as quickly as I can, step back to get my feet through the window, and let go, falling down to the grass below. The edges of the window scrape at my sides as I fall, and when my ankle touches the ground, it twists with a loud *crack*.

I cry out in pain, but I can't stop for it. There are voices calling out in anger now, and the light to the bedroom turns on, creating a rectangle of light on the grass. I dodge to get out of it, not wanting to be recognized.

The outside door bangs open, and I hear footsteps running. *There's two of them.* I dodge behind a dilapidated fence along the woods, ducking in and out of the shadows.

I don't stop, even when the sound of pounding feet fades.

—

I limp through the doorway into Uncle Jeremy's—my— home. My ankle throbs with painful heat, but I know I've lucked out. I haven't broken anything, and I made it home without being recognized.

I let the door slam shut behind me, turning the deadbolt and hanging the chain before kicking my boots into the corner. There's the cherry-colored stairwell with the beige runner to my left, but as always, I make a beeline to the right, away from all the memories that part of the house would ignite.

I pull off my jacket and hang it on the standing coat rack before flicking on the light to the living room. I barely register the hanging photos and well-worn couch as I walk into the kitchen. I flick on the kitchen light and open the door to the fridge, grabbing the pitcher of water and an apple before letting it shut sharp enough to cause the shelves to clang.

Dropping my haul onto the small kitchenette table, I open the cabinet nearest the fridge. The first shelf holds plates and bowls, all mismatched and nicked from years of use. On the second shelf, I grab a clear glass, ignoring the Disney and Looney Tunes cups that I keep because I can't stand the thought of letting them go. Not yet.

I slump into one of the chairs, pouring myself a glass of water and biting a chunk out of the apple. The juice feels like a balm on my tongue and throat, rough from the panting as I ran most of the way back to my home. Afraid I was being followed.

It had been a stupid idea that left me with more questions than answers. I don't know what I'd hoped to find, but it certainly hadn't been anything leading to Leigh. I knew her from school. She was a few years older than me, but in such a small town, that made little difference. She had been quiet but kind. She mothered the younger girls, with a quick wit to combat the advances of the more adventurous bullies. But she'd also been emotionally distant. As if nothing could touch her. As if she didn't want to let anything touch her.

Turney's other grandchildren were scattered among nearby

towns, but Leigh had stayed. Last I knew, she was renting a home with her fiancée. When Turney had his surgery, Leigh had been taking care of him, and the rumors about her burnout weren't unknown.

Could she really have killed him?

I finish the apple and chug down the rest of my water. I throw the core into the tin for the compost pile and wash my hands in the sink, relishing the cool water running over my fingers. I'm sweaty. Beat.

Drying my hands, I walk through the living room, intending on making the sharp right in the hallway to my room where I can collapse in my own bed. A twinge in my ankle stops me cold, and I lean a hand on the wall. As I wait for it to pass, a photo catches my eye.

It sits on a blocky shelf on the wall, the first woodworking project Uncle Jeremy and I had undertaken together. It was uneven, the polish sloppy. But he'd smiled crookedly and declared it 'perfect' before showing me how to hang it.

The photo is similarly in a frame I'd made, this time when I knew more of what I was doing. It had a shallow, beveled edge, made of a cherry wood to match the decor in the room. The photo showed a younger me with uneven bangs and jean overalls with an oversized blue shirt tucked in, and Uncle Jeremy, forward on one knee, holding up a carp we'd caught in the Francis River nearby the community center. It was small, nothing to brag about. But he had anyway, insisting we get a picture for 'his kid's first big catch.'

It had been the first time clear in my memory that he'd

called me his own. I had been his niece, his sister's kid, anything but his for so long that the memory is burned into my mind. That was the first time I'd had any sense of belonging to someone. That I belonged somewhere.

I took the frame from its perch, fingers caressing every nick and flaw, knowing my Uncle Jeremy had seen none of them. He'd thought it was perfect.

And then the other memories. Some not so happy. Because for all our days of bliss there were those when we butted heads. Time's when I hadn't been perfect enough, smart enough, fast enough. And all of it comes crashing into me like a waterfall.

I set the frame back down on the shelf with a harsh knock, not fully registering the crack as I do because my breaths are coming fast again. *Not now, not here.* I grab the door jamb in a clenched fist, nails digging into the wood as I try to let in big gulps of air. I see the photo of me first signing the Trickster record, me at a holiday recital, Uncle Jeremy and I on Aunt Lilah's boat, all of it swimming together with the times he'd yelled at me for being too stubborn, lacking foresight, being too aggressive.

My breath is like a metronome that's been set too fast, and it takes everything in me to make the steady tick slow inside my chest. I balance myself on the doorjamb with both hands and force myself to exhale once. Twice. Three times. I study each curve in the paisley wallpaper, count each shade of the muted tones like paint by numbers. My breathing slows, and with it my heart, and I turn away from all the photos.

Not wanting to risk another attack, I drag myself from the room, taking the sharp right down the hall towards my own bedroom, hand tracing the wall as I go.

TWELVE

MY ANKLE STILL HASN'T FULLY RECOVERED by the time I go back to the records office the next day. I'm like a caged bird, startling at everything with the guilt weighing like bricks around my ankles.

Justified or no, and whether the information I gathered was worth it or not, this was not a conversation I was looking forward to having with Jethro.

I've come to the realization that I can't do this without him, that he's my partner in this as sure as any Citizen. I know I'll have to weather his fury at my objectively stupid runabout last night, but there's determination set in my jaw.

He's already in the office, as I expect, and I deliberate on which would seem more laden with guilt- walking with my head high or lowered. I settle for a nod in his direction as we lock eyes, and I open the hatch to enter through the other side.

"Afternoon," he says, and his voice sounds drained. Resigned.

I set my bag behind the counter and take a deep breath. "There's somethin' I gotta say. And I'm gonna tell you upfront, I know it was stupid. I know it was wrong. But it's done, and now we gotta figure out what to do with what we got."

He squirms in his chair at that and pulls his hands away from the keyboard. His mouth is in a grim line, his eyes focused on mine. "Okay...I don't like the sound of that. But I'll listen."

I pat my bag, take a deep breath, and let the rest out.

"I broke into Turney's house last night."

His eyes widen, and he stands from his chair. "You wha-"

I hold up my hands and stare into his eyes until he sits back down. "I know. I was desperate. You don't have to tell me how wrong it was. I get it. It was stupid, and I let my pride get the best of me."

He calms at that, but he still holds the edge of the chair in a tight grip. "That doesn't really make me feel any better, to be honest, but you have more to say, so say it." He says it in a tone that's terse, barely held at a stable volume.

I rub my neck with my hand, then lean back against the counter, cross my arms. This was going worse than I'd hoped. "I found some things. Not a lot. But enough to give me questions. For one, Turney had cancer. It was terminal."

He straightens at that, face softening. "Seriously? How long?"

I shake my head. "It looked like a recent diagnosis. He'd a hell of a time medically lately. A recent hip replacement surgery where he was laid up for a while and couldn't pay his bills. Then cancer? He picked up small whittling work at the shop, but not enough, and how long could he do that undergoing chemo? He'd have been drownin' in debt, if not already then soon."

Jethro bites his lip and taps the side of his chair with his fingers like a drum. "There was a lot of medical debt that was dismissed when he died. Not the worst I've ever seen, but a lot still. But is that enough for someone to want to kill him? And who? Next of kin?"

I pull myself up to sit on top of the counter, something I'd never get away with if Mrs. Delaney were here. The thought tugs at my heart as I briefly wonder how she's doing. Better that she be resting, though.

I lean forward on my arms as I talk. "His next of kin is his granddaughter, Leigh. I knew her growing up, though we don't talk much these days. I found letters that seem full of love on the surface, but there's somethin' naggin' at me. I know Leigh's been talking 'round town lately about the stress she's been under. I wonder if it's related?"

I cross my legs onto the counter, knowing Mrs. Delaney would have slapped my arm. I do it anyway. "There's one last thing, though. Turney had heart issues and was prescribed Warfarin for high blood pressure. Uncle Jeremy had that too, and you ain't supposed to go without it. But his bottle was empty. Maybe I missed it, maybe he had it on him. But the pharmacy he used is a town over, and Turney didn't have a reliable car. Meaning Leigh would have had to refill it. What if she didn't?"

Jethro's eyes meet mine, and the look he gives me is sour. "They say he had a heart attack. So what if it wasn't an accident?"

I shrug. There's a lot of pieces, but no smoking gun, and we both know it. "I say the best way to figure it out is Leigh herself. We should ask around about her, see what she's been saying."

He suddenly turns the chair around, wheels it towards his bag, and pulls out his laptop. "I got a better idea," he says, opening the case and turning it on. "Leigh got a Facebook? Twitter? Any social media?"

I tilt my head, trying to think back. I rarely go on myself, and we don't run in the same circles. Well. I don't run in any circles. If she does, I have no idea.

"A Facebook, I think." I uncross my legs, hop down from the counter, wincing at the twinge in my ankle, and look over his shoulder. "Why? What're ya gonna do?"

Jethro turns his chair to me. There's a dangerous look in his eyes, something I've not seen before. Face as tough as granite. "I'm going to hack into her Facebook account and see what she's been saying."

I raise my eyebrows towards my hairline in surprise. "You're…what? You? Why?"

He turns away for a moment and I can't read his expression, but I notice the stiffness in his shoulders.

"You remember why I'm here. My grandfather. I'd do

anything to help him through this, even knowing he's not going to survive. I want it to be as easy and as peaceful for him as possible." His shoulders quake for a moment, but with his face turned away, I can't read if it's a sob or anger. "If Leigh was involved, I want to know. And I want her to pay. No one should do something like that to someone they love."

The room is quiet for a moment while I process this. After a few seconds, he starts typing on the keyboard, pulling up first a web browser and then Facebook. As he starts searching for the right 'Leigh,' I make an irrational decision, one of many I'm sure the chatterbox will have me making.

Facing his back, I put my arms around his shoulders, bury my face into his neck, a soft 'thank you' falling from my lips.

—

Getting Leigh's number had been easy enough when we already had access to her Facebook and email accounts.

The call went about as well as you'd expect given we told her nothing about what we needed to talk to her about or why it was so urgent. Since Leigh doesn't know Jethro, we decide I should field the call. I'm not exactly subtle, so it's a miracle we get her to appear in the records office the next morning. She is hesitant and short with me over the phone; her mind wanders at the oddest moments.

I can't blame her. Those first few days, I'd been much the same.

I try not to think too hard on why Leigh would do this.

Adrian Turney was a congenial, kind old man who made me
feel at ease. He could have been like a grandfather to me, if
we'd had time. I would have done anything to have family like
him, even for just a little while longer.

When she comes into the office, I try to school my features. Her brown hair is pulled back in a low ponytail, frayed
and loose; a stark contrast over her light skin. She's wearing a
black knee-length dress and black dress shoes. Her under-eyes
look sunken, her face blotchy, pale around her features, red
around her eyes and nose. She told us she'd be coming straight
from the funeral home where she's making preparations, which
leaves my gut with a terrible ache. I'm at war with myself
between accusation and empathy. I've stood where she stands
now, like a sailboat in a maelstrom.

But I've also seen the emails, the Facebook messages, the
cruel, self-absorbed lack of empathy when she talked about
him while she thought no one else was looking. It's hard to
reconcile the grieving woman before me with what I'd seen.

I nod at her, keeping my face solemn and unreadable.
Jethro leans on the counter, reaching his hand over it as she
draws near to take hers in a firm grip to shake. We agreed that
though Leigh doesn't know Jethro, he'd be the best person to
handle the talking. I could normally lie if pushed, but there was
no guarantee I could keep my temper in check. And I know
how I come across. I may be bullheaded, but I'm self-aware.

"I'm so sorry for your loss, Ms. Johnson. Thank you for
coming," he says, and there's a soft, empathetic expression on
his face. "I'm Jethro. I've been working here with Mrs. Delaney

and Wren while I'm in town." He places his other hand over hers as they shake, and she gives him a small smile in return, eyes watery. *Is it real or a deception?*

"Thank you," she says, and she sounds sincere. "You can call me Leigh."

He lets go of her hand and leans back. His grin is broad now, a thank you. "It's nice to meet you, Leigh, though I wish it were under better circumstances."

He pulls open a folder we purposefully placed on the counter, Turney's name written on the side tab, and filled with the paperwork we'd filed. "We were going through the paper-work you'd filled out about your grandfather's medical debts, and we had questions."

She turns her head sideways in question. "I went through all of it with my lawyer. He said it was all taken care of. Is there somethin' wrong?"

The suspicion rankles. *Is she on to us?* I grasp the shelf under the counter in a white-knuckled grip, gritting my teeth hard. I want to speak up, but I know I need to trust in Jet.

"Oh, nothing's wrong per se. There was one copy that was smudged in the fax machine, so I wanted to go over the copy we have and make sure it's all correct. I know it's a lot of red tape, but the last thing we want is for this to come back in a few months and make you go through it all over again. Better to have you confirm the information now when it's fresh. Then you can sign it and be on your way."

Nice save, I think, hoping the relief doesn't show on my face. Especially because Leigh looks over to me at that.

I shrug, figuring she's looking at me for confirmation, not trusting the outsider. "You know how Mrs. Delaney is. Crosses her 't's and dots her 'i's. Nothing gets past her without being perfect."

Leigh looks around, and I force myself not to wince at my mistake. "Where is Mrs. Delaney?" she asks, as I was afraid she would.

I open my mouth to answer, but Jethro beats me to it. "She's sick right now. She's been having a rough time the past week or so. We've been hoping to get everything set and settled for when she comes back so she doesn't stress herself out more than need be. You know how she is better than me." He gives her a crooked smile, one that's somehow both self-deprecating and endearing at the same time.

Leigh buys it, her shoulders relaxing, and she holds out her hand for Jethro to pass her the paperwork he's holding.

As she looks through it, Jethro starts asking the questions we'd gone over with a fine-toothed comb. "The main thing is the question about his health history. He had a diagnosis of heart disease, correct?"

She doesn't look up from the paperwork, and I assume she's reading the copy line by line for mistakes. She'd been diligent to a fault in school. She answers in a voice that sounds distant. "He had high blood pressure and heart disease, yeah. He was on blood thinners. The doctor said-"

She stops then, closes her eyes, holds the papers in a tight grip. "The doctors said he should be okay, though. Had a clot after his surgery, so we were being careful with his medication.

I don't know why this happened." She sniffles, and there's an ache in my chest. Guilt. Empathy.

But there's fire too, knowing that someone in this equation is lying.

"This must be really difficult. For them to say that and then to lose him. It sounds like you loved him very much and did everything you could to take care of him."

She nods, sets the records on the counter, and looks up at Jethro. "It was hard, the past year. With his hip, and he kept gettin' infections. He was in and out of the hospital for a while before he got settled in." Her words stutter, and she bites her lip as she takes long inhales before continuing. "He was supposed to give me away at my wedding. My fiancée and I...we were waitin' till grandpa's health was better when we could pay off his medical debts. Then we were going to get married. He was supposed to be my first dance." The tears fall, and Jethro grabs a tissue from a box nearby and hands it to her. She nods at him thankfully before wiping at her eyes and nose.

My chest feels constricted, and I grip the shelf under the counter with my nails now. I know what it's like to have the future you planned taken away in a moment, and there's a part of me that feels for Leigh. *Are we wrong about this?*

But it's too late and we've dug in too deep. This could still be an act—she could still be guilty. We need more, but we won't get it here, not now.

I risk a glance at Jethro, trying to think of a way to signal him to back off, afraid of going too far, but in his eyes, I see determination. I wonder if he's so blinded by his own grandfather that he can't see past it.

"So you were on good terms with your grandfather?" It's the wrong question, and I know it as soon as it's past his lips.

She stands straighter, tilting her head to look down at Jet. "Of course. We were two peas in a pod."

Jethro nods and leans forward onto his elbows, arms crossed in front of him. When he looks back up at her, his expression is shuttered. "That's not what I've been hearing."

She startles at that, taking a small step back. She grimaces at him. "What's that supposed to mean?"

He looks down for a moment, avoiding her eyes. "Around town they've been saying that you were sick of taking care of Grandpa."

I clench my jaw at the revealing of our hand, his words like fire and smoke in the small room. *Jethro is beyond my reach now.*

She clenches her fists at that, her face flushing red. "Who's been saying what? Who you been talkin' to?"

"Jet," I say, setting my hand on his shoulder. "Leave it alone."

He shrugs off my arm and stands straight. His eyebrows are furrowed over dark brown eyes behind his silver-rimmed glasses, but I can see there's fire in them through the glass. "You've been saying you wish it was over and done with so you could move on. That you were tired of paying off his medical bills and waiting on him hand and foot."

She pales, holds her arm to her chest. "Who told you that? You been talking with Meredith? No, she wouldn't tell you anythin', never. What did you do?" Her eyes widen, and her face transforms into disgust. "It was you, wasn't it? You broke in last night!"

"So you don't deny you said it?"

She throws up her arms, and I can see tears starting to well in her eyes. "So what if I did?! It was tiring—he always needed somethin' and I been workin' two jobs trying to pay down those debts. I just needed to vent, that ain't no crime. But he was almost better. We were so close to everythin' being okay!"

Jethro slams his hands onto the counter, and Leigh and I both jump back. "So you admit to wanting him dead?"

Her face mottles a beet red, eyes slitting. "What the hell you talkin' about? I didn't want him dead, I wanted him healthy!"

With a sinking feeling, I realize the depth of our mistake, but it's too late as Jethro keeps talking. "Fat chance of that happening when he had cancer!"

There's silence as the words echo in the room, Jethro still holding his fists on the counter. The sound of the A/C drowns out our breaths, but the dust particles in the air are the only things that move. I see wetness in his eyes too, and I suddenly know deep in my bones this was a mistake.

And now I've hurt both of them.

"Jethro-" I start, but Leigh interrupts me.

"He had cancer?" Her voice is soft and ends in a shuttered hiccup.

Jethro straightens, and I know he's caught on too. "You didn't know?"

She moves her hands to cover her mouth, choking on an inhale. She shakes her head.

I slowly move through the hatch in the counter and move to Leigh as if I'm approaching a spooked horse. She looks at me, still in shock. I hold out my arms to her, and she walks into them. I enclose her in an embrace, and she leans into me, sobbing.

I look over her head and see Jethro fling his hands up, look up at the ceiling, then cover his eyes with his hand. He's trying to stem the tears, and I wonder how this all went so wrong. *Way to go, Wren. Now you're losing both of them.*

I sigh, still holding the bundle of Leigh sobbing silently onto my shoulder. "All right y'all," I say. "I think we gotta take a moment and think this through."

Leigh pulls back from me, and I remove my arms from her shoulders. She wipes at her eyes with her forearm, looking up at me with betrayal in her eyes. "Why did you bring me here?" she asks, and my heart breaks because I know I can't lie.

"We're trying to figure out who killed your grandfather." There's a choked sound that comes from Jethro, but I don't look at him.

Her eyes widen, and she takes in a quick breath. The splotches in her face are a violent red now, but the rest of her is paled in shock. "Killed?"

I raise my eyebrows, suspicion forming. "Yeah, we been lookin' at who attacked him. To try and find the killer or at least who wanted him dead." I pause. "He meant a lot to me. To Uncle Jeremy. I have to know what happened."

She's taking in shallow breaths now, and I'm suddenly certain the Sheriff hasn't been entirely up front with her. I'm already tired of being surprised, but it seems one more is in store.

"You think someone killed him?"

I grit my teeth, suddenly furious at Sheriff June. "No one told you about the wounds?"

She shakes her head, and I offer my hand out to her. She takes it, and I lead her to one of the chairs in our makeshift waiting room.

"Come on, Leigh. I'll explain everything."

THIRTEEN

I'VE NEVER SEEN SHERIFF JUNE SO ANGRY.

It's a few hours later, after I've calmed Leigh and Jethro down enough for them to realize they are on the same side. It should have been left at that, but once we explained what we'd found to Leigh, she'd gone on a tirade, nearly busting down Sheriff June's door.

It had been nearly an hour of yelling muffled through her office door before Leigh stormed off, face spotted red and fresh tears on her face.

Sheriff June stands at the door and gives me a look that near turns me to stone. She motions me into her office, and I barely make it to the seat before she lays into me.

"I have never in my entire career dealt with someone as

stubborn and misguided as you, Wren." She is pacing, eyes not meeting mine, tipping her hat up and down on her forehead subconsciously as she paces. "She said you told her that Turney's case was a murder. That he had wounds from an attack."

"Isn't that true?"

She stops pacing, leans forward, and slams her hands onto the top of the desk.

"We *think*, Wren. But she's a granddaughter who's grieving, and the case is still open. Ya really think she needed to hear all that right then instead of when he's buried and she has time to breathe?"

Her eyes are dark, near black in her rage, and her hair is tousled out of her normal ponytail. She grits her teeth as she continues. "I'll have you know we knew about Turney's cancer, and as I told her and I know word gets around, you should know he was refusin' treatment. He didn't want his granddaughter going into any more medical debt. You got nuthin', Wren. You got no leads. Back. Off."

She straightens, pulls off her hat, and drops it with a fwap onto the table. She pulls the hair out of her ponytail and sets about pulling it back again proper.

"This is your last warnin'. I will not have you interferin' again. If you so much as step foot near Leigh, I'll have you detained until I'm sure you can keep your nose out of where it don't belong."

Hair back, she puts her hat back on her head and looks back at me. "Do you understand me, Wren? No more leeway. No more games. Back off before someone else gets hurt."

I let my gaze drop to where I'm clenching my fingers into my knees. My chest is a tangled knot of guilt, anger, and grief. I have to get her to understand, but I don't know if I have the words to express myself. What little connection there is between us, friendship even, is strangled, taught, ready to snap at any moment. I don't want to be the one to break it, so I say nothing. I nod instead.

"Good," she says and nods back. "Now get the hell out of here before I ban you from the town hall."

I stand up slowly. There are words on the tip of my tongue, but I don't say them. They seem weak and frail against the fortress that Sheriff June has built around herself.

I force my bones to move toward the door even as I feel pinpricks in my eyes. Opening the door, I spot Jethro hanging by Sean. He offers me a sad smile, and Sean avoids my gaze.

No. This is not the person I'm going to be.

I back up into the room and close the door behind me. I turn around to face where Sheriff June is looking at me quizzically.

"She deserved to know," I say. I puff up my chest, push my shoulders back, and stand up straight. "I know the case is open, and I know it's hard to hear. But she needed to hear it. She deserved to know why, that there's someone to blame." I swallow. "He was like a grandfather to me. *I deserved to know.*"

Sheriff June sighs, removes her hat, and this time, sets it down on the desk more gently. She waves me towards the chair in front of her desk and settles in her own behind it with a creak that breaks the silence.

I sit, waiting for her to speak. She's staring at the top of the desk, eyes far away.

"Wren. I been doing this a long time." Her voice is gentle now, tired. "Let me tell you the truth. It don't matter why. What matters is that the person you love is gone. Learnin' the how and the why don't change that. If there's someone to blame, it's my job to bring them to justice. But that's not healing. The only healing is through it. You understand?"

She looks up at me, eyes tired. I wonder if she knows this from personal experience or many years on the job. I remember that Sheriff June was not born and raised in this town, and I wonder what she's been through.

"She deserves to have someone to blame. That person deserves to be brought to justice."

She shakes her head, taps her fingers on the wooden desk as she speaks. "Right this moment? By *you*? You think that instead of rememberin' her grandfather as they lay him in the ground, she needs to be thinkin' of revenge? His killer will be caught if there is one. But right now, her family is gone. By whose hand don't matter. He's gone, and she needs to learn what that means first."

I let out a deep, exasperated sigh. "So it's more important to let her bury him blindly than to catch his killer?"

She looks at me, eyes piercing. I stare right back at her. She shakes her head. "Wren, is this really about Turney? About Leigh?"

I startle back, furrowing my eyebrows. "What's that supposed to mean?"

She leans her elbows on the top of the desk, and her gaze is softer now. "I know you blame yourself for Jeremy, Wren. We've talked about this. The important thing isn't to take blame or ask what-ifs, because what good will it do? He's gone, Wren. And that is the truth ya need to make peace with."

The pinpricks in my eyes are back, and I stand up suddenly, the chair tumbling back half a foot before it settles back on all fours.

"This ain't about me," I say. But my heart is beating too quickly. My exhales stutter, and I start gasping in air that won't seem to get into my lungs.

Sheriff June stands up and walks around the desk in a few steps, and part of me wonders at how quick she can move, but the rest of me is fading into a swirling mass that's blurring my vision.

I feel arms around me, her scratchy Sheriff's uniform against my cheek, the cold metal of her badge on my forehead as she lays my head into her chest. She's taller than me, and I wonder at how she'd never seemed to tower before when now, she is like a monument.

"Breathe, Wren," I hear, and the voice sounds tinny and far away, muffled. "Deeper, Wren. Let it out."

I do as the voice says, lengthening my inhales, and eventually managing to exhale. She squeezes my shoulders and mumbles numbers to me, syncing our breaths.

It feels like both minutes and hours when I start to come back, lightheaded but aware. Everything in my vision is distant and surreal, but I can think again.

Sheriff June sets me down in the chair carefully, and I choke back a laugh as it creaks again. It bubbles out of me unbidden, but that only causes the burning in my eyes to worsen.

Sheriff June takes to her knees in front of me, sitting back on her boots. She holds my shoulders in her strong grip still, and I look into dark eyes like black holes that feel more life-giving than draining.

"You with me, Wren?" she asks, and her voice is gentle. Soothing.

I nod, still feeling far away.

"I'm gonna drive you home tonight. No buts. My shift is near over, and it's on the way."

I shake my head, remembering what day it is. "I have the Citizens meetin' tonight. I don't wanna miss it, not with everythin' messed up like this."

"Then I'll go with you. About time I attend one of these meeting's, anyhow."

I raise a single eyebrow, a protest hanging on my tongue. "You? At a Citizen meeting? Afraid we're gonna try to overthrow ya?"

She wipes at her eyes. "I deserve that. No, to make sure you're all right and because I shoulda reached out a long time ago. Y'all are people of this town, and it's my business to lend a hand where I can. Ya'll have been through a lot lately. Least I can do is show support." I nod again, no energy to protest.

She stands, and I grab her forearm before she can remove it from my shoulder. I look up at those dark eyes.

"Thank you," I say, and I find that I mean it.

She smiles a crooked, lazy smile at me, her cheeks dimpling with the change of expression. I realize I haven't really seen her smile before.

"You're welcome. You can be a bull in a china shop, Wren, but that don't mean I don't like you. You got a good heart for all the mess you've caused. Take care you don't shatter it."

I smile tersely back, nothing left to say.

Maybe that's enough.

—

Despite the insistence that she is there to keep an eye on me—to which I'd had to explain no, it wasn't in a detrimental way but in concern for me, bless Sheriff June for her wording—the rest of the Citizens give the sheriff a wide berth as we find our seats.

The sheriff takes a chair to the back, arms crossed and settled deep, almost asleep within the first ten minutes. I take the opportunity to study her: the tan face with more wrinkles than I remembered; the bruised under eyes from lack of sleep; the hair in disarray now that she'd removed her sheriff's cap. She's burning the candle at both ends, and I feel guilt over my own addition to her problems.

And yet, I can also envision the devastated face of Leigh. I find myself pulled between two monoliths, twisting my arms between them.

The meeting goes without a hitch, however. A total for the

fundraiser for Leigh is shared, and it causes a burst of warmth in my chest to know how much it will mean to her to help cover the costs of burial. There's a follow-up from the vigil for Turney, a summary for those who had missed the event.

That's when the talk devolves into the normal, petty bickering and differences of opinions that the meetings typically end up in. Declarations of where the Trickster has been seen last and what the current best way to spot it is. Talks of air currents and humidity, and how it is affecting bird sightings in the area. Arguments over the best way to do bird calls. It's petty, but we thrive on it, our own little obsessive world that brings us together in a strange way.

"If that's all," Molly interrupts Tom, "I think we gone on long enough, and I'm sure we'd all love to be in our homes soon so we can get out early tomorrow mornin'." There's a knowing chuckle among a few members who were the 'early birds' of the crowd. "Anyone else have *important* matters to bring up instead of bickerin'?"

"I have somethin'." The sound comes from the back of the room, where Sheriff June is settling her cap on her head and eases out of the chair. I don't miss that she does so slowly, with care.

Molly's eyebrows shoot up, and she frowns but acquiesces. "Of course, Sheriff. You have the floor."

The sheriff comes up behind me, hands settled on her sides. To my surprise, her expression betrays bashfulness.

"I gotta say, I owe y'all an apology," she says, then scratches the side of her face in distraction before continuing.

"I had misgivins about the Citizens since I came to this town. I'd heard things, and there's wariness about the whole group. But seeing you tonight, knowin' what y'all have done for Leigh and others in this town, I don't see any reason to be mindful 'round you."

She crosses her arms in front of her and huffs out a breath, as if letting go of the tension in her body. "But I gotta be sure, and this is me talking as the Sheriff. Is this all you do? Have these meetings always just been about birdwatching? Or is there somethin' I'm missin'."

It's Nathaniel who speaks up, lip curled in annoyance. "I'll have you know this isn't *all* we do. This is a typical meeting, of course. We have bylines, rules. I'm the secretary, and I allocate all our funds. We do food drives for the town, and ain't no one turns up their face when they need help. We have picnics that are, of course, open to the public, though we're usually given a wide berth. And yes, we watch the birds, of course. The Trickster especially."

Sheriff June frowns at him in confusion. "So you do all that...then why is the rest of the town so afraid of you?"

There's quiet, gazes turning away from the sheriff. Hurt. Not from the sheriff, who was at least trying, but from being outcasts in our own damn town when it was convenient.

It's the thing I've never understood about the Citizens, and Uncle Jeremy never had a satisfying answer for either of us. Adrian Turney was our longest surviving member, and when questioned, he'd deferred the question. Now he was gone.

Maybe the knowledge was lost with him.

"I don't rightly know," Molly says at last, breaking the silence. "We do what's best for the town. Some people don't agree on what exactly that means."

The reasoning is the best I've heard, but there is something she isn't saying. If Sheriff June notices she doesn't let on, nodding and tipping her hat to Molly in reply.

She turns to me, hand sneaking to her pocket, and I hear the jingling of keys. "Sorry to cut this short, but I gotta get Wren home. Been a rough day for both of us. Wren?"

I debate arguing, but it's not a fight I would win—or want to partake in. I gather my bag, wave at the rest of the Citizens, and we walk out the door side by side.

For the first time, I question the Citizens and my part in their story.

FOURTEEN

WALKING INTO THE COMMUNITY CENTER the next morning feels surreal. A night's rest shines light on our mistakes. We jumped the gun, made assumptions, and acted on faulty or missing information. I feel embarrassed and exposed, caught out in the worst way. What's worse is I dragged Jethro into it, and it brought up buried wounds in him. I have amends to make with him, but first, I have a sheriff to talk to.

When I get to the front desk, the first thing I notice is the sheriff's door is closed, which means she is either away or in a meeting. Sean is already at the front desk, and when he notices me looking over at the doorway, he waves over at me, still half looking at his computer screen. I walk the remaining way to his desk then around it before I hop up on the edge where there's no paperwork, knowing it'll get on his nerves. I'm not wrong.

"Hey!" He glares at me, and turns the screen away, which immediately sets alarm bells off in my head. "Don't be comin' back here like you own the place, Wren. And get off my desk. I don't know where your ass has been."

"Why you all actin' madder than a wet hen?" I say and slide off obediently but twist around so I'm behind him, looking at his screen dead on. I expect to see pornography or a dating site with how he's cradling the screen, but I am dumbfounded by what's there instead.

"Private investigator licensing requirements? What's all this about, Sean?"

He sighs and clicks the window away, revealing a desktop that needs a good organizing. He swings around in his chair, arms crossed over his chest. Even sitting, he's nearly my height—the man is a giant.

"Believe it or not, some of us don't plan on stayin' administrative assistants forever." He holds his chin up, rotates his shoulders back, and speaks with a passion I'd never heard from him. "I wanna be a private investigator. I'm lookin' at the requirements and the training, and I think I can do it. I got all the experience helpin' the sheriff, and if they won't take that, I fit the education requirement. If I can get the other stuff together, I could be an investigator in a few months, I bet."

The notion is outrageous. Sean has been sitting in the same chair doing the same job for years, near as long as I've been volunteering at the records office. He'd come in with a lot of spunk and sass, though I had to admit the spunk had diminished as of late. Maybe this was his way of bringing back his passion for law enforcement, but I can't help but wonder at how he thinks he'll accomplish it without real training. And to make a career change like this so suddenly?

I shake my head, hands on my hips. "Nothing against ya, Sean, but it kinda came out of nowhere, ya know? And why exactly you wanna be a private investigator anyhow? Plus, don't' we already have some here? We don't need *that* many. It's a small town."

He shrugs, but I see him deflate at my lack of enthusiasm. "Who says I gotta stay in this town? And why not? I see what the sheriff does. I don't think I can handle the guns and all that. But the detective work, sneakin' around, getting all that gossip…I can do that easy peasy."

I can't help it I snort at that. His glare intensifies, and I can't stop a giggle. He's large as all hell but not intimidating at all.

"You're an ass, Wren. You know that?" He turns around in his chair, conversation over.

It occurs to me that he's not wrong, that I should have been supportive of him. My reaction hadn't been purposely mean but it had been.

"Come on, Sean. I'm sorry I laughed; it was the look on your face, that's all! You can be an investigator, I'm sure of it."

He doesn't respond, just opens up Excel and pulls a file towards him, presumably going back to his real work. I sigh. I don't know how to recover from the damage I've done, and I'm kicking myself over it. When did I become such a terrible friend, such a terrible person?

"I'm sorry, Sean. I'll talk to you later." I don't know what else to say, so I walk around the desk toward the hallway that will lead me to the records room. Right before I round the corner, I look back at him. On his face, I see furrowed eyebrows and downcast eyes. A look of sadness I put there.

God, I am an ass, I think, and I'm left with the inkling that I need to make this right somehow.

—

By the time Jethro drops his bag behind the counter next to me, I've worked myself into a tizzy. I'm sitting in the squeaky office chair, swaying back and forth in it, leg twitching all the while. I can't sit still, and I bite my lip in frustration.

Jethro notices my tension right away and leans against the counter in front of me to observe my scattered self. I must look a right mess to him, but I've worn myself down thinking of how we'd put our foot in it this time. It's unlike me, the self-confident, brash Wren he knows, but then again, he hasn't known me long. I wonder what's going through his head, but his face is a blank sheet.

"Hey," is all he says, and I hold back a snort at how little that tells me.

"Hey," I reply in kind, trying to keep the edge of wariness out of my voice. I don't fully understand why I'm so nervous. Yes, we messed up. But who am I holding myself accountable to? I'd made amends with Leigh, with the sheriff. Why is it that approaching Jethro again face to face feels like looking over edge of a cliff?

Because I care what he thinks, and I don't want to lose him, I realize, and the thought catches me off guard enough that I nearly miss what he says next.

"So. About yesterday." He leans further back into the counter, holding himself up by his elbows and leaning his head back to look at the ceiling. It looks uncomfortable, and I wonder if he's asking God for forgiveness for what we'd done. "Man. We messed up. Bad."

He finally looks back down at me, sighs, rubs one hand into his eyes. He looks defeated and slumped into himself now. Uncertain. It occurs to me he's as unwilling and scared to have this conversation as I am, and that's okay. We were in this together and we can muddle through it if we work as a team. Something I hadn't been part of in a long time. Since…well. I won't think of that.

"Yeah, I guess we did." I stop shaking my leg and pull both of them up until I'm sitting cross-legged on the chair and rest my arms on my knees. I slump into the position, relaxing a little bit as we talk.

"I didn't like being the bad guy, Wren," he says. "I don't ever want to feel that way again."

"Me either." I nod in agreement. *At least we're on the same page, no surprise there.*

"I shouldn't have hacked into her accounts. I'm amazed I'm not in jail right now. Honestly, the sheriff must really like you, because if it was just me, I'd be in a whole world of trouble."

His words make me pause. I wonder that he's taking more blame onto himself than he should. But he's not wrong. Had he been working alone, he would have been jailed sure enough. And yet…

"It wouldn't have been just you though, Jet. I'm the one that pushed you. Ya wouldn't have done all that on your own."

He sits on the counter and leans forward, his arms perched on either side of his legs. Attentive. He towers over me, and I have to crane my neck up, so I unfurl from my chair and follow his lead, jumping up onto the counter too. *Mrs. Delaney would kill us if she saw us doing this. Good thing she's not here.*

"I'm not so sure. I think the second it got into my head that it might be Leigh, I was a goner. I kept thinking about my own grandpa, and I couldn't think straight."

His grandfather. I haven't heard much lately about him, which leaves me wondering if there is more to it than Jethro had been letting on. He seemed upset yesterday when we talked with Leigh, and I have to know.

"What's goin' on with him?"

I can see him slump further into himself, head downcast.

"He's getting weaker every day. They think it's a combination of his heart and the diabetes. He's close to needing dialysis. They thought about surgery, but he's not a good candidate for it. And Grandpa…he's like Turney. He doesn't want to put anyone through that, though at least we can afford it."

No wonder he over-reacted. I would have done the same. I pat his shoulder for lack of anything else to do.

"But I thought of Turney and all he was going through,

and all I could see was my grandpa, and it made me so angry, I wanted her to be to blame. But we were dead wrong."

We're quiet for a little bit, the opening and closing of doors echoing through the hallways outside along with the mechanical hum of the air conditioning. What's there to say? We made our mistakes, and now we have to deal with the consequences.

"How do we make this better, Wren? I don't know where we go from here."

What do we do? There was one thing I could think of that mattered.

"We find the killer, whoever it is."

He lets out a low hum, then is quiet for a moment. When I look over, his head is tilted in that way he does when he's thinking about a problem. I noticed it when we were looking through the records and when he was hacking into Leigh's accounts. I wait for him to process whatever it is he's thinking.

"About that, Wren. I think we may be going about this all wrong."

I frown, unsure how to take his words. "What you mean?"

He shrugs, picking away at his fingers, avoiding my gaze. Not wanting to push my reaction most likely.

"Well, we keep assuming there's a killer. But shouldn't we at least be open to the possibility that it was an accident?"

Part of me becomes agitated, like I'm being called into question...but is that what's really happening? Jethro is only calling into question our assumptions on the case. The defensiveness has a tight grip in my chest, though, and it's hard to buck.

"What about the knife wounds?"

He crosses his arms but still doesn't look at me. "We don't know for sure it was a knife. He could have been sliced by any kind of metal. He could have got caught on something out there and lost a lot of blood."

He sighs, and carefully climbs down the countertop before facing me, challenging me this time now that he's said his piece. "I'm just saying we can't know for sure. We shouldn't discount the possibility that there was no one else involved."

I can't deny that his words make sense. A part of me believes, almost wants it to be a murder, but there's another part of me that questions *why* someone else would have to have been involved. It's not unheard of for the forest to be a dumping ground for trash, metal included. It's why everyone in town is religiously up to date with their tetanus shots. But the coroner thought it was a knife wound, so doesn't that mean something? Still, I can't discount the possibility.

"I suppose that makes sense. We'll keep our ears open for now then."

I climb off the counter and spy a relieved smile on Jethro's face. He looks relaxed, and there's a tension that's dissolved between us. We've made mistakes, but we're going to work through the rubble.

"Oh, by the way, Sean said Mrs. Delaney called, and she's coming back in a little bit."

The calm atmosphere changes in a moment.

"And you're just tellin' me now?! Jet, we gotta get all this taken care of before she gets here, or she'll think we been wasting time!"

"Oh crap, I didn't think of that."

—

It's several hours later while Jethro is out on an errand for his father when Mrs. Delaney returns. She still looks quite sick, and the worry itches beneath my skin. "I'm fine," she swears and putters around with the current files to be sorted stacked on the counter. "I got a little overexcited the other day and needed to lie down a bit. Nothin' to worry about."

I do, though. She hides it well, but I see her sit more than usual, pausing at odd times to hold herself up on the countertop.

"I can get this," I say. I grab the folders and start to sort them. The pile is higher than usual; Jethro and I set aside the organizing I'd normally had done to look further into a motive for the killer. I feel guilt, knowing that Mrs. Delaney won't take a break until they're all organized.

"Come, child. I'm not useless, you know. I just stove up, that's all." She takes a few of the folders back and pauses for a second as a they drop from her shaking hands. I pat her hand as gently as I can, trying for reassurance.

"Jet and I can get this. It's our fault for foolin' around these past few days anyhow."

My referral to him by his nickname gets her grinning, as I

knew it would, and she allows me to get her to sit down in one of the rickety office chairs because of it. The slight hit to my pride is worth it.

"Well, now. Sounds like you and our young Jethro are gettin' along then?" Her smile is wide enough I wonder if it'll slide off her face if it goes any wider. "Enough that you haven't gotten nuthin' done while I been gone?"

I nod, avoiding her gaze as I sort the piles by type—something I should have done days ago. "Enough, I suppose. He's not such a terrible chatterbox once you get him calmed down."

"And about him being an outsider? How has that changed?" The tone is somewhat icy, and I turn back to check her expression. There's a cautious frown on her face, one eyebrow raised in question.

"I suppose he's not so bad for a city boy." The admission doesn't hurt to say as much as I thought it should. Not after all he's done the past few days.

She beams wide again, showing her missing teeth. "I'm glad to hear it."

We sit in silence for a while, me sorting while Mrs. Delaney leans her head back onto the side of the shelves, resting her eyes. I make quick progress on the files—probably because I've already been through them before.

"Hmmm. Ya know who you two remind me of, child?" I don't look up from where I'm sorting. We have a rhythm, Mrs. Delaney and I. This isn't the first time she's needed to stop for a break due to her Parkinson's, and it won't be the last. I'll keep sorting, putting files away, doing the grunt work while she regales me with stories of the town. It's one of my favorite parts of volunteering here. She's the records keeper in more than one way—she knows everyone in town, their family history, passed down from records keeper to records keeper.

"Who?" I ask absent-mindedly, listening but also focusing on alphabetizing the pile for February.

"Your Uncle Jeremy and his friend Moses when they was teens."

I pause at her words. Moses is a name I haven't heard before, and I've heard many a story of Uncle Jeremy's childhood. I set down the files and turn around to see a mischievous smirk on Mrs. Delaney's face.

"Who was Moses?"

She grins wider—she knows she has me by the collar—and motions to one of the stools by the counter for me to take a seat. "Sit down, child. Take a break. You can finish that when young Jethro gets back. Heaven knows he shouldn't get away with you doin' all the work 'cause he been foolin' around for days too."

I snicker and jump onto one of the stools as I'm told, hunching forward in anticipation of the story.

"When your uncle was about nine or ten, a new family moved into town—the Hutchinsons. They was accountants, going to take over for the Leroy's when their grandfather passed. The father in the family decided to become a doctor instead of keepin' in the family business, so he had no one to give it to. So, the business was going to go to them instead."

She takes a deep inhale, eyes closing for a moment, and I

hop off the stool to grab her water bottle from the counter. She smiles at me gratefully when I give it to her, giving her time to recover before she continues her story. I've spent enough time with the woman that I know when she is struggling, and I'm not about to push her for a story I can get anytime.

"They had a son, Moses, about your uncle's age. Sweet kid, shy but once you got him goin', he was like a bird chirpin'. Kinda like your Jethro."

I scrunch my nose up. "He's not *my* Jethro. He's his own."

She chuckles at me, and I stick out my tongue at her. I'm glad I can make her smile even if she's not feeling her best. It gives me a sense of pride.

"Well, yours or no, he and Moses were alike. Your uncle and Moses got along like peas in a pod. They was close, always making trouble. Your uncle was the one doing the convincin', but Moses was the one who got things done. Then your uncle could charm a snake, so he'd get 'em out of trouble. They were a good team."

Her expression is far away, and I can tell she's lost in the memory. "Eventually, they used their talents for good. They got up to mischief, but they had good hearts. Would stick up for the little 'uns and take care of neighbors yards. They'd make a game out of it and get all the kids in town involved. One time, they got all the kids racin' to see who could trim the most lawns in one day. The whole town got their grass cut, and the kids who won got a free lunch at the diner. Of course, Moses and your uncle were among them, but at least they shared the glory."

I'm beaming and I don't care. There are tears in the corner of my eyes, and I can't tell if they're from happiness or grief. This is a part of my uncle I'd never heard of before, and my heart is fit to bursting hearing about it. It's too much all at once, and too little, as I hang on every word like it's a freshwater spring and I'm dying of thirst in the desert.

"Why ain't I ever heard about this?" I ask, and her smile falters. *That can't be good.*

"I'm afraid young Moses broke your uncle's heart. It wasn't his fault. The Hutchinsons decided that they wasn't making enough to stay in the town with everythin' going downhill. His pa got a better offer a few towns away, so they moved. Now, it's not like they couldn't have visited every now and then, but I think your uncle was heartbroken that someone he was so close to was leavin'. They had a fight, to this day I don't know what about, and they never saw each other again."

My heart breaks for my uncle, and sudden understanding dawns on me. *The outsiders don't stay long. Don't get cozy; they'll be gone soon.* It's what my uncle had always said, and I'd believed him to this day. Now I know what made him so sure, so set in his ways. He'd been burned, and he didn't want to see me hurt the same way he'd been hurt. *Oh, Uncle Jeremy. I'm so sorry.*

Mrs. Delaney is looking at me with curiosity in her eyes. "A penny for your thoughts child?"

"Jethro said once his grandfather... Once he's gone, they'll be movin' back. So he'll be leaving too. I'm settin' myself up for heartbreak too, ain't I?"

She hums an affirmative, her eyes holding back something

I can't quite decipher between the wrinkles and crow's feet.

"Ain't we all though, child? None of us will be here forever. *I* won't be here forever. Does that mean you should keep away from me?"

I straighten on my stool, my voice gruff. "Never. You mean too much to me."

She nods slowly. "Then why would Jethro be any different?"

I frown, my thoughts twisting and turning in my head, not making any semblance of sense as much as I try to put them in a straight line. "Because—"

I'm interrupted by the sound of the door opening, and when I look over my shoulder, Jethro is carrying several brown paper bags in his arms.

"I got us a late lunch," he says, as if that explains it all. "My treat!"

For the moment, I'm saved from having to make any decision at all.

—

"So I was thinking."

I look up from dipping my french fries in ketchup, pausing before I can shove them in my mouth. "Yeah? Does it hurt?"

He grabs a fry from his own plate and throws it at me. I duck and look around to see if we've been caught out throwing food again by the waitress. Fortunately, she seems to be busy with a toddler screaming across the room.

"About the case," he continues without missing a beat. "Maybe we need to write down what we know. It might help us come up with ideas of what to do next."

I shove more fries in my mouth, thinking as I chew. It's not a bad idea, but I didn't bring my bag, so I have nothing to make a list with. "You got any paper?" I ask after I swallow. "Or can we use your laptop?"

He scrunches up his nose at me, horror in his eyes. "No, I don't have paper, and no way am I pulling out my laptop when there's food all around. It's expensive."

I shrug and turn around to wave the waitress over, who's now finished with the toddler, her apron covered in chocolate milk. I feel bad for her, but at least my ask doesn't involve getting covered in dairy products.

"Whaddaya want?" she asks in a not very polite tone. We've burned that bridge apparently.

"Do you have any blank paper? And a pen?"

"This ain't a store," she says, but she goes to the bar and gestures for the waitress holding down the shake machines to come over, presumably to ask about our request.

"She didn't seem happy," Jethro points out as if it's not obvious.

I shrug. "Only so many places to eat around here. Not like they have much competition. You eat here or you eat at home. Take what you can get."

He frowns but goes back to eating the last of his burger.

It's not long before the waitress comes back with a children's menu and crayons. "Best I can do," she says, and she's gone.

I shrug and flip it over, clearing a space where my plate used to be. When I look up, Jethro has an incredulous look on his face. "What?"

He leans forward and whispers, "We're writing down clues for a murder on the back of a children's menu? In *crayons*?!"

I grin at his horror. "Not a fan of the irony?"

He pushes his plate away, face grim. "That's not irony. That's just...*wrong*. On so many levels."

I shrug again and write 'Clues' at the top of the page. "I'll take what I can get. If it makes you feel better, we'll take a photo of this when we're done and toss it so you don't have to see the Teletubbies on the back every time you unfold it."

He covers his face and groans into it, and I can't help the laugh that bubbles up. I write, but even after I've written the first few clues—heart attack, knife wounds—he's still got his face covered. I sigh, drop the crayon, and lean over to pull his hands away from his face to reveal furrowed eyebrows.

"Are you seriously that freaked out about it?"

He exhales brusquely, then drops his hands to the table. "No, no, I can handle it. What do you have so far?"

"I have heart attack, knife wounds, I was gonna add crazy handwritten notes." I start writing, while still listening as he lists off the few other things we knew.

"He had a heart condition, high blood pressure. We found blood, gauze, and bandages in the deer blind. You said he was walking in circles instead of towards the town."

I write it all down as he speaks, trying to keep up while writing with a dull crayon, then realizing he's stopped.

I look up. "What else?"

He rests his head on his hand. "That's all really, isn't it? We didn't get to the end of his trail. I guess you can put down that he was found by a body of water, but we don't know which one."

I look down at our list. It's not very long. "Do we want to add in his cancer?"

Jethro groans and puts his head back in his hands. "You can if you want. But the more we look into this, the more I think it was an accident."

I tap the crayon against the paper, then write down the part about his cancer and his medical bills, to be thorough. But I have to admit, Jethro is right. The case for murder looks thinner and thinner the more we look into it.

"What I don't understand though is why the coroner would think it was a knife wound," I say. It's the linchpin that has me confused. "You'd think he'd know the difference between a ragged cut from metal and a cut from a knife."

Jethro pulls his plate towards him and picks at his fries. Not eating, but pushing them back and forth on his plate, using one like a poker. "Maybe it was really sharp? Or maybe he was attacked by someone, but it was happenstance, and he got a blood clot? Or maybe he accidentally cut himself on his own knife somehow."

My mind is spinning, so many what ifs and none of them fitting into any sort of picture. I set the crayon down.

"I don't think we can solve this with what we have," I finally admit. "We need more information."

"Hmmm," he says, noncommittally. "I'm wondering if we can solve it at all."

I hate it, but I'm wondering if he's right. "Maybe not," I finally admit, "but we can still keep our eyes and ears open. Maybe somethin' pops up in the records office or around town that gives us a clue. We gotta stay alert."

He drops his fry and uses his napkin to wipe his hands. He pulls out his phone and motions towards the list. "Take a photo on each of our phones then. The least we can do is have it handy."

I do as he asks, and later, when I rip the paper up and crunch it into a ball to toss it in the trash bin, I wonder at the feeling that I'm letting Turney down.

FIFTEEN

WAKING UP IN MY CHILDHOOD BEDROOM no longer
surprises me. I grip the faded Mulan sheets in my fingers,
remembering their worn texture and coolness in the hot summer air.

I'm equally unsurprised to see Uncle Jeremy back in the
plush chair. He's unchanged for all that I'm taller and pudgier
than I was last time I was here. My feet under the covers reach
further down, and I bend my toes back and forth to watch
them under the sheets.

"You ready for our story, Little Bird?" he asks. I missed his
voice, his heavy southern lilt and deep tenor. There's a tightness in my chest and throat, but I have to push through it. I
have to know.

"What did you argue about with Moses, Uncle Jeremy?"

He'd been turning the pages, but he looks up at the question, caught off guard. It feels like there's a disturbance in the dream, like it's been put on pause but the actors are still moving despite the frozen landscape. "Who told you 'bout that name, Little Bird?"

"What did he say?" I press, not wanting him to change the subject because I don't know how much time we have.

He hums to himself, then flips through the book, shaking his head as he goes back and forth through the pages as if he's looking for something and can't find it. I'm about to ask the question again when he stops and clears his throat.

"I'll tell you about Moses, Little Bird. But first, let me tell you a story."

I grip the sheets in frustration. "I don't want a story. I want you to answer my question."

When he looks back at me, his face is a mixture of hurt and nothingness as if someone tried to erase the area where his face should be, and suddenly, I realize my mistake. *He can only tell me stories in these dreams.* I resign myself to it, not wanting to waste the time but knowing it may be the only way I'll learn about my uncle's childhood best friend.

"There was a little bird, a beautiful little wren, who lived in the forest. They lived there alone for a very long time. One day, a starling flew into the forest and decided to make its home in a tree there."

The wren is obviously meant to be me. *The starling must be Jethro,* I think. I settle back in the pillows, entranced in his storytelling as I always have been.

"The little wren didn't trust the starling at first, but soon enough, they became fast friends. They did everythin' together; they ate bugs together, they flew through the clouds together, they huddled away from the rain together.

"But the starling became home sick. They missed their family dearly. One day, they decided they wanted to go home. The little wren was devastated—how could the starling abandon them like that? Wasn't their friendship enough? The little wren offered to have the starling stay in their own tree with them, but the starling insisted. They wanted to return to the forest where their family still lived."

Is this me and Jethro, or is it supposed to be Uncle Jeremy and Moses?

"The wren was so angry they said things they didn't mean. The starling was hurt and left the forest, never to return. To this day, the little wren regrets that they lost a good friend to their hurt and temper."

He closes the book and settles his hands over it, looking down at it somberly.

"Is that what happened to you and Moses?" I ask. "You got angry at each other and said things you shouldn't have said and never saw each other again?"

When he looks up at me, his crow's feet are crinkled in a squint that meant he was holding back tears and didn't want anyone to know.

"This isn't my book, Little Bird. These stories are made of echoes, memories, and could be's. Whichever one it is isn't for me to decide. That's up to you."

I nod, not understanding but knowing I won't get a straight answer. But there's something else I need to know.

"What exactly did the wren say to the starling?"

He smiles at me, but it's sad.

"That's up to you, isn't it?"

The dream ends in a flutter of lights, smoke and questions.

SIXTEEN

THE FOLLOWING DAY, it's Mrs. Delaney and me for the morning, Jethro in a meeting with his father, grandfather, and his grandfather's doctors. I worry about him, but I know there's nothing I can do, so I push it from my mind. Instead, I focus on finishing organizing the last of the paperwork we'd meant to organize while Mrs. Delaney was gone.

I'm almost through when the door to the office is thrown open. I jump, then calm when I see it's Jethro.

Until I see his face.

His eyes are wide, and he looks sick to his stomach. I immediately move toward the opening to the counter and lift it open. I walk to him before I have a chance to think clearly.

"What's wrong?" Mrs. Delaney asks, her voice laced with concern.

"I think you should come see this," he says and holds the door open wide for me. I hadn't heard it before with the door closed, but there's yelling down the hall down toward Sheriff June's office.

I turn back to Mrs. Delaney and motion her to remain seated. "It's fine, Mrs. Delaney; I'll go with Jethro. You stay here—it's probably nothin'." She sits back, but she's frowning in worry.

We move through the door and down the hallway, Jethro whispers an update as we go. "Sheriff June brought in this guy. It sounds like he shot someone! The guy he shot, his daughter is here, and they're making a scene."

My eyebrows shoot up in surprise. "Sounds like somethin' a killer might do," I say. Jethro nods at that, and we quiet now that we're closer to the yelling.

When we near Sheriff June's office, we hold back, close enough to see the woman yelling but far enough away that we can say we were making sure it wasn't anything we needed to be involved in.

There's a woman—Ellie, if I remember right—who is all but screaming at someone hiding behind Sheriff June. I'm unsurprised to see its Tom, his chin held up in defiance at her.

"You know him?" Jethro asks. I lean a little closer to be sure, but there's no denying it.

"It's Tom," I say. "He's one of the regulars at the diner. ·
He's always braggin' about one thing or another. He's a Citizen,

too, though Heaven knows how he's managed to spot anything with his head up his ass."

"So, he shot someone? You think he's the killer?"

Ellie leans over Sean, who's doing his best to keep her pushed back as Sheriff June moves Tom into her office.

"You could have killed him, Thomas, I swear! Stop hiding behind the sheriff and come out here, you asshole!"

The door closes behind June, and Ellie collapses onto Sean to sob into his shoulder.

The scene is heartbreaking, but I shake my head. "Nah, Tom's a braggart but not a killer. Besides, he's a Citizen. He'd still pay Turney respect if nuthin' else."

Jethro sighs and grabs my forearm. He pulls me back towards the records office but stops me short of the door. I pull my arm away and move to look him in the eye. He looks consternated. "You're the one that thinks this was a murder. Well, if it was murder, I think you have to accept that it's possible someone you know is a killer. And there's a good chance that whoever it is, they're a Citizen."

I balk at that. Every part of me denies the notion. "Can't be. A Citizen wouldn't hurt another Citizen like that. Trust me."

Jethro grabs at his curled hair with his hand, digging it through to the ends. "Wren. You were so quick to blame Leigh, but not Tom? Because he's a Citizen? Sometimes people do bad things. Whether they've seen some stupid bird or not."

I stretch to my full height and lean into his personal space. He moves back at first, then digs in his heels. "Don't forget, you're an outsider. You don't get it. You just moved here. You're no expert on what we will or won't do around here."

I see his chest rise, and he holds it for a moment before he lets out his breath in a huff. He leaves his hands on either side as he locks his gaze on mine. "Wren, if someone killed Turney, don't you owe it to him to consider all possibilities? It could have been a Citizen."

I shake my head as if that will stop the notion from taking root. "It's not a Citizen. I know it. But there are others, people who are jealous of us. Maybe it was someone targeting Turney, because we did something they couldn't?"

I can see his jaw clench as the muscles tense in his face. "That is crazy talk. You think someone would kill someone for not having seen a bird?"

I throw up my arms at him, at the limits of my frustration. "You said we should consider all possibilities! Well, I'm considering them. It's just as likely as a Citizen targeting other Citizens."

"I didn't mean that they were targeting others for being a Citizen. They may happen to—you know what, never mind. You're not listening to reason. Forget it."

He turns and begins to walk away, and in a moment, I know that if I let him go, that's it. No more help, no more chatterbox, no more whatever he is to me.

There's a part of me that feels relief at that. But to my surprise, it's a very small part.

I grab his arm to hold him back from leaving. "Jethro, wait."

He stops and turns back to me with a curious look on his face. As if saying, *go on.*

I growl at him—literally growl—and he snorts.

"All right. So it may be possible that a Citizen did it. Fine. But I don't think it's likely."

He sighs at that but doesn't leave either.

"And I can show you why. If you see the Trickster, I bet you'll understand."

He turns to me fully. I can see interest underlying his uncertainty.

"I thought it was super hard to find that bird and that's why you have this underground secret society of birdwatchers?"

I roll my eyes at him and move closer so I can nudge his shoulder. "It's not a secret society, and yes, it's hard to find them."

I smirk, and I'm relieved when he slightly smiles back.

"That is, if you don't know the secret."

His smile is broad, and I try not to think about how relieved I feel.

SEVENTEEN

THERE IS NOTHING BUT trees and leaves surrounding us, the sounds of birds and insects a blanket of noise. The sun shines through the edges of the canopy, the fresh smell of greenery a twinge in the air. The ground is dappled shadows, the occasional ferns and bushes breaking up the mottled browns of twigs and dirt. Leaf litter lies across the ground at random, the top of it green but underneath yellowed or brown in decay. *This is my home.*

"But if I don't look down, I'm going to run into something." He states it with incredulity as if I haven't passed down an important secret to him. *Ungrateful.*

"Take it slow," I say through gritted teeth, trying to remind myself to be patient. "Keep checkin' in front of you with the stick I gave ya. If you flat out have to, you can look down for a second. But keep lookin' up otherwise."

We're back in the woods again, this time on the hunt for the Trickster. We've been hiking for about twenty minutes, and we're leaving the last sounds of the town behind us.

It's still too early to see anything. But I knew I would have to give him a crash course if there's to be any chance of him seeing the most elusive bird there is to see out here.

It's the leaves that are giving Jethro trouble. They mask the areas where the ground suddenly dips, hiding branches and tree trunks. I hear a yelp behind me but don't dare move my gaze from the midline of the trees.

"Tap it on the ground ahead of you if ya have to. We can go slow as you like but keep your eyes up. They'll disappear on you before ya know it."

We walk in silence, the sound of the breeze and the occasional songbird breaking the quiet. I risk a look back at him and see he's closer than I assumed, about ten feet back. I'm impressed but don't show it on my face when he meets my gaze.

"Am I doing okay?" I do smile at that, a small one. Barely a hint, but I can tell from his toothy grin that he's taken it as intended.

I turn back around to gaze at the treeline. I've seen plenty of other songbirds so far—a few different warblers, a grosbeak, and even a woodpecker. But no finch. It's not surprising this close to town yet, but the longer I have Jethro out here, the sooner he'll lose his patience.

I consider my choices and decide on distraction.

"What kind of birds do you have back in..." I let the sentence runoff, realizing I'm not quite sure where Jethro lived before. He talks plenty of his family but not where they had lived.

"Ohio," he says. I can hear the embarrassment in his tone. "I know, I know, the land of corn. We lived in Columbus, though, so at least there was more to see than cornfields."

"I don't know all that much about it, to be honest. Nothin' wrong with corn. Lots of hawks and crows." A dip in the ground catches me off guard, and I tip forward, my ankle twisting in the small crevice. I cry out, more in surprise than anything.

Jethro is suddenly at my side, holding my arm to his chest. I'm able to settle back onto my other leg, staying upright but barely.

I look up at him, and his forehead is creased in worry, bushy eyebrows over concerned brown eyes.

My initial instinct is to pull my arm away, but I let it go. "Thanks," I say. And I surprise myself that I mean it.

I try putting weight on my injured ankle and grimace at the pain, gritting my teeth. "Crap."

"What happened?" *He sounds so concerned.*

I shrug, grabbing his shoulder to hold myself steady while I try to take a step. "It's still raw from when I jumped out of Turney's window."

I can feel his shoulders tense under my grip. "From when you... What the hell Wren?!"

I glare at him and take another step. "It was necessary," I say, only halfway convinced myself. His shoulders slump, and he grimaces.

"Should we go back?" I expect him to sound eager to get out of the woods, but instead, he sounds disappointed. "I can carry you if I need to."

I roll my eyes at that and swat at his arm. "No, I don't need you to carry me. Let me try givin' it a rest and see if that helps."

He considers, looking from my ankle back to where we'd come from. I wonder if he realizes how difficult it would be to carry me back—we are nearly the same height, after all—because he acquiesces.

"Alright. Let's sit down, then we'll decide."

I look around for a good place to sit and spy a fallen tree further into the forest. I point toward it with the arm not in Jethro's grasp. "There. We'll sit, then I'll try walkin' on it a bit. See if I can get it settled down."

It takes some figuring out, but we manage a system of him holding one arm under my shoulder and me grasping his other arm with my hand to steady me as we limp towards the tree. It's slow going, and we're both too busy looking ahead to bother watching for the Trickster.

When we get to the tree, he lets go of my shoulder, and I twist my body to sit back on the dried-out trunk. It shakes for a minute when I sit but holds.

"You sit too," I say. "It should hold. I ought'a teach you how to spot the birds anyhow."

He sits down slowly as if afraid the tree will collapse beneath him. It doesn't.

"Is there a trick to it?"

I nod towards an area of the forest to our right, opposite where we'd come from. "Tell me, what do ya see there?"

He squints to where I nodded, moving his head back and forth, gaze moving through the trees. "I see nothing."

"You gotta give it more time than that, Jet. Look over there, but don't look at one point. You kinda look at the general area. Got it?"

He leans back, eyes moving around the area, but I can see the frustration on his pursed lips.

"I am looking, but I don't see anything."

I put my hand on his forearm, squeezing it gently. His body tenses at first but then relaxes, closes his eyes.

"Take a deep breath," I say. "Relax. Stop tryin' to see 'em; let them show themselves to ya."

He takes in a deep breath and I feel the rigidness in his body, his stance, melt as he exhales audibly. When he opens his eyes again, I can see the difference in him.

"Okay. Look again, but don't be in a rush. We ain't going anywhere; they ain't going anywhere. Let the sight come to ya."

He nods slightly, and I turn my gaze back to the trees, where the warblers dance from limb to limb. They're far enough away that they're not easily seen, but to a trained eye, they might as well have neon feathers.

I wait, practicing the patience I'd impressed upon Jethro. They're Magnolia Warblers, not very common this time of year but not unheard of either. Their backs are gray, black, and white, with bright yellow underbellies. I wait for them to show their colorful bellies to Jethro, knowing that's when he'll finally see them.

It's a few minutes later when I feel Jethro tense again, and I remember I'm still holding his forearm. I let it go as he points towards the two birds as they flit around the trees. "There, I see them!"

His exclamation startles the birds, and they fly off. I sigh in disappointment. It's time he learns the first truth of birdwatching.

"Rule one: if you see somethin', point. Quietly. Birds will hear you before you see them. They already knew we was here, but they didn't see us as a threat. You startle them, they're gone. They have a lot of predators out here wanting to snatch 'em up."

He leans back, eyes still wide with excitement but frowning in embarrassment. "Sorry. I guess I should have realized that."

I shrug. "Better you learn now than when we see the Trickster."

He tilts his head at me, eyebrows furrowed in confusion. "You mean that wasn't him?"

I shake my head and slowly stand up, carefully easing pressure on my ankle. It holds, but there's still a twinge. "No way. We have a ways to go before we're likely to see one of them. Better to get practice in, though, or it'll be gone before you spy the wind from its wings."

"Can I try the binoculars now?" he asks, starting to reach

for them where they hang around his neck.

I slap at his hand. "No. That's level two. You're still a beginner."

I take a small step and wince. Another one. "I'm gonna pace a bit, get my ankle movin'. You keep watchin' around. Tell me if you see another bird but don't yell about it. Grab my arm and point."

He nods, so I walk forward toward where we came from. It hurts, but it's already beginning to ease off. I'll be nursing it for a while, but provided I don't make any more stupid moves, I should be okay.

I move back to Jethro and see him pointing back where we'd come from. I pause in my pacing and look to what he's pointing at. I grin, wide this time, then sit down next to him.

"Good," I whisper, barely a breath. "Time for your next lesson."

I clench my teeth, open my lips, and let air out between my teeth saying 'pish' several times in a row.

Jethro jumps and grabs my arm, moving his head toward my ear to whisper. "What are you doing? I thought we were supposed to be quiet."

I nudge him back. "Watch what I do. This is different."

I turn back to where we'd seen the birds, making the high-pitched noises again, pausing between bouts.

Jethro's hand clenches my arm as the birds start to flit closer in the trees. And then two more appear. I can tell that they're Tufted Titmice from their black beaks and slightly burnished yellow under their wings.

"How are you doing that?" The whisper is close, awed.

"Easy enough. You clench your teeth and say pish a few times through 'em. Here, you try."

He shakes his head, but I nudge him in his side. "Come on, they're Titmice; it's not the Trickster. What's the harm?"

He lets go of my arm—I'd forgotten he'd been holding it—and I see him flex his jaw. He clenches his teeth, opens his lips wide, and attempts to pish.

I let out a snort behind my hands, and he glares at me. "What? Keep trying."

He shakes his head at me but tries again. It's better this time. I turn toward the birds and watch as they turn their heads back and forth, aiming their eyes at us to try to discern what we are. It brings a genuine smile to my face, and I realize how much I'd missed watching with someone, not alone.

The thought sobers me when I remember why.

I let him pish for a while longer while I stand to pace and move my ankle a bit more. I keep my gaze to the ground, grinding my teeth to hold back the tears. The memory has ruined the moment.

When I look up, he's watching me with concern.

"Are you sure you're okay? If your ankle is hurting, we can go back, try again later."

I walk to him and sit back down on the tree. My weight pulls it down again, but it's still holding strong.

"It's not my ankle."

I consider what to say. I could change the subject, but I don't think I want to anymore. He's met me halfway in everything so far. I have no reason to believe he won't in this, my hidden shame.

"It's been a while since I've done this. Watched with anyone." I avoid his gaze, but I know he's watching me. "My Uncle Jeremy and I used to do this together. Before."

"You never told me what happened to him. Do you want to talk about it?"

I snort, unamused. "I'm surprised you ain't heard the whole story already. This town is full of gossips."

I turn to him, trying to read him. He shrugs, and I see no dishonesty in his eyes. "I don't listen to gossip. People say things they don't mean when they don't have someone to be accountable to. Rather hear it in person."

I smile at that. "And I suppose that's what you're doin' now?"

His smile back is warm, not the excited flash of teeth of his normal beam but a subdued, gentle upturning of his mouth. "If that's what you want."

I turn from him then, easing back onto my feet. My ankle is near back to normal, and we need to get moving. But still. I look down at him.

"I'll tell you the story soon. For now, let's make you a Citizen."

———

I can tell from his slowed gait that Jethro is reaching the edge of his patience. The initial excitement from learning how to spot the birds in the trees and how to pish has long since passed. In its place is annoyance, harsh criticism, and long sighs.

"Are you sure we're going in the right direction?" he asks. Again.

I don't look at him remembering the cardinal rule myself even if he's long since abandoned it, but I can hear the venom in his voice. "I'm sure that if we keep goin', we'll see him," I say, considering. "There's no hard and fast rule on where. We may not see him the first time."

The sounds of his hiking stop. I want to scream at him to keep moving, but it's no use. He's met the end of his patience.

I start to turn around to talk him through it, but I see something out of the corner of my eye and pause. I don't turn away but motion with a wave of my hand for Jethro to come to me. He does so louder than I would have liked but with as much caution as he's capable of.

"Look," I whisper. I point northeast to a gathering of trees about ten yards in front of us. "I think I see one, right there."

There's no response at first, and I debate the risk of looking at him.

"I don't see anything," he finally says. "Are you saying this so I won't get mad?"

I hold back a screech at him in annoyance but instead grab for his hand. I pull it in front of me, using it to point to where I see not one but two of the Trickster finches in the trees.

I wait for him. Wait for him to become a Citizen, an honor that few in the town, let alone an outsider, have ever been gifted.

RUE SPARKS

I wait, but nothing comes.

I dare a look at his face. His jaw is slacked in awe, and for a moment, I think that he understands. But then he looks back at my face, into my eyes.

There is no moment of understanding, no feeling of life-changing awe. It is only the face of someone who's seen a pretty bird. A rare, exclusive bird. But a bird.

I try not to let the disappointment seep into my face, but by his frown, I've not succeeded. "What?" he says.

I turn away, relieved to see that the Tricksters are more interested in each other than fleeing. "It's just..." I say, not sure what I'm trying to say. "That's not the reaction I usually get."

The birds are dancing between the branches, their eyes held to each other. "What were you expecting?"

One of the birds braves a lower branch, and the other one—a female—follows.

"It's usually a lot more impactful, I guess." I can hear the disappointment in my own voice, and I wince. He takes my hand and gives it a squeeze.

"Of course it's not the same. You're right, Wren. I'm an outsider."

I turn to him at that, suddenly furious on his behalf. "You're not just an outsider."

He smiles though, not taking offense. "I didn't say *just*. But I *am* an outsider. I didn't grow up with these stories. Of course, it would mean more to you, to someone who grew up with them. The history. And that's okay. It doesn't have to mean the same thing to me."

His smile turns sheepish. "Honestly, it means more to me that you wanted me to see them than actually seeing them in person."

There are tears in my eyes, and I turn away quickly. The birds are close to the ground, closer than I've ever seen them, but then again, I've never seen two together.

"Don't say things like that." I try to punch him lightly in the shoulder, but I miss and hit the air. "You big softie."

I don't get to hear his response because there is a sudden loud trilling from the finches, a sound I've never heard in all my years out here. It's a sound of *wrong* and *danger*.

I look around, but I see no other wildlife, nothing that would cause a sudden change in mood.

"What's going on?" Jethro asks, sensing my tension. I keep searching the landscape, stepping forward to try and find the culprit. The finches have flown off, their discordant song echoing before the woods become silent in their wake.

"Got no idea," I say. I'm near where they flew from, and though there's prickling up the back of my neck, my curiosity wins out.

I turn around to look where Jethro still stands, eyes turning back and forth through the trees, following my lead.

The bite catches me off guard.

I look down immediately, crying out in surprise. There, nestled in the leaf litter and making its way quickly towards a nearby hole, is a large black viper.

"Wren?" Jethro's voice comes from far away, my mind quaking with the shock. I reach my hand up and hear my voice in the distance saying something about stopping, waiting for the snake to leave.

When it's disappeared below the ground, Jethro runs towards me, leaning forward to look at the bite.

"Oh my God," he says, voice rough. "Are you okay Wren?! What do we do?" He looks up at me, and for all my Uncle Jeremy's training on snake bites, I draw a blank.

"I don't know," I say. "I don't know. I've never seen that kind of snake before."

He looks back where the snake disappeared as if that will give us any answers. I can see him panicking, and I try to calm down enough to think clearly. I can feel the panic bubbling up, but not panic for me. No, panic for Jethro because I can't do this to him.

I breathe deeply then, thinking of Jethro and what I can do to make this as easy on him as I can.

"I need to get to the hospital. But if I walk, I'm afraid the venom will spread faster. You need to go get help. Run. Go to the office and tell Sean what happened."

He shakes his head, running his fingers through his hair. "I'll never get there alone—it'll take too long! I need to carry you."

I walk as far away from where the snake disappeared as I dare to with the bite. "No. Absolutely not. You can follow our trail, and you'll get help. I know you will."

He follows on my heels, and before I can sit down on the tree trunk I'd been eyeing, he has his arm under my legs and starts lifting me, pulling my other arm around his shoulders.

I gasp at the sudden change and look at him incredulously.
"What the hell do you think you're doin'?!"

"I'm going to carry you. I can do it. You tell me where to
go, and I'll take you. It'll be faster."

I shake my head at him, the adrenaline and possibly the bite
making me light-headed. My heart is beating too quickly. "You
won't make it. I'm too heavy. Leave me here and come back."

He hikes me up higher into his arms and starts walking.
I slap his chest with my hand, but with every moment, I feel
more and more lightheaded.

"You gotta put me down." It comes out a slur, and there's
a metallic taste in my mouth. Not a dry bite then. The place
where the viper bit me is swelling, the pain a pulsing at my calf.

"You gotta listen." I pause, feeling bile rise in the back of
my throat. "When you get to the tree broken at three o'clock
on the east side, take a left. Follow that path all the way to the
diner."

Jethro doesn't reply, and I stop resisting. I watch the sun
shining spots through the canopy above, white and greens and
yellows that blur together. *Maybe I'm not doing as good as all that.*
The pain hadn't started so bad, but now it feels like my calf
might burst, the muscle white-hot with pain and tight, burning.

There's more I need to tell him, but I can't form the words.
I choke on my own spit as my vision blurs and my tongue
becomes numb and awkward in my mouth.

I don't want him to be like me, I think, and then everything
goes black.

EIGHTEEN

I EXPECT TO WAKE UP GROGGY and sore in a hospital bed if at all, but instead, it's as if I breathe into my room, each heartbeat bringing the vision clearer.

There are no cartoon posters or comic book character bedspread. The hardcover children's books have been replaced by well-worn, yellowed paperbacks. The stars that were hung above the bed are gone, replaced by vinyl silhouettes of swallows.

The room is as I left it this morning, complete with my t-shirt and sleep shorts on the floor. But unlike this morning, Uncle Jeremy still sits in the plush chair, book clasped in his hands. The juxtaposition shatters my heart and brings tears to my eyes. I can't hold back a choked sob.

"Now, Wren, you let it out," he says, and his voice holds the same gentle timbre that it always has. That smile, that tone, the rasp of the words in a room of familiarity and loneliness... The tears cling to my lashes, but I clench my eyes tight. I'm buried in the moments with my uncle like an avalanche, and I cling to every bit of debris like a lifeline.

Riding Eleanor's mares together, trying and failing to mimic the dressage we'd seen the previous week. Driving an hour to the nearest pet store to get my one and only hamster that would escape from its cage not two weeks later. Dying Easter eggs the most awful color combinations we could imagine, cracking them against each other to see which egg won. Birthdays with chocolate cake and trinkets that Uncle Jeremy found or made.

And over and over again, the moments where the Trickster would come into view as we'd sip our thermoses of homemade sweet tea, sitting on the forest floor cross-legged and side by side. The memories all come to me like a swarm, and I'm drowning in them.

A cold hand on my arm makes me jump. I look up to see Uncle Jeremy holding me steady, his eyes as warm as his hands are cold. But as I look, for a moment, they're the glassy emptiness of death as he lay in the morgue. I jump back away from his grip and wrap my arms around myself as I shake with the strength of the sobs I can no longer hold back.

"Why?" I ask, though there's no answer he could give that would make it easier. "Why did you have to die?"

It's the question that has held me trapped in my own skin

for so long that I forget what it's like to connect with anyone but myself. The bars that have kept Jethro at bay when there's so much of me that wants to embrace everything he has to give. It's what keeps me at arm's length whenever someone reaches their heart toward mine.

"I don't know," is his soft answer, and though I expected it, I shiver at the cold truth of it. "I don't think anyone knows, Little Bird."

I cling to the silence. At this moment, all I want to do is exist with my Uncle Jeremy for a few more minutes before I have to face reality. I startle to realize that I don't want to go back to a world where Uncle Jeremy doesn't exist, that I'd rather follow wherever he goes. The thought leaves me with an icy longing.

"There is somethin' I can tell you though, Wren." I look up at his dark eyes and notice in my periphery that he's opening the book, further along in the pages this time.

He pretends to read. I know he's memorized every page, as he had done with the books he had read to me over and over as a child.

"The little bird was sad. Their family had left for another life, but the little bird blamed themselves. They tore themselves away from the helpin' hands around them because they didn't want to get hurt anymore. None of them was enough to make up for what that little bird had lost."

After he turns the page, for the first time, he turns the book around for me to see.

There are no words. Only small, watercolor drawings. I

gasp in a shallow breath, wet with tears, and reach out a hand
to trace the figures in the pages.

It's Jethro. And Sheriff June, Mrs. Delaney, Sean, Leigh.
They're all reaching out a hand to the center of the book where
a small, yellow wren stood clinging to a shattered pink heart.

"The little bird was afraid. They didn't want to be hurt
again. So they fluttered away like the passing wind, away from
their friends. The sheriff, like an older sister. The memory
keeper, a grandmother. Friends, friends that cared deeply. And
one, in particular, that would risk his life to save them."

He looks into my eyes and gives up the pretense of reading. My vision swims, but his voice is clear.

"Don't run away from them. You can't run away from
the people who love you. Because Wren, one day, you'll find
yourself alone. And that would be a tragedy more terrible than
heartbreak."

I blink through my tears, and the watery view of the room
dissolves into black.

NINETEEN

I OPEN MY EYES to a familiar ceiling, and a memory hits me in my gut. In my mind, I see Uncle Jeremy on the gurney, face pale and lips purple, waxen. Panic bubbles in my chest, and I grasp at the sheets, knuckles clenched tight.

"You're awake," someone says, and I recognize the voice as Jethro. There's suddenly a hand grasping my wrist in a gentle hold, a body close to my side. I try to turn my eyes toward him, but I feel weak and overwrought.

"Hey, hey, it's okay. Relax. You're safe." He rubs his fingers along my forearm and grabs my hand in his. I feel it like a tether, grounding me in the moment. It brings me back from the dark place of my memories.

I look up into his face, and though at first it's blurred out of focus, when I concentrate, the vision clears. His mouth is creased in a frown, eyes wet. *He must have been terrified.*

"What happened?" It comes out rough, my throat raw from lack of use. I focus on my breathing—deep inhale, longer exhale, like my social worker told me. If I was in the hospital, alive, the last thing I needed to do was overtax my body with a panic attack.

I look around. There's an empty bed to my right, the curtains drawn over where I suspect there's a window to the outside from the light seeping around its edges. I'm hooked up to an IV, and the steady beeps become a lullaby that ticks in the back of my mind. There's a vase with lilies on my side table with a card—from Mrs. Delaney?—along with Jethro's bag. There's a pillow and a blanket on a reclining chair in the corner. How long has he been staying here?

There's silence for a moment. He rubs his other hand up and down my arm, barely a touch at all. It tickles, but the sensation sets my mind back in the present. The panic sits in my throat, and I choke out a sob. The events of the day—yesterday?—come back to me like a flood.

The finches. Their song. The snake.

And Jethro, carrying me through the trees until I passed out.

"You're safe now," he says, a whisper. "They got you the anti-venom in time, though I had a hell of a time describing the snake. I'm not nearly the wildlife expert you are."

I let out a half-laugh, half huff at that, but it sends me into a choking fit. My mouth feels dry, eyelids caked. He puts his arm under my head, around my shoulder, and I allow him to help me to lean up to get it all out.

After a while of coughing, I'm more aware, and Jethro sets me back down on the bed. He rubs my arm again, and though the feeling has become rough and mildly annoying, I let it go. I'm simply glad for his presence, the comfort.

"I don't think I woulda been much help either. I ain't ever seen that kind of snake before in my life," I say.

Jethro nods at that and pats my arm one last time before he lets my hand go. I try not to miss the comfort. "That's what the doctor said, too. They haven't seen anything like it before. But they said it was similar to a coral snake, and they found something that worked. Took a few tries, though, so you should stay put a while. No hiking for a month, they said."

I grunt, annoyed at the restriction but understanding the necessity. Lynn was bitten by a cottonmouth a few years back, and it took her months to recover fully. Anyone who stepped foot in those woods knew the danger and was willing to take the risk. I was lucky to have my life.

Then I remember exactly why I have my life, and my face heats.

"You saved me." It comes out a question. "You coulda left and saved yourself, but you didn't. You dragged me here all on your own. Why would you do that?"

He scrunches his nose and frowns. "Why wouldn't I? You're my friend, Wren. I wouldn't let you die. Yeah, it sucked carrying your ass here, but I would never leave you like that."

From his tone, I sense his hurt at my questions, but I don't understand. Sure, if something happened to Sean or Mrs. Delaney or Sheriff June, I'd do what I could to save them.

But that was it, isn't it? I couldn't. I couldn't save Uncle Jeremy, though he was my lifeline, my foundation. I couldn't save him, but Jethro saved me and doesn't even understand what that means. The remembrance clenches my throat tight, and for a moment, I choke on air, eyes tearing up.

"I saw him die." The change of subject is abrupt, but I need him to know. "We were in the woods when he suddenly went down. My Uncle Jeremy. He raised me since I was little, when my parents passed away in a car wreck. Taught me everything I know. He's the one told me about the Trickster, told me the key. 'Don't look down.'"

I inhale deeply, and I can feel the grief choke me. "I couldn't save him. He passed out, had a stroke. I tried so hard to drag him back, but he was so much heavier than me. I couldn't. I couldn't carry him."

I let my head fall back, close my eyes, and idly pick at the sheets at my side with my fingers. Jethro notices and takes my hand back in his, squeezes it once.

"I ran as fast as I could. I got to the diner, called Ned to bring a stretcher, and Sheriff June came as quick as she could. Between us and a couple of guys from the diner, we got him to the hospital, but it was too late. He died here, in this building."

The pain overflows, cleansing through the tears that fall down my face. I hiccup, and Jethro pulls me up the bed by my shoulders and leans my head on his.

I cry until the tears run dry. We sit there silent but holding each other in quiet understanding.

For the first time, I don't feel the guilt. I feel understood. Loved.

I don't want to ever let that feeling go.

—

When Sheriff June comes to visit me in my hospital room a few days later, I fully expect to hear a version of 'I told you so.'

Instead, she looks haggard and worn down, eye sockets purpled from lack of sleep and stress. I debate saying something like 'you look worse off than I do' but figure that would be pushing her boundaries.

"I'm glad you're okay," she says, and it sounds sincere if tired. "I put out a notice that there's been a bite in the area, so hopefully no one else follows in your footsteps." The last quip sends a flood of annoyance through me, though it's probably an unintended slight. Considering the haunted look in her eyes, I let it go.

"Thank you," I say instead. "I'm lucky Jethro's as strong as he is or it may have ended differently."

She nods and pulls off her cap. Her expression is serious.

"Wren. I know you still carry guilt about what happened with your uncle."

I open my mouth to protest but close it with a snap. Maybe it's okay to be reassured. *Maybe I want to be.*

"Your uncle knew the dangers of trekkin' into those woods. He knew 'em better than you did at the time. And he'd been in those woods plenty of times without you. What do you think would have happened had you not been there at all, Wren?"

I'm silent. I understand what she's getting at, but I need to hear it. My chest constricts around the pain, and there's prickling in my eyes.

"He wouldn't have made it, but we wouldn't have known. For days, weeks, we may never have found him. Even if you couldn't save him, Wren, you gave him dignity. You gave yourself closure. In a bad situation, sometimes that's all you get."

She taps her cap against her knee a few times, a dull rhythmic thud like a heartbeat.

Like healing.

"It ain't ever going to go away. The pain. It'll change, sure, but it will never go away. And that's gotta be okay. You gotta be okay with letting the pain in because if you don't, it will swallow you whole."

She settles her cap back on her head and pushes it down until it hits her low ponytail. I watch her, mesmerized by her words, unable to speak for the clench in my throat.

"You have people that will listen, Wren. You gotta let 'em in." She smiles with her teeth, and I realize I've never seen her smile more than a closed mouth upturn of her lips. "I'll listen too, though you and I both know we're like oil and water."

I let out a wet laugh. My voice is muffled and my nose stuffed like cotton. "Yeah, I appreciate the offer Sheriff June,

but I think I'll stick with Mrs. Delaney and Jethro if that's okay
with you. You got your own business to worry about."

She sobers at that, and I miss the smile. Her frown is deep-
set, thick wrinkles on either side. "You could say that."

I know it's not my place, I know Sheriff June has been
kind and I'm pushing my luck, but I can't stop myself from
asking. "How is Turney's case going? Do you think Tom did
it?'"

She shakes her head and rubs her cheek with her hand
before it slaps down to her knee. "You know I can't talk to
you about an open case, Wren. As I said, you're a civilian." She
stands up, pats down her jacket to push out where the air had
gathered it in bunches, and avoids my gaze. "Though between
me 'n you and the fence-post, our dear friend Thomas was on
a huntin' trip in Avery County the past few weeks with six of
his pals. Got a twelve-point buck and a six-pointer. Sure you'll
hear all about it in the diner."

There's a sly smirk on her face, and she gives me a wink.

I suppose sometimes oil and water can mix.

—

Jethro comes not long after Sheriff June takes her leave,
arms bogged down with food from the diner and several
books.

When I look up at him, he hesitates. I wonder what kind
of expression I have on my face. I'm feeling a mix of amusement and annoyance—so the annoyance must have won out. I

send him a tired smile, and he relaxes, sets the books on a chair and the food on a side table.

"I wasn't sure what you like, so I got a few things." He unpacks the food and sets a few Styrofoam containers on the bottom of my bed.

"Exactly how much do you think I can eat? And how long do you think I'm gonna be here? I definitely don't need that many books!" I try to let my amusement seep in my tone, keeping it light. Teasing. I'm still unpracticed in the art of having a friend.

He shrugs and pulls plastic silverware out of the bag. He points at one Styrofoam container, then another. "Meatloaf or country fried steak?"

"Meatloaf," I say. "Jay makes the best meatloaf in town. I'll even let you try it if you want." He hands me the container, and I take it gratefully, glad to be able to have something besides the hospital fare.

We eat in silence, me in my hospital bed and him on one of the squeaky plastic hospital chairs. The meatloaf is a welcome change, juicy and covered with Jay's famous secret sauce on top—which everyone knows to be ketchup and brown sugar. I'm thankful to Jethro for the kind gesture, but not sure what to say to him now that he's here.

"I saw Sheriff June in the lobby," Jethro says, and I'm thankful for his chattiness. "She seemed tired. I hope everything is going okay on the case."

I take the conversation starter for what it is, glad that he's able to sense my need despite my inability to start.

"She said that Tom ain't the killer. Well, not in so many words. He wasn't in town when Turney was murdered."

There's silence for a while, and I wonder if I've said something wrong. He's got his fork in his mouth, looking up at the ceiling in contemplation.

"We have no other leads," he says, mumbling around the cutlery.

I shrug. After my own near-death experience, I'm not in a hurry to get back on the case. The whole thing is a little silly in retrospect, to think that I could succeed where Sheriff June failed. All because I thought I was the superior tracker and took offense to a murdered Citizen.

"I think we should hold off on investigating further," I mumble in the direction of the food, and I realize how out of character it must seem. "What else can we do?"

He's silent for a while, and I sneak a glance back up at him. But he's turned his attention to the food, concentrating on where he's trying to cut up the chicken and failing.

I turn back to my own food. The case was what had brought us together, but maybe that's all our friendship was based upon. Without that, can it survive?

Although, there is one other thing we share a passion for. Knowledge.

"Hey, seems how you're one of us now, I should teach you how to read through the back books. You could learn more about the town, and it might be useful for your degree."

He doesn't say anything, and I try not to show my disappointment as I deflate. Maybe that's all it was, a friendship of necessity. I try not to be sad about it.

I hear him set down his plastic cutlery and look over. He looks down at the remainder of his meal with brows furrowed in a thoughtful expression. "Jet?"

He turns towards me, and his face is full of excitement, the kind he gets whenever he sees a challenge.

"While we're at it, let's see if we can find out what kind of snake bit you. Sheriff June said she's never heard of the like before. Surely the town records or the library should have something."

I smile in relief, a crooked thing that feels barely there.

—

It doesn't last long—the relief, or the smile.

It's not quite a week later when I get discharged. The doctors are surprised at my slow recovery, and I bristle at the implication of my weakness, but they reassure me it's possible I may have developed an allergic reaction or complications. Neither of those possibilities soothe my nerves.

Jethro comes to help me home, and though Mrs. Delaney offers, I know it would be like the blind leading the blind, us trying to get each other to a car. But I can tell immediately that something is off. Jethro is scattered, nervous. He keeps checking his phone through my discharge instructions, while we wait for the prescriptions, and while I pack my meager belongings. Any conversation is stilted and one-sided. The normally exuberant chatterbox has gone nearly silent.

It's when I'm ready to go and he's nose deep in his phone that I've had enough.

"Can you grab my bag?" I ask, exhausted from the exertion of packing but wanting to get out of there.

"Huh?" He doesn't raise his eyes from where he's texting.

I resist the urge to smack his arm, but he finally looks up. I point to where my bag is on the hospital bed. "I said, can you grab my bag? Geez, Jet, stop checkin' your phone and help me out"

He frowns at me and puts it in the back pocket of his jeans. I can see a temper like a storm cloud brewing.

"It's my phone. I can check it if I want." He grabs the bag and slings it over his shoulder, takes a step, then pauses when the telltale ding alerts him of a new message. He doesn't hesitate in pulling his phone back out.

I grunt in stewing frustration. "Okay, fine, but you're here to help me, not check your phone."

"I'm helping you, aren't I?" Again, he doesn't look up, the phone shining an eerie glow on his face in the low light of the hospital room.

"*Now* you are. *Before* you were checkin' your phone." I lean up against the wall, my limbs still weak from not being used.

He turns off his phone with a click but doesn't put it away. "Come on, Wren. Give me a break."

I throw up my arms, wincing as the motion causes a wave of dizziness. "I'm not the one's come in here with an attitude."

"I didn't have an attitude until you got on my case! I'm distracted today, okay?" He seems frustrated, but there's a tinge of apology in his tone that soothes me. Only a bit, though.

"You're not the one getting discharged from the hospital. What have you got to worry about?"

It was the wrong thing to say. His face transforms from near apology to fury, stature lifted back. He drops my bag on the hospital bed.

"A lot, actually. My grandfather was taken to the hospital because he had a bad fall. Now we need to see if he broke his hip and if he has, whether he'll recover. So excuse me if I'm worried about whether we'll be planning a birthday party or a funeral."

My heart drops to my stomach, and I feel weak for a moment. Long enough that my response is slow.

"I'm sorry, Jet. I didn't know."

He shakes his head and rubs his fingers over his eyes. I can't tell if he's rubbing away tears or tearing away at the anger in his eyes.

"You would have if you'd asked. But that would mean you'd have to be thinking about someone other than yourself for once."

It feels like an arrow in my heart. "Hey, that's uncalled for."

He drops his hands and the look he gives me makes me feel the smallest I've ever felt.

"Is it? I've helped you with your panic attacks, with this stupid investigation which, may I remind you, nearly got you *killed.* But asking your friend why he's so upset, that would be too much. And I can't call you on it, why?"

Every word feels like a punch to the gut, but it's blowing

air on embers and smoke too, and I feel a rage building inside. But I also remember those first few days after Uncle Jeremy died, and I won't begrudge him his own fire.

"Come on Jet. You're upset, and I said I'm sorry. But you're gettin' out of line."

He stuffs his hands in his pockets and looks down at the floor. "Am I? Maybe I've had it. Maybe I'm too goddamn patient all the time and I need to get a backbone. I thought you were my friend, but it's only ever about *Wren.*"

The words sting their way into my eyes and burrow in. "Jet. Knock it off." But he isn't finished.

"God, I'm so stupid. You've got your head in the past with your uncle and those goddamn birds; you never see the people trying to help you. Mrs. Delaney treats you like a grandchild, Sean's been trying to be a friend to you for as long as I've known him, and me, I've been bending backwards trying to be there for you, but you keep *pushing us away*. Like you don't give a damn about any of us."

He runs his hands through his hair and holds it there, and in the low light of the room covered by the shadow of his arms, I can't see his expression.

"I wish I never came here. I'm so sick of this stupid town with your stupid birds and this stupid forest where everyone goes to die."

The fire burns, and it doesn't hurt anymore. Now there's rage.

"Get. Out."

He drops his hands, and I can see his face, eyes shining

with signs of held back tears, but I'm too angry to care.

"Fine," he says, shaking his head. "Not like I was wanted in the first place. Not really."

He walks past me, and for a nanosecond in time we're shoulder to shoulder, me facing the room, him facing the door and the light shining through it. I see through the window the forest and its trees, green leaves swaying in the wind, their silver undersides flashing like shuttered lights. A storm is coming, so it's all a dark blue hue, the wind strong and blowing dirt and dead leaves and twigs through the air. I see no birds, but I know they're further in, huddling down to weather the storm.

I live in that world, that storm. I always have.

Behind me is the light of the Jethro's world, where there are people I don't understand. People who *want* things from me I don't understand. People who came and left like storm clouds, and was that what I wanted my life to be? One never ending wait for the storm cloud to pass, where I'd be left to my calm but lonely world, the chaos and life and joy only ever a fond memory I was waiting to experience again?

And there, a memory: *One day you'll find yourself alone. And that would be a tragedy more terrible than heartbreak.*

"Jet, wait."

I hear his footsteps come to a stop behind me.

"Just wait."

I walk to the hospital bed with shaky legs and collapse onto the edge. I blink against the light after having stared into the darkness of the room for so long, but Jethro is still there, looking at me with curiosity now. I point to the chair where he'd sat just a few days ago.

"Sit."

He frowns at me. "I don't think-"

"Sit. Down." I don't give him another moment to debate. He sighs and rubs behind his neck but does as I ask.

"Now." I run through my head, trying to figure out what to say, how to make him *stay*. I don't know how to be a friend.

Maybe honesty is best.

"I'm sorry. I don't know how to be"—I wave a hand between us uselessly—"*this*. A friend."

He snorts. *Off to a good start, then.* I sober, biting my lip until I taste blood.

"I'm sorry about your grandpa. I saw that you were upset, and I shoulda asked. A friend would have asked." I can see his shoulders slump as if he's been holding them tense, like they've been holding the foundations of something. Maybe they have been.

"I get so in my head. You're not wrong. I'm gonna try to do better. Give me another chance?"

He smiles, fragile and tenuous, and I've never been so glad to see those pearly-white teeth. "Yeah. I guess I over-reacted too."

I glare at him, and his smile vanishes, wincing in embarrassment. "You did."

"Yeah, I did. I shouldn't have said those things about this town. I didn't mean them."

I shrug. "You did. Or you've thought them, at least. But

you wouldn't have said them if I hadn't hurt you first. So that's a start."

He stands up from the chair and flops down next to me on the bed, bumping his shoulder into mine after a moment. Up close, I see the tear streaks, and it hurts to know I put them there.

"Truce?" I bump a fist against his shoulder in reply, but I know we're not done yet.

"I really am sorry about your grandpa. I'll be here. No matter what happens. I promise. I don't break my promises."

"I know you don't. And thank you."

TWENTY

ONCE I'M SETTLED AT HOME the days bleed into each other. I feel a bone deep exhaustion I've never experienced, and it saps my resolve. My savings dwindle, despite the occasional drop off of groceries and food from Jethro and his family. I meet his father, a short and stocky man with short, curled hair as bright as the moon in contrast to his dark brown skin. He has an easy smile and the same joyful personality as Jethro. I feel after the first few days that I've been adopted into their family. After our argument, it makes my stomach turn sour, guilt eating me from the inside.

My need to make income while I'm bed bound leads me to pulling some pine blocks into my room, and I whittle scraps into a plastic bin over my knee. But every piece wrecks my self-confidence. Broken off pieces, unseen cracks in the wood, or simply failed attempts. The wood shavings multiply but at the end of the week, I only have two good pieces, a turtle and a swallow. They're simple, and my fingers are uncharacteristically full of splinters. *At least they're sellable.*

It's the following Tuesday when the repetition of the hours is broken by a knock at the front door, barely audible through the hallway. "Come in!" I call out, hoping they can hear me. After a few minutes and another knock, I set down the plastic basin and begin the slow, stuttered trek towards the doorway.

I'm surprised to open the front door to find Leigh on my front porch. She's holding a basket covered in purple iridescent plastic and topped with a purple bow. I catch her gaze turning to the right, to where Uncle Jeremy's carving station is still intact. When she pulls her gaze away, she looks at me with a small, understanding smile.

I turn away, leaning heavily on the door jamb. "I couldn't move it," I mutter. "Doesn't seem right."

She shrugs, her grin turning sly. "I was the opposite. I couldn't stand to see everythin' how he left it."

I raise an eyebrow at her in question. "That why you wrecked his bedroom?"

There's a look of horror on her face, then she laughs, surprisingly bright. "I forgot you snuck in, you jerk. I got angry. I wanted to start packing things, and then I got so overwhelmed, I had a bit of a fit. It's better now. Billy is helping."

I open the door so she can come in, my leg aching from

the extended standing. "Billy's your fiancée, right?"

She bites her lip but takes the cue, stopping in the hallway to gaze around at the space. I realize she'd never been in here before. *After I broke into Turney's, I suppose it's fair she gets an in-depth look at my space.*

I close the door and turn toward the living room but stop suddenly as my balance begins to tip. She catches my arm with one hand, looking at me with concern.

"You're still hurt," she says, looking around. "Where were you sittin'? Let's get you back there so you can relax."

I nod towards the bedroom down the hall. "Second room on the right, but really, we can sit in the living room. I'll be fine."

She shakes her head, sets the basket in the crook of her right arm, and takes my forearm with her left. "Nonsense. You're hurt. Let's have ya lie down and we can chat."

I mutter to myself, and she giggles in return. The sound echoes down the hall, breaking the dull silence. We stumble down the hall slowly, and Leigh glances at the photos on the walls as we go. I can tell she's itching to speak, but she focuses on holding me up.

When we get to the bedroom, I ease down onto the edge of the bed, and Leigh sets the basket on a nearby chair before she opens the drapes on the window. The sudden light makes me blink, and I let out a huff in protest.

"None of that," she says. "It's so dreary in here. You need light and air to heal." With that, she slides open the window, keeping the screen down to keep out the flies. The wind that rushes through is hot but it brings with it the smell of freshly mowed grass.

She steps back to admire her handiwork, rubbing her hands on her skirt before turning to me. "Now, we need to talk."

I drag my legs under the covers, placing the plastic bin back on my knees and starting to whittle again. If we're going to talk, I need the comfort of my hands to be moving.

She sits on the edge of the bed, back to me. I wait for her to start, the only sound in the room the chirping of crickets from the window and the scraping of the knife on wood.

"I need you to find out what happened to my grandpa."

I pause in my whittling, the knife half notched into the wood. I look up at her back, but she's got her gaze fixed out the window.

"Why me?"

"Because I trust you."

I turn back to my whittling, cursing at the new nick right where the birds' face was supposed to be. "I broke into your grandfather's house. We hacked into your social media accounts and email. We lied to you to get you into town hall. Yet you trust me? Why?"

"You did those things because you would do anything to find out what happened to Grandpa."

"Hmm." I try to continue my whittling, but my hands are shaking, and the last thing I need is to cut myself. I set the half-finished bird down on the side table. "Why not look into it yourself? Or talk to Sheriff June? Don't you trust her?"

There's quiet, the silence strangely calm, unhurried. I let my head fall back and study the vinyl swallows on the ceiling.

"I trust Sheriff June to do her job and what's right for the town." She turns towards me, then reaches a hand to grab at mine on the sheets. "I trust *you* to do what's needed for my grandpa. For me. I trust you to know this town better than anyone. And I trust you because you're in the same place as me."

"And what place is that?"

She squeezes my hand, and her smile burns itself in my memory. It sends an ache in my chest.

"Lost."

—

"Get up, Wren."

The voice eases into my mind, but I curl deeper into the sheets, seeking the coolest part to ease the ache in my leg. I mumble something incoherent, sticking my face hard into the pillow.

"Wren. Up. Now."

I shake my head, then suddenly the sheets are pulled from my torso, but they stick between my legs, and I let out a yelp. When I turn over, I see Jethro, red faced in shame but with a determined look.

"How did ya get in here?!" I yell, pulling the sheets back around me. I'd fallen asleep in my clothes, fortunately, but having him see me sleeping sets me into rage.

"You gave me a key, remember?"

"But I never said ya could come in without asking!"

"Then why give me a key?"

I wad up the sheets and throw them at his face, but he catches it with a laugh. I mutter to myself, stretching my leg carefully.

"You northerners and your weird sense of propriety. You don't come into someone's house unannounced. It's not done."

Jethro folds the sheet, and I yank it from him in annoyance and fling it to the end of the bed. I stop myself from crossing my arms and pouting like a child but just barely.

"Why are you here?"

"To stop you from moping," he answers, then after a pause, "and to get you groceries. You're coming with me this time."

I stifle a yawn but swing my legs over the edge of the bed. "I don't need any more groceries. I don't know how much y'all think I eat, but I have plenty."

"Then to get you out. I'm not letting you stay in this bed one more minute."

I glare at him. "I'm *injured.* Remember? Snake bite? You having to carry me all the way to town? Your memory can't be that bad."

He rolls his eyes, but there's a concerned edge to his expression.

"Seriously, Wren, you have to get out of here. The doctor seemed to think you should be more recovered than you are—maybe you need some fresh air? Let's go into town. I'll get you a few treats for shits and giggles, or we can get ice cream. But you need to get out of here."

"Really? You think fresh air and a brisk walk will cure my snake bite? Since when did you become an expert." I pick at my fingers, at the splinters still caught in them. "I'm not here because I wanna be. I'm just...healin'."

He grabs for my hand, but I pull away and look at him in question. He wiggles his fingers, and I let him see. He tuts as he looks at the raw skin and splinters.

"You've done a number on your fingers. Let me get the tweezers and we'll fix these up first." He looks to the basin full of wood shavings still sitting on the chair at the side of the bed, then back at me with a raised eyebrow. "And you say you're fine?"

I nod my head towards the small army of figures I've carved. After more frustration, I got into the zone and managed several more pieces—a raven, a small bear, a pony, a few fish. "I gotta make money somehow. These won't make much of a dent, but it's a start."

He hums noncommittally but drops my fingers. "Let's get you fixed up and we can go out."

I grimace, stuffing my fingers under my armpits. "Nope. Stayin' here."

"Wren—" He stops and rubs at his eyes, leaving his hands covering his face. "Wren, please. Just this once, please, let me help you." He drops his hands to his sides and sighs. "I hate to see you like this. Air will help, I promise. Plus, we never do anything for *fun*. Can't you stop being stubborn for five minutes?"

There's an edge of frustration but also hurt to his voice, and he stands hunched as if he expects I'll swat him out of the room at any moment. I grit my teeth in frustration, my thoughts a jumble as I try to form the words to make him understand.

"Leigh stopped by," I finally acquiesce, and I hope he'll understand. "She asked me to find out what happened to her grandpa."

His face twists in confusion, brow furrowed. "We were already doing that, weren't we?"

I let out a harsh breath and throw my head back. "You don't *get* it. She's asking. *Us.* Not the sheriff, not anybody else. Us." I look back at him, but I have to turn away quickly lest he see how fickle my thoughts are at the notion. "I don't think I'm the person she wants me to be."

There's silence that stretches, broken only by the cicadas outside—a steady orchestra that plays an unharmonious tale of impermanence. *Do they know how fleeting they are?*

I feel a dip in the bed, and he starts fiddling with the sheets, gaze not meeting mine. "Gotta say, I'm not used to you being the uncertain one. It's weirdly comforting that even you feel unsure sometimes."

"Not. Helping," I grumble, pulling the blankets away from his hands.

He stands from the bed, looming over me, closer than I would like but I won't be the one to flinch. "Wren. I'll be here to help. We'll figure out what happened to Turney, together. But not today. Today, you're hurting, and I don't mean physically."

I look up at that, and though he's closer than I'd like, his smile is sunshine. "I'm not telling you, I'm asking you: can I take you to town for ice cream? Heaven knows we deserve it."

I bite my lip and nod. The grin he returns is worth it, wide enough his dark brown cheeks bulge with it, freckles like constellations. He adjusts his signature aviator glasses, and the motion is so familiar it hurts.

"Alright. Let's get those splinters taken care of and head out."

—

The town is as quiet as ever, the streets near empty. We're at town center, which is little more than a gas station, the grocer, a farm supply store, bakery, and a thrift shop. The bakery, also the ice cream parlor, looks the newest—it used to be a pizza parlor, but they had a fire and the whole facade had to be replaced.

We decide to stop for ice cream, me getting a plain vanilla cone and Jethro deciding on mint chocolate chip. Nancy, the owner, eyes Jethro warily, but after seeing me inch closer to him in clear acceptance, she beams unabashedly. She sneaks an extra scoop on his cone to appease me. It's when I mention Jethro's grandfather though that she loses all suspicion and inquires about how he's doing—apparently old friends with the man from their school days.

"I never thought of my grandfather in school," Jethro says thoughtfully as he tries to tackle the towering cone once we've left. We're walking down the street, the sun shining bright in my eyes, and I use my free hand to shade them. "Especially down here. No offense, but I can't imagine growing up black in the south, especially back then."

I wrinkle my nose. "None taken. People are assholes. Not gonna lie to you, I'd be careful in some of the towns 'round here. We were one of the last towns to integrate back in the seventies from what Mrs. Delaney told me, and some towns around here haven't changed much since then." I bump him in the side, and he fumbles to not drop his cone. "You stick with me. I'll tell you what places to watch out for."

I sigh, dropping my hand from my eyes as we pause under the shade of a tree to finish our cones. "I was kind of pissed off at Nancy at first to be perfectly honest. It never bothered me before, but having you here, talking with you more…I guess it's making me see things differently."

He hums to himself, in the middle of trying to stop his cone from dripping on his hands. I snort in laughter, and he gives me a half-hearted glare. "What kind of things?" he asks when he gets it under control.

I shrug, letting my eyes wander down the empty sidewalk. There's a trickle of people here and there now that the sun is easing down the horizon. "I've not much talked to outsiders before. My Uncle Jeremy, he warned me off them. Said they never stay long, that there's no point. Never had much respect for anyone outside the town."

Jethro is down to his cone and takes a bite and chews thoughtfully before he answers. "I have noticed this town is pretty insular, isn't it? You said that it was partially because of the issues with the town losing a lot of its income, right?"

I nod, but the action causes my arm to move enough for the ice cream to drip down my fingers. "Ah, napkin, napkin! Gross!"

Jethro laughs, the sound melodic, and hands me a few from his pocket. "Wow, that has to be the most afraid I've seen you of anything. It's just ice cream."

I grumble, wiping down my hand. "It's *sticky*. I hate being sticky." I drop the offending napkin in a nearby trash can, and we walk again, ice cream almost gone.

"And yet you live where the air is like sticky like syrup when it rains." Jethro finishes off his cone and tries to talk with his mouth full. I lightly slap his arm, but he continues. "You know, you said that the fracking stopped and that's why the town started losing income. Why did it stop?"

I finish my cone and wave my hand at him. He snickers and gives me his last napkin.

"They coulda ran out of what they was looking for? I don't rightly know. It did a lot of damage to the area, though. We started havin' issues with the groundwater is what Mrs. Delaney said. We aren't supposed to drink the tap water now."

"That's what grandpa said too, that we aren't supposed to drink the water. Made me really nervous when we first got here." He frowns, looking down at his feet. "Speaking of Mrs. Delaney, I should tell you … She's been out of the office for a few days. She says she'll be fine but, well, I don't know her so well, so I don't know what to trust."

My heart beats a harsh rhythm in my chest, but I turn my thoughts to all the times she'd left and come back no worse of the wear. It could be nothing. *I can't lose her too.*

We're in front of the grocery, and I see Sophie's husband outside, fluffing up bouquets of flowers on a shelf on the sidewalk. Jethro gives me a mischievous grin and runs up to him. The grocer jumps at first, but Jethro puts his arms up to assuage him. There are words exchanged that I can't hear, and then Jethro is pulling out his wallet. *Oh no, he isn't...*

He is. I make it over, hobbling faster than I probably should, determined to protest, but I'm too late. He sets the bouquet in my hands with a sheepish smile. "I wanted to give you flowers when you were sick," he says, "but I wasn't sure where to get any. And I was too worried to figure it out at the time. Better late than never, right?"

I peek through the plastic wrapping at the flowers—lilies and baby's breath—and let out a sigh at his antics. The look he's giving me is that of an excited puppy, and the last thing I want is to proverbially kick him. "You're such a weirdo," I say, "but they're nice. Thank you."

He holds out his arm, and I do roll my eyes this time before taking it. "Off to your ball! Er—grocery!"

He makes me smile. The thought catches me off guard. And then, *You would have liked him, Uncle Jeremy.*

The thought of my uncle turns my stomach, but I won't let anything sour the moment.

Not today.

—

I know the second we pull up to the sidewalk in front of Uncle Jeremy's house that something is wrong. Where there should have been darkness seeping back behind the house, the backyard is lit by the humming of the back light, bright and casting shadows in the near darkness so soon after twilight.

"Stay here," I whisper to Jethro. "Somethin's up." I undo my seatbelt and get out of the car, careful to quietly shut the door lest I tip off the intruders.

"Wait, Wren—" he starts, frantically trying to undo his seatbelt. I raise my hand to him.

"The light's on in the back, and I haven't been there in weeks. I'll grab somethin' and see who's snuck back there. Stay here, have your phone ready in case we need to call the sheriff."

"Wren, I don't think you should—"

I don't wait for his answer. I'm still weak from my recovery, but I won't let anything happen to Uncle Jeremy's home. I cross the grass at a slow, stuttered gait, listening for any indication of an intruder. There's the telltale sounds of creaking wood and hushed movement which sends my heart racing.

Sneaking to the side of the porch, I grab part of a two by four leaning against the side of the house in the wood pile and inch my way around the yard. Everything is cast in a blue hue, and it takes my eyes a while to adjust between the dark of the side of the house and the light in the backyard.

Around the corner there is—

"A surprise party."

I jump, nearly whacking Jethro with the two by four in my shock. I use it instead to steady my balance at the sudden movement, glaring at him.

"It was *supposed* to be a surprise party," he continues, "but you kind of ruined the surprise part."

I try to calm my heart, eyes wide as I take in the balloons, streamers, and Citizens milling about in the backyard. "I'm *surprised*," I whisper. "I am very surprised. And confused. What the hell is goin' on?"

Jethro slowly, carefully, reaches for the two by four I'm still holding and sets it against the side of the house. He holds out his arm, and I take it, still in a daze. We round the corner, and there's a chorus of 'Surprise!' and noisemakers before we're surrounded by people. Though expected, the sudden noise puts my teeth on edge, but a greater part of me is awestruck.

Along with the Citizens, there's Sean, Mrs. Delaney, and the sheriff makes a (brief) appearance as the night goes on. Apparently my entirely self-induced isolation had not gone unnoticed, and it had been Sean's idea to break the tension with a potluck. It leaves me with a warm feeling in my chest that I try not to dissect. I think idly on how strange it might seem to someone on the outside for me to be my age and count so many older adults among my found family and friends, but I'd never much gotten along with my peers at school. I'd been an outsider, and happy to be so.

Apparently the outsider role doesn't fit me anymore.

As glad as I am for the support, eventually I become worn out at the crowd. Jethro takes it in stride and asks if I'd like to retreat to the workshop for a breather, excusing us by saying he's not had a chance to see it properly.

We sit in comfortable silence, Jethro drinking a beer and me a canned soda. He teases me for being too young to drink, to which I glare and remind him he's only *just* old enough but still call him an old man for my trouble.

Jethro sneaks glances at me that he thinks I don't see but mostly entertains himself by staring at all the wood working tools and miscellaneous half-finished projects. It's comforting to know we don't have to say a word.

That is, until there's a knock on the workshop door. I yell out a 'come in' before Nathaniel peeks through the entryway.

"Party's finishin' up," he says, then hesitates. "Before we leave, I have a question for ya."

"Shoot," I say, and finish out my soda with one last gulp. Jethro nudges me in my side, and I roll my eyes. "What?"

Nathaniel doesn't react to my curt reply and walks cautiously toward the half-finished bear Uncle Jeremy had been working on. It towers above even his height, ferocious in its jagged edges and roaring maw.

"I want to talk to you about the bear, actually," he says, reaching towards it but looking at me in question before I shrug. Taking it as permission, he touches one of the rougher areas, mouth open in awe.

"It's not finished," I say, as if that isn't obvious. Regardless, he circles it, turning his head back and forth as if evaluating.

"Finished enough."

"Finished enough for what? It's not even half done, it's not no count. What's this about?" I'm uncomfortable at the scrutiny. It was one of Uncle Jeremy's last projects, and the intense stare is getting to me. It feels like it should be private somehow.

He straightens and inhales as if to gather his courage. "I've taken a shine to it. I'd like to buy it."

I scrunch my nose. "Buy it? Why?"

He looks down at his hands, playing with the cuffs of his jacket as he avoids my gaze. "I like it." He shrugs, and I can sense he's uncomfortable with the question.

"Not good enough" I say and stand to stumble over to the recycling bin where I deposit my soda can before turning my back to him. I feel a flicker of unexpected hurt that he would ask.

"What's not good enough about liking something?" he asks.

I cross my arms. "It's not *done*. He never got to finish it. He never will, okay? I don't know what ya want from me."

Nathaniel turns to Jethro, as if he'll be able to translate my words, but he shrugs and shakes his head.

Nathaniel approaches me, hands out. "Look, I know you don't like me. Jeremy never did either. I haven't been your biggest fan either in the past, to be perfectly honest. But I'm being truthful here."

I throw my hands up, simmering now. "Telling me you don't like me is not the way to get me to sell you something, especially not something like this. Don't you get it? It's the last thing he touched, for all it's not done. It's not for sale."

He frowns at that but nods curtly. "I see. I can understand that." He turns to Jethro, then back to me. "I'm sorry for botherin' you."

He walks past me and out the door, careful not to slam it but I can feel the frustration coming off him as he passes.

I stumble back to where we'd been sitting and lean back all the way on the table until I'm laying across it, staring at the beams that hold up the workshop.

"Can you believe that?" I say out loud, not expecting an answer. "How dare he," I mutter.

"You know, Wren, maybe you should sell it to him. Maybe not yet. But eventually."

I lean up on my elbows, eyebrows raised at Jethro. "What's that mean?"

He sips at his beer, staring at the bear. Except for the parts that are half completed, it feels real enough to come alive.

"You have to figure out something eventually. And you do have a lot of work from your uncle. You don't have to sell everything, but you have to figure out how you're going to take care of yourself."

I sit back up and lean on my elbows, taking in the workshop. "I know."

"So what do you think? What do you want to do with yourself?"

I pick at my fingernails as I speak, not wanting my hands

to stay still. A bad habit. "I don't have the grades for college. Don't have the money anyhow. I thought I'd take over for Mrs. Delaney and take over the shop. But I don't know anymore. It all feels like too much."

Jethro finishes his last sip of beer and stands up to drop it into the recycling bin. Walking back, he offers his arm to help me up.

"You don't have to figure out now. But you do have to start thinking about it." He pauses before we get to the doorway, patting my arm with his other hand. "We can think about it together, if you want."

I'm surprised not to feel the overwhelming panic I've come to expect on the subject, and my expression softens. "I'd like that."

TWENTY-ONE

THE LIBRARY IS IN A SMALL BUILDING across the street from the community center, all harsh lines and stained concrete. It's newer than the community center, but that doesn't mean it's new.

It feels more like a second-hand car—new enough to be useful, but not new enough to be reliable. The roof leaks every time it rains, so the librarian, Allison, is always moving books and shelves around to stop anything from getting ruined.

But considering the lack of funds, Allison runs a tight ship. New books are rare, but what we have is well kept and organized. She kept records of every publication and firsthand written notes we had on microfilm along with handwritten books from residents.

The strip of grass leading up to the entrance is overgrown in the shaded areas and yellowed where the sun hits. We walk up the sidewalk cautiously, Jethro hovering near my arm as we navigate the hairline cracks and fractured pavement.

I'm still recovering, but I won't be stopped. Jethro knows enough of my stubbornness by now and resigned to come along so I don't collapse.

The cool air greets us as Jethro holds open the glass door for me. I scan the room for Allison. The doorway opens to a long, yellow counter with a white laminate top that serves as the courtesy desk, but there's no one there.

"Allison?" I call out, but there's no reply. I hobble towards the counter, Jethro offering me his arm again, but I wave him off. When I lean over the counter, I spot her in the adjacent room, an archway leading to what serves as the office. She has headphones on and is sorting books into piles, completely oblivious to both of us.

I wave my arm wildly, waiting for her to turn towards me. When she does, she jumps, immediately pulling off her headphones and putting a hand to her chest.

"Wren! You scared the livin' daylights out of me!" She sets the headphones down, and I see they are attached to a CD player. She presses the pause button, then turns to walk towards us. She's willowy, alabaster skin and greying brown hair lying flat along her shoulders and back. She wears a long, flower print dress with a white bolero. She has all the making of a quiet, soft-spoken librarian, but I know better.

"I'm sorry, hun, I was listening to an audiobook. Stephen

King is quite talented, isn't he? I'm listening to The Shining, and I've been immersed." She gets a faraway look as if still dreaming in the horror-filled world she'd come from.

"I need your help with somethin'," I say, knowing I'll get a long-winded love letter to one book or another if I don't keep her on track. "We're looking for records."

She nods, pulls out a binder from below the counter, and places it on the white laminate. "Around what time period? And do you know the title? The author?"

I hesitate, knowing the request is going to be near impossible. "It's not a specific newspaper or book we're looking for. We're looking for a reference to a certain kind of snake, something we ain't seen around here lately."

She leans back to look at me with eyebrows raised, forehead wrinkled. It makes her look older—and even more skeptical.

"A snake? Do you know what it's called?"

I shake my head, biting my lip. The sheer impossibility of the request hits me then, and I wonder how to explain what we're looking for.

It's Jethro that saves me. "It has to be something endangered or not common around here. Don't they have records of what kinds of snakes have caused injuries or deaths in the past?" He says it with such authority and conviction that though the request is still outlandish, Allison's face transforms into curiosity rather than dubiousness.

She taps her hand on the binder a moment, staring off at the wall behind us. She then closes the binder and replaces it into the shelf behind the counter.

"If it's a snake you're looking for, we used to get biologists around here that would track animal populations about thirty or so years ago. Before all the funding dried up. We have some of their written records. Death statistics might help too..." She walks back towards the office, making a turn out of the counter space and into the library proper. She beckons us to follow with her hand, and Jethro helps me with the tenuous journey by holding my arm.

We round the corner into the small desk with the bulky microfiche reader situated on the desk. It takes up nearly the whole table, a Frankenstein configuration that consists of the scanner connected to a computer monitor. It's one of Allison's prized innovations.

"There are handwritten logs that were scanned for the library. We used to use them in the classrooms to get the kids interested in science. They're so outdated now, though. Not much use for anything but taking up space." She pulls out and then pats one of the chairs for me, Jethro helping me ease into the plastic and metal seat.

"There's a lot of them. Though a lot of them are records of bird populations. Do you know we used to be a hub for birdwatching? There were articles in state newspapers about it." She starts up the monitor, getting a glazed look in her eyes, lost in her head.

"What changed?" Jethro asks. It would have been my next question were I not winded by the trip to the chair.

She shrugs, leaning back against the side of the desk. "Not

sure. The records start getting' slim and then there's nuthin'."

I frown. "Around what time was that?"

She looks up at the ceiling, placing her hand on her hip. As if the ceiling will give her the answers to the universe.

"About twenty, thirty years ago. Like I said, it happened slow."

There's something significant about the two dates, but I can't quite put it together.

"Can you get us the records a little bit before they declined and then the last few you have? To start?"

She raises a thin brown eyebrow at me, crossing her arms over her chest. "To start? Exactly what is it you're looking for?"

I sigh, unsure of the answer. I look over at Jethro, but his frown is as lost as I am, unhelpful.

"I think they may be connected somehow. Sheriff June needs us to identify the snake first but bring us anything you see on the birds as you go through."

She waves her hand at us in mock annoyance. "Come now, Wren. Do I look like a maid?"

I smirk at her, all teeth. "You look like a librarian."

She lets out a short laugh and leans forward, hand on her chest as she follows it with a giggle.

"Now, Wren, I don't think I've ever had a nicer compliment."

She winks at me at me before turning. As she walks away towards the back room, I look over at Jethro. "You ready?"

He grimaces. "Something smells fishy about this whole thing. But we have to get out a bulletin to warn the town about the snake, so that has to be our priority."

I nod in agreement. "Of course. But after that? I want to know what happened to the birds. Uncle Jeremy said when he was a kid, that's when things started to get worse. The timing is too coincidental, for birdwatching to start going out and the biologists to stop coming at the same time? Something's wrong in all this."

He nods in agreement and straightens his shoulders. He cracks his knuckles and gives me a sly smirk. "Ready Mr. Holmes?"

I snort at him. "Don't be ridiculous. It's Mx. Holmes to you."

We wait for Allison, and with each passing moment, my unease grows.

—

The endless loading, scanning, unloading, then reloading of the microfiche becomes a rhythm over the next couple of hours. In between half-hour segments of staring at the harsh light of the microfilm, we move on to boxes and boxes of records that Allison found from local birdwatchers, donated when the birdwatching society in the area closed its doors decades back. We slip on the soft white gloves and are only allowed to look through them under Allison's careful gaze, but I can't help the excitement bubbling up in me as I read. These are my people.

We're looking at microfilm from one of the biologist's

studies when a sketch of a snake loading on the screen causes
Jethro to sit up straight, nearly knocking over a box to his right.
We're both huddled near the screen, boxes surrounding us like
a fort. I inwardly groan, knowing we'll be the ones to put them
back.

"What is it?" I ask him. He's leaning forward, adjusting his
glasses.

"This is it," he says. "The snake that bit you. I'm certain of
it."

I take a closer look. The date says April 12, 1973, scribbled
in hand lettering on the bottom of the sketch. It's clearly taken
from a notebook, ragged edges on one side. The drawing is
beautiful—the snake winding into itself, each pattern along its
back visible over its scales.

As I look at the head, I tilt my own head sideways. I intake
a shallow breath.

"It looks like a skull," I say. "Looking at it from its back, it
looks like a human skull."

Jethro grunts and tilts his head back and forth. "I don't see
it."

I click my tongue at him and lightly smack his side. "You
have no imagination."

He leans in closer to the image, then draws back with a
grimace on his face. "Well, someone else agreed. It's called The
Reaper, or the Eastern Dusky Blacktail."

It's my turn to grimace. "That sounds familiar." I shake my
head as if that will help put the pieces in place.

Jethro scrolls through the microfilm until he gets to the

end, then loads the next one in line. It's all about the same snake, including death rates and effects. My vision blurs, and I rub at my eyes, trying to rub out the strain.

"Wren." Jethro's voice is tight, and I open my arms to see him pointing at a section of the film.

"What is it?" I ask, trying to focus my eyes on where he's pointing. The text is small, barely legible.

"It reads, 'The effects of a bite seem to include disorientation, pain at the site of the bite, and in the worst cases, heart attacks.' Turney had a heart attack, right? What if this is what killed Turney? He could have got bit and we missed it. They go on to say that the yearly toll of attacks had begun to decrease though."

Leaning back, I try to order everything in my head, but it's all muddled. "We could Google it, see if we can find anythin' on the species."

Jet's phone is out immediately, the screen bright in the semi-darkness of the room. It shines on his face, and I spy the darkened skin under his eyes, but I can't tell if they're shadows or if the skin's taken on the hue of a bruise from sleepless-ness. *He's been really worried about me*, I think, and am suddenly ashamed for dragging him out to the library instead of letting us both rest more.

"There aren't many results," he says. "There are two references on a Wikipedia page, one of them saying it's extinct. There were studies done in the 70s to try and track the population, but a few years later, it's declared extinct."

Shaking my head, I turn off the desktop and stand to pack

up the loose records. "Can't be it, then, if it's extinct." I set the lid on one of the cardboard boxes and move on to the next.

He stands up quickly enough that the chair rocks. "No, I'm sure this is it! It fits. I found another link, a study. I can't see the full article without paying, but the abstract says the name of the town. It's too coincidental—it fits everything!"

I sigh and set the lid on the last of the boxes. I know Jethro is going to have to put them back himself; I'm useless with my leg. One more thing to feel guilty about. "Then what about the knife wounds? And how can an extinct snake kill someone? Might as well blame it on the dinosaurs."

He paces, hitting his phone against his leg as he walks. "I don't know. Maybe he got cut by a tree or something? He could have been unsteady. And just because it was declared extinct doesn't mean it is extinct. Maybe they couldn't find them; maybe there was a bad year."

I sit on one of the tables, stretching my leg out carefully as I speak. "Jet. We're here because we were curious about the snake. And now you're lookin' for evidence of a killer snake that's gone extinct and saying that Turney's death wasn't murder. I'm starting to feel sorry for bringin' you along in all this. You gotta let it rest."

He stops at that, gives me a look of betrayal. His eyebrows are low, his mouth slack. "How could you say that, Wren? You're the one that's wanted to do this from the start! You've been adamant about it this whole time, broke into the victim's house, had me hack into someone's private accounts, and now you're telling me it's enough? And after Leigh herself asked us to help? What's gotten into you?"

I flinch at the reminder, avoiding his gaze. *She'd never forgive me, but if something happened to Jethro, I'd never forgive myself.* I look down where my hand rests against the table. "I think we need to cut our losses and duck out. I nearly got us both killed, and I've run you ragged trying to solve this. The sheriff was right. It's not our business and we're not cut out for this."

He walks up and leans his back against the table I'm sitting on. We both stare out the windows at the far end of the building where the sun is still shining, the leaves on the trees swaying in the wind, a few of them showing the silver undersides of leaves as if waving at us. It feels peaceful and reminds me of days spent with Uncle Jeremy out in our backyard around the fire pit. Home.

"You don't have to protect me," he says. "If anything, I should be the one trying to protect you. You're the one that got bit. You nearly died, Wren. And if we hadn't started on this harebrained adventure, we wouldn't know each other like we do. I like you. You're brash, impulsive, confident. You're badass, and this town wouldn't be the same without you."

I chuckle at his declaration of my badassery, but it turns into a choked sob. But I hold it back in my throat. I won't break down here. "Friends protect each other," I say. "Not just from getting' physically hurt but emotionally. I know what it's like to lose someone, and even if you aren't the one hurt, if I'm hurt, you'll hurt too. I'm tired of hurtin' other people. I don't want to be asking for trouble because of my pride."

I catch him shaking his head out of the corner of my eye,

crossing his arms in front of him. "That's it, Wren. Being in a relationship—a friendship, I mean—with someone means getting hurt. It's part of it. You can't ever be close to someone and not hurt. If so, you don't really care about them, do you?"

I hum at that, massaging my bad leg as I keep my gaze out the window. Listening, but unconvinced.

He sighs with his full body, slouching into the table. "Look. I know you're not going to like this, but I think we should go find the snake."

I turn towards him, already shaking my head, disagreement on my tongue. But he interrupts.

"It's no more dangerous than any other walk in the woods, and if these things are back, the town needs to be aware. Especially if they've already killed someone. We'll be careful—high boots, not get too close. You're the best tracker around, right? You'll find them no problem, and then we can head back. No repeat of last time."

I clench my lips tight, eyes narrowing. It's true that I'll have to face my fears and go back to the woods eventually, and regardless, we should be aware of what type of snake it was so we can let the townspeople know it's become aggressive. Normally, snakes don't bother hikers, cautious by nature, but this one struck with no warning. It's possible I got too close without noticing it in my interest in the Tricksters, but it's unlikely. I don't make those types of mistakes.

But I also know what Jethro has on his mind. He wants to prove me wrong, prove to me that The Reaper had been the one to attack me and likely Turney. But the coroner found no snake bite, and it doesn't explain the cuts.

I let out a sigh in defeat, realizing that another trek may need to happen soon anyway, and that Jethro was right—I'm the best person for the job.

"Alright," I say. "Give me a week to recover a bit more, then we'll go out and find the snake. Deal?"

He smiles that wide, toothy grin of his and holds out his hand to me. "Shake on it?"

I roll my eyes but grab his hand. We shake, then suddenly, he pulls me sideways into a hug. He squeezes my shoulder twice, then let's go.

We both move off the table, Jethro reaching to pick up the first box. He pulls it off the table with a grunt, and I see an opportunity.

"Oh, by the way. Mrs. Delaney is doin' better. She's coming back to the records office tomorrow."

His grip on the box slips, and he nearly drops it. "That's great news…but she's going to be pissed at us, isn't she?"

I grin at him in fake innocence. "Us? Oh no, Jethro. I'm injured, remember? She wouldn't want to give me a fright. No, she'll probably take her anger out on someone else."

I see his throat move as he gulps, and I laugh.

TWENTY-TWO

EVERY RUSTLE OF LEAVES, every chirp from nearby birds, every creaking of a tree limb has me on edge.

It has been a week since the library, and a promise is a promise. Yet I find myself regretting it. It feels too soon, though this is the world that I love. It nearly killed me, and I'm not in any hurry for a repeat performance.

But Jethro is right. I am the best tracker we have. If anyone can find the snake—The Reaper, as he is convinced—it will be me.

It helps that I remember the general area where I was bitten. There's a tree that was downed several years ago during a hurricane in that area, and Jethro's track could have been an elephant for how much he hid his steps. We'd had a dry spell since our excursion, and I can still see his large boot prints in the mud.

It doesn't take long now that we aren't looking for the Trickster. We keep our eyes low on the ground, watching for any sign of snakes. So far, no luck, but we are still a ways away from our goal.

"So what are we looking for exactly?" Jet asks from behind me. He is close, in case I trip and injure my bad leg. It is better than it was last week, but it still throbs the more I use it. I am determined, though. To prove Jet wrong, to warn the town.

"Holes they can crawl into, areas where there's direct sunlight, mostly on rocks. This time of year, they may sunbathe to keep warm. And eggs. Be careful; they're not super creative where they lay their eggs, so it may be under the leaf litter. I doubt she'll protect her eggs from us, but you don't wanna step on her 'cause ya weren't paying attention."

He nods, face blotchy from the sun. "And once we find her?"

I grimace, scrunching my nose. "We stay away, take a picture, mark it on the map, and leave. No use gettin' bit a second time. I wouldn't recover, and I can't carry you."

He nods, eyes wide at the warning. "Right. Stay away, picture, run. Got it."

I smile at him, hoping it'll ease his nerves. "Relax. I was caught off guard that time. Now we know to watch out for her."

When we come upon the clearing, I shake my head at the obviousness of the issue. In retrospect, it had been the perfect

place for a snake—plenty of leaf litter to hide, patches of
sunlight to sunbathe, access to water, and plenty of prey. But
normally, snakes leave hikers alone, so it hadn't occurred to
me to be extra cautious beyond the typical safety measures. We
know better now.

"Watch your feet, but start looking for holes, eggs, any
disturbed leaves. It's late in the day, so it'll probably be active
'round now. We only have so long to look though before it
becomes dark."

I cautiously look through the scattered leaves and brush,
using my walking stick to push aside any suspicious greenery.
I find a few holes for larger animals, but nothing small enough
that a snake would be comfortable in. I find a patch of sunlight
on some rocks and look around all the edges to find any places
where a snake may hide, but with no luck.

The longer it takes, the more frustrated I become. *This was
a dumb idea* echoes in my mind. Chances are the snake freaked
out and left, or if it is here, that it'll stay as far away from us as
possible. And if we do find a snake, what are the chances that
it's The Reaper?

"Wren?" Jethro's voice reaches me from my left, and it's
edged in panic. Walking towards him, leaning on my walking
stick after my crouching down on my leg, I come to a halt to
see where he's pointing.

In the shadow of a rock, tangled up in branches and
decaying leaves, is an Eastern Dusky Blacktail.

The Reaper.

"Well, shit."

It's stationary except for its forked, pink tongue tasting the air. It must have seen us and frozen, luckily for Jethro. We've already seen how aggressive the snake can be, and I'm glad we spotted it before it spotted us.

"Pull out your phone," I order, my gaze not leaving the snake. "Take a photo, and let's get outta here before it takes a strike."

Jethro fumbles in trying to pull his phone out of his pocket, and I feel the air around me closing in like a fog, like there's no oxygen left. I hold back the need to breathe in shallow spurts, thinking *not now, please*. Jethro finally aims the camera on his phone at the snake, taking a few pictures at different angles—all quite far away from the dangerous predator—before holding my arm and backing us both away, facing the snake at first, then at a steady hike.

We're about a hundred feet away when I can't hold down the panic anymore. It bunches in my throat, blocking my airways, and I gasp in spurts of oxygen.

Jethro is at my side immediately, pulling me down to sit on a nearby rock, careful of my bad leg. He grabs one of my hands, and like he's done so many times before, he starts to talk. His voice is a steady tenor, a balm on my throat, and it almost itches as I feel it opening enough for me to gulp in more air with each breath.

But the more the panic attack dissipates, the more devastated I feel. Jethro looks alarmed when after my breathing comes back to normal, I break into sobs.

"Wren?" he asks, voice not betraying his panic. "Are you okay? Are you hurt?"

I shake my head and bury my face into my hands, digging into my eyes with my palms. "No, I'm not okay! This is not okay—nothing is okay! Why does this keep happenin' to me? Why can't I be normal? I hate this, I hate this so much, and I want it to stop!"

My shoulders shake, and the moment drags. I don't expect an answer. Jethro may be intelligent, sweet, and wise for his age, but he's no miracle worker. In my heart, I know there's nothing to be said.

The silence continues, and I hate that too. I feel a steely part of me wanting to throw that anger in Jethro's face, but I'm done being the person who has to make others feel pain when they're hurting themselves. And so I cry.

Jethro squeezes my hand, and I'm thankful for the closeness. As I expected, there are no wise words. No comfort for things that can't be comforted. Nothing changes that day.

And maybe it's not meant to.

—

"You sure you're going to be okay?" Jethro asks again.

I sigh at his worry. "Yes," I say, "I'll be fine. Have fun with your family."

It is late. The light outside is dimming, heralding a thunderstorm. "If you don't get going soon, you'll get caught in the rain."

He nods at that and straightens his collar. While he normally would be wearing an oversized t-shirt and a pair of sagging jeans over sneakers, today he wears a fitted button-up and a nice pair of slacks. The sneakers stay, though, and I have to smile.

When he came in this morning, he informed me he had to leave a little early to make it to his grandfather's birthday party. As morbid as it seems, everyone in his family knows it'll probably be his last one, so they're going all out. They rented the banquet hall in town, and family from all over the country is driving or flying in to celebrate the occasion, and for some of them, to say goodbye.

But if he doesn't leave soon, he'll be late rather than early. I hurry him along, nearly pushing him out the door despite his protests. He gives me a side hug before he leaves, something I am still getting used to but appreciate.

Once he is gone, I turn back to the empty room, a bit lost. Mrs. Delaney left a little before Jethro, tiring out earlier than normal. It's to be expected after her Parkinson's flare. I see it as an opportunity to have time to myself in the records room and even got permission from Sean to stay after hours. It means that Sean has to stay later too so he can lock up, but he didn't bat an eye at the request.

He's been extra sweet after the snake bite, going so far as to bringing in a batch of his homemade sugar cookies for us to snack on. There are two left, a testament to how great a baker he is. It leaves me with a warm feeling to know that Sean is more of a friend than I expected.

I lift the latch to get behind the counter again and locate my go-to's on the shelves. I line them all up on the counter, browsing between them, lingering in the overwhelming feeling of home and family they give me.

Uncle Jeremy's birth certificate. My parents' marriage certificate. The purchase agreement to Uncle Jeremy's—to my—house. The log citing my great grandmother's passing. Whether the record is something joyful or sad, it makes me feel like I belong.

There's a knock at the door. I jump, caught by surprise. I walk over cautiously, open the door, and blink.

"Oh, I hoped you'd still be here," Mrs. Delaney says. She's using her rollator, and I immediately help her walk over to one of the chairs to sit. "I left my purse under the counter and didn't realize until I got home! My memory isn't what it used to be. Can you get it for me, child?"

I nod and move behind the counter. It takes me a few tries looking on different shelves before I find it somewhat hidden behind a cardboard box. I pull it out and hold it up so she can see. "This is it, right?"

She smiles wide, nods at me. "Yes, yes, that's it! Oh, thank you, Wren. I don't know what I'd do if I had lost it. It has everythin' a woman can need, you know."

I giggle at that, which makes her eyes sparkle in mirth. I make my way back to where she sits, setting the purse down in the basket underneath the seat of her rollator. When I straighten, she grabs my wrist in a gentle grip.

"Now, Wren, come and sit with me for a moment. I want to hear all about what happened with the Sheriff today."

I nod and take a seat on the fabric-covered, beige plastic

chair. The top of the seat is curved higher than my neck, and it's uncomfortable to turn towards Mrs. Delaney, but I do it anyway.

She's heard much of our adventures before the snake bite already and had been rightly furious with us. But after some cajoling, she calmed down and put us to work in retribution.

I told her what happened at the library and Jethro identifying the snake from the biologist's notes, our trek into the woods, and how we'd gotten a photo of the snake for Sheriff June. The sheriff had been quiet when we'd explained it to her, and I was thankful she hadn't been mad. She had talked to the coroner about looking through Turney's autopsy for a final time to see if there was any evidence of a snake bite that could have at least caused the heart attack. The wounds were still a mystery.

Mrs. Delaney listens quietly, nods, and gasps alternately at the story. She seems engaged with my retelling, which makes my cheeks hot but also gives me a sense of pride to be able to keep her intrigued. Like I'm not as terrible with words as I think.

When my story is done, she tilts her head, staring at the ceiling for a moment before she responds. "You never met him, but the man who ran the records office before me was Lance Sheppard. The name won't mean anythin' to you, he passed on long ago, but I remember some curious records in our files as he was showin' me how to organize them. They were from biologists that were studying the wildlife in the area."

My eyes widen, and I tilt my shoulders and head back in surprise. "You knew about that?"

Her grin is mischievous. "Oh, Wren, you kids didn't think you were the only ones with a streak of curiosity, did you? Heavens yes. By the time the records were passed on to me, they had already packed up and left, but we still had to file receipts, permits, ordinances, everythin'. In my younger years, I was fascinated by them. I read through anything I could find. They're somewhere around here; it's been quite a while since I looked, but I do remember some of how it all went down."

I frown, eyes narrowing. "What do you mean?"

She turns more towards me, hands folded in her lap. "Well, we once was the place to go for birdwatching. We had birders coming 'round from all over the country to see 'em all. The town thrived as well as it ever has. We've always been quite small. That's why the biologists came originally, to study the different species."

She lets out a sigh and lowers her gaze. "But all things come to an end, child. After a while, we started treating more and more snake bites. The more people out in the woods, the more disturbed the animals became. The biologists started to study the snakes too, to try and see how they could prevent or treat the bites. The venom was especially toxic, they said. Worse than a rattler.

"That's when the gas company come in. Started a fracking operation partway up the mountain, by Buckmore Creek. When the snake population started goin' down, we thought it'd be a good thing. But then the birds left too. Even the Tricksters."

She turns away from me, leaning back against the chair. I can see from her face she's feeling pain, and I debate telling her she can tell me the story tomorrow. But a big part of me wants her to continue.

She takes the choice out of my hands. "After a while, the biologists left, and so did the birdwatchers. It was the Citizens who did the gas company in. They protested and proved the fracking was poisoning the water. It's a time long past in everyone's memories, but it's my job to remember our history. One day, it'll be yours too."

"The Citizens did that? They're the ones who drove off the gas company?"

She shrugs, which sends her shoulders into quaking. I rub at one of them to try to ease her tremors as she speaks. "Who knows? Maybe they figured there wasn't enough left to make it worth their while to stay. But as far as the town is concerned, it was the Citizens that started the slow fall of the town by driving them off."

I'm silent in thought. So many pieces of the puzzle now fit, but there's still so much I don't know.

"Was The Reaper one of the snakes? The Eastern Dusky Blacktail?"

She shrugs. "Can't say I know one snake from the other. But could be."

I sigh, unsatisfied with the answer but knowing Mrs. Delaney was reaching her limit. "Let me help you get back to your car."

When I go to stand, she pushes me back down lightly by

my shoulder. "Now, child, that wasn't what I came here to talk to you about."

I raise a lone eyebrow at her. "I thought you came here to get your purse?"

She smiles sheepishly. "Well, that too. I think It's time I stopped coddling you, child, and there's somethin' you need to hear."

I lean away from her, not liking where this is going. "Like what?"

Her voice is firm despite her physical tremor. "Child, it's time that you learn to trust in other people. I see what's on that counter. I've seen it a million times, whenever you're afraid or doubting yourself. You love what's on those records more than you love the ones around you. You trust in them. They never change, never hurt you. They remind you of home."

I open my mouth to protest, but she holds up a hand and I quiet.

"Relationships ain't what's written on those papers, Wren. You need to learn to start letting things behind ya stay behind ya so you can live what's in front of ya."

I grimace. "I can't forget, Mrs. Delaney. I can't forget them."

She places a hand on my shoulder, pulls me sideways into a hug. "Oh, child, you should never forget. But letting go doesn't mean forgetting. It means letting the right ones in too."

We stay like that for a while, enjoying each other's company. Outside, we can hear the thunder like a drum echoing through the town, the rain pattering against the window. Inside,

my heart aches, but the feel of warm arms around my shoulders remind me of home.

TWENTY-THREE

WHEN I COME IN EARLY THE NEXT MORNING, I'm on a mission. I spot Sean getting settled, setting his bag underneath the desk and turning on his desktop and monitor. He looks tired, eyes blinking away sleep, and by the time I'm standing in front of his desk, he's on the tail end of a yawn.

He ends the yawn on a small smile when he sees me, and I wonder that I've made such good friends without knowing it. I straighten my posture, determination like a pillar in my spine.

"I owe you an apology," I say, not waiting for him to greet me. "I teased you 'bout being a private investigator a while back, and you didn't deserve me bein' an ass about it."

His smile withers, and there's a hooded look in his eyes. Like he doesn't want to be reminded of it and would rather the conversation go anywhere else. It hurts to know that such few words seem to have done so much tarnish.

"You weren't wrong, Wren. I looked into the requirements more, and it's not possible. I fit the education and experience requirements, but you need liability insurance, and I'd probably have to start off working for someone else. Who would hire me in this town? It was a pipe dream." He turns on his monitor and starts typing, signaling the conversation as being over.

My nostrils flare as I try to reign in my frustration. This isn't how it was supposed to go, but I'm not giving up yet. I drop my backpack and lean down to dig in the front pocket. I pull out a small pine figurine I'd carved overnight, my fingers raw and bearing the slivers to prove it.

I'm not going to give up without a fight.

I set the figurine in front of Sean, letting it touch down with a loud thunk to catch his attention. It's a carving of an owl on a tree trunk, wings open as if it's getting ready to fly. It's small enough to fit in the palm of my hand, so smaller yet to Sean.

"When you become a private investigator, I want this to be the first thing on your desk. You're gonna get that liability insurance, you'll work for someone or work for yourself, you'll get certified, and you'll do what you need to do. Because you're one of us. The people in this town, we don't give up. My *friends* don't give up, not because somethin' is hard or seems impossible."

Sean's no longer typing, staring at the owl with an indecipherable look on his face. He gently picks it up and looks it over, twisting it around in his hands to see it at all angles. "You made this?"

"Course. Owls are supposed to represent knowledge, truth. Thought it'd be a good bird for you to keep handy."

He sets it down on the table, and this time when he looks up at me, I can see the mirth and joy in his eyes. "That's the nicest thing you've ever done for me, Wren. The nicest thing I've ever heard you do for anyone."

"Hey!"

"You better watch it, or someone might think you got a heart in there." He grins and picks the owl back up again, admiring it openly as he turns it in his palms.

He's quiet for a moment, and I'm content to let him admire the token. It warms something in me to know that he likes it, that it means something to him, and if he decides he doesn't want to pursue being an investigator, I know I did what I could to make amends.

When he speaks, his voice is so soft, I can barely hear it. "You think I can do it? You're not just being nice?"

I snort and cross my arms. "You hear what you're sayin'? You just said so yourself earlier. I don't do *nice*. I mean it."

He wears an expression I've never seen on him but it's one I think I'd like to see more. "Alright. I'll give it another go."

Internally I'm relieved, but I won't show it. "Good. I think you can do more than be the sheriff's assistant. If it takes time, so what? What matters is you get there."

I swing my bag back on my shoulder and get ready to head down the hallway. "I'll see ya, Sean."

I'm turning to go when I hear him call me back.

"Wren, wait. I wanna say somethin'."

I look back at him, wary I've done something wrong, but he's looking at me curiously, head tilted, not with anger.

"You know, I've always admired you, Wren."

I blink, then frown. "Me? What about me?"

He looks down at the owl and rolls it between his fingers as he speaks. "You seem untouchable. Steadfast. Like you know who you are and ain't afraid to cut anyone down who tries to steamroll ya." He shrugs and looks back up at me. "But I think I like this Wren better. That's the problem with being untouchable. It's gotta be lonely, ain't it? This Wren is still brave. But this Wren cares."

I don't know what to say that, so I say nothing, I nod and walk back to the records room with his words ringing through my head.

—

What Sean said is fresh on my mind as Jethro and I dig into our plates at the diner. I ordered the meatloaf, my favorite dinner from the entire menu, and yet it might as well be watered down sawdust for all I can taste it.

I sneak a glance up at Jethro and see him immersed in his phone, which sends me flashing back to the hospital. The memory is still a fresh wound, for all it had been a while. I'm not entirely convinced I've been a good friend since, though I've made an effort as much as I know how. *This is a chance to change that.*

"How's everythin' going with your grandpa?" I ask, hoping I'm not stepping on a landmine but genuinely wanting to know the answer to my own surprise.

He looks up, then down at his phone, before frowning and setting it on the table. *Smooth, Wren.*

"You don't have to put your phone away," I say quickly. "It's fine. I just wanted to know, promise."

The frown stays, but he picks up his fork and pokes at his mashed potatoes with it. In my head, I'm kicking myself, thinking I must have ruined his appetite.

"He's not doing any better but not any worse either. He's kind of in limbo, I guess? It could go either way. He's in a wheelchair right now, and they have hospice coming to take care of most of his needs. It's like…"

He stops fiddling with his potatoes and drops his fork onto his napkin with a *thunk.*

"He's really going to die, isn't he? I'm going to lose him." He's staring at his plate like it can give him the answer. My heart hurts to hear the crack in his voice, the joy seeped out of the exuberant soul I consider a friend.

He's quiet for a long time, and I push back the need to fill the silence. There's nothing for me to say, and a part of me thinks he needs to process this out loud, on his own. I watch his face, the tremble in his lips, the flaring in his nose as he inhales deeply, how he clenches his eyes shut to stop the tears.

When he speaks again, I lean close, the words so quiet it's like they don't want to be heard.

"I remember visiting as a kid, him teaching me all about

his radios and reading old poets to me. Keates, Whitman, Frost. I'm who I am because of him, and he'll just be gone? It feels impossible."

The last word trembles, and he covers his eyes with his hands, rubs at them with the heels.

"And then it reminds me that someday Dad will be gone too, and Mom, and then I'll be all alone. I've never lost anyone like this, not that I can remember. My parents got a divorce when I was young, but that was different. I can still see my mom; she didn't *die*. How can the world possibly keep turning without him in it?"

He drops his hands on either side of his plate and finally looks up at me with deep brown eyes like chasms that pull me in, full of sadness and fear.

"I don't know what to do or how to feel. I'm so scared. It hurts to be around him because I know soon enough, I won't have the chance."

I push my plate aside and lean over the tabletop to grab one of his hands in mine, grip firm. I hold his gaze, brokering no resistance.

"He's not gone *yet*. Don't bury him until he is."

I squeeze his hand and try to push every hope and every bit of love I can through to him.

"I'll tell you what you do. You go home and you spend time with him when you can. When you're there, you're there one hundred percent. You make these memories matter. That's all any of us can do."

He rubs at his eyes with his other hand with a slight upturn of his lips. I give his hand one last squeeze and let it go. He lets out a weak, self-deprecating chuckle that catches me off guard.

"I yelled at him the other day. I was mad because he ate my bagel, and afterward, I couldn't believe I did that. Who yells at a dying man over a bagel?"

I shrug.. "You do, apparently."

He chokes on a laugh.

"Seriously, though. Bein' with someone means all the emotions that come with it. Arguments too. Yelling at him over a bagel doesn't mean you don't love him, and he knows it. If the last thing you ever said to him was to scream at him over a bagel, he would still know you love him. That's what matters."

I sober. "Uncle Jeremy…I don't remember the last words I said to him. I try to remember but I can't. I don't remember the last time I told him I loved him. But I gotta believe he knew, ya know? I have to believe that."

"What was he like? Your uncle?"

I tap the table, trying to think of how to describe him. He'd been such a presence in my life, and someone everyone else had always known, so I've never had to describe him before.

"He was outgoing, more than me. He could be funny. But mostly he was a storyteller."

"How so?"

Memories of bedtime flit through my mind.

"I remember when I was a kid, him telling me bedtime stories. He'd do the voices, gesture with his hands, really get into it. He'd memorize the books, all of them, by the time they'd wear out. When I got on to chapter books, he stopped memorizing them, but he still did the voices.

"When we'd have bonfires, he'd tell stories around the fire for the kids. Even hearing him tell tales around town, you could tell he got excited sharin'. When he talked, you couldn't help but listen. He knew how to get your attention."

Jethro takes a fry from our communal side and chews it with a thoughtful expression. "I bet you could do that if you tried."

I snort, unconvinced. "Me? No. I'm too...*me*. I don't like people much, if you haven't noticed yet."

"I noticed."

I grab a fry at throw it at his head.

"Hey!"

We get a few fries in before a glare from the waitress stops us, but with that, the tension has broken, and we're laughing freely. It feels good. Like something is healing between us.

Well, it's as good a time as any.

"Oh, about your grandpa. I have somethin' for him."

I dig into my bag where I put my gift, wrapped in newsprint. I hand it to Jethro over the table, careful to be gentle with it though I know it'll take more than that kind of drop to break it.

"What's this?" he asks, but I only smile.

He moves his plate away so there's an empty spot in front of him and unwraps the present carefully. Eventually, he reveals the pine carving of a dove, hanging from a green ribbon.

"It's a dove. It's supposed to represent peace, which is what I want to wish him. It's not much. I wanted to get it done for his birthday, but I couldn't. Sorry it's late."

Jethro holds it up by the ribbon with a look of awe on his face, and I can feel my cheeks heat.

"Wow, Wren. This is great. You did this? This is amazing."

I rub at my beck in embarrassment and try to convince myself not to hide down into my t-shirt.

"Uncle Jeremy taught me woodworking and carving. I'm not as good with the big stuff, can't hold a chainsaw for the life of me. But I can do the little stuff."

He puts it back in the paper and lovingly wraps it back up again. "It's beautiful. He'll love it. Thank you, Wren."

The thought brings a smile to my face. When he's done, he puts it in his bag, and pulls his plate back to finish eating, but I reach over to stop him.

"Hey," I say, licking my lips out of nervousness. "When it happens…I'll be here, you know. I promise."

He takes my hand and squeezes once before letting it go. "Thanks, Wren."

—

The next day finds me in the records office alone with only the sound of the air conditioning and the faint pattering of rain on the windows.

Mrs. Delaney has a specialist appointment to evaluate the progression of her Parkinson's a town over, and Jethro offered to take her. Neither of us thought it was a good idea to have her drive that far on her own, and Jethro isn't quite up to speed on the protocols enough to hold down the fort without me here.

We're caught up with all the filling, and with the rain we're going to be getting today, it isn't likely that we'll be getting many, if any, new records to process. Usually that means I do whatever task Mrs. Delaney assigns me or I wander my way through the back records, but after my talk with her, it leaves a bitter taste on my tongue to rely on old habits.

But sitting on my hands isn't in my personality. Instead, I decide to do a little research of my own. I call Allison to pull the dates on a few of the microfiche records on The Reaper we'd left out, looking to see if I can find anything that relates in our own records. If we've had issues with the snakes in the past, there's a good chance there were precautions taken at the time that we may make use of now. Plus, anything new in the town I know like the back of my hand is asking to be investigated.

I start around the date of the sketch, April of 1973. At first, I find unrelated records —noise complaints, property purchases, hunting and trapping permits. I skim through each, setting them aside when nothing stands out.

Eventually I come across an invoice that makes me pause. It's from the Spastoke Birding Society. The state charged them for facility usage. Apparently, they met in the community center every two weeks, signed under the name of their co-founder, Troy Miller. The name is immediately familiar, and I go back to the previous pile.

Sure enough, Troy Miller had applied for a hunting and trapping permit that same month, but it's the subject that catches me off guard. I hadn't looked that far down in the document at first. Usually, they were signed off for deer or game birds. This one was signed for snakes—specifically, the Eastern Dusky Blacktail. The Reaper.

"Why on Earth would he want to hunt a snake?"

I look through the rest of the files for that month, but there's nothing more for Troy Miller in April, or in May.

I consider Googling him on my phone, but the chances of finding the right Troy Miller without more information are low. I choose another approach.

Allison doesn't seem very happy to be hearing from me again so quickly. "We aren't a busy library, but I do have things to do you know, Wren."

"What could be more important than savin' the lives of the town's population?"

There's silence over the phone, and I can't tell if she's skeptical or considering it. "Is that what you're doin'?"

I huff, unable to keep up the pretense. "Not sure yet. I'll let you know when I find out."

I hear a long sigh, but she acquiesces. "What do you need now?"

I pull up a piece of blank computer paper from the stack under the counter and a pen. "There was a Troy Miller who ran the Spastoke Birding Society in the 1970s. Do you know if we have any records from him in our system?"

I hear a tapping on the receiver, then the click clack of keys. "Nice to have a specific request this time. Makes my job easier."

"Don't be silly," I respond with humor in my tone. "You love the hard cases."

She sighs again, longingly this time. "I really, really do. But you're in luck. There are quite a few records from *Dr.* Troy Miller. He was a co-author on the monthly newsletter the Spastoke Birding Society released locally. We have those on microfiche. But he also has several papers in scientific journals available online. He was a biologist outside of being an avid birdwatcher. He left in the eighties, though."

I write down 'biologist', 'newsletter', and 'scientific journals' on my sheet. "That's perfect, Allison. Can ya email me those links? I'll come by the library some time to look at those journals."

She hums noncommittally, but I know she's already doing it. "What is all this for, hun?"

I tap the pen on the paper, unsure how to answer. I'm not entirely sure myself. "Just a hunch, I guess. And boredom. Jet and Mrs. Delaney are off to her appointment."

"You worried about them?"

I stop tapping the pen and consider. I am worried. I'm incredibly worried, actually. I've never seen her this bad for this long.

"Yeah," I finally say. "Yeah, I am. Her Parkinson's been getting worse lately."

"It's okay to be worried about someone you love, Wren.

And it's okay to distract yourself, too. We all do it. I got these emailed over to you, so keep yourself focused on something else until you hear what the doctor says. There's nothing you can do for Mrs. Delaney. You'll drive yourself batty trying to solve somethin' can't be solved. Focus on the things you can do somethin' about, alright? This bird, snake, whatever it is you're up to. It gives you a focus. Just make sure you can put it down when you need to. Don't lose focus of what really matters when you're with them."

I feel a loosening in my chest at her words. It feels freeing, like something untied inside me, and I can breathe easier.

"Thanks, Allison. I'll remember that."

We hang up, and I spend the next several hours going through the links she'd emailed me, letting myself get lost in the study.

TWENTY-FOUR

I FALL INTO THE DREAM like a bird landing in water, a moment of weightlessness before the cool welcoming of belonging.

When I turn my head toward the chair, there is Uncle Jeremy, still smiling, still holding the mysterious book. But instead of the exuberance I've seen in previous dreams, tonight his smile is gentler, calmer. He looks at me so deeply, I wonder if he can see to my bones. I try to rearrange the guilt, sadness, and anger inside my chest so he won't see it, but I know he does. I could never hide anything from him.

"You seem different tonight, Little Bird," he says, leaning back into the chair and tilting his head. "We're almost at the end of our story, you know. I don't need to tell you how stories end; you've been a storyteller since you were little. You know the acts, the climax, the hook. You sing stories like a bird and people flock to hear you. You just don't know it."

Opening the book, I'm unsurprised to see that he's right; we were nearing the end. The thought curdles in my stomach. What will reaching the end mean for the dreams?

When he finds the right page, he clears his throat, looks down at the book, and starts to read. "The little bird learned to trust. To trust the ones they love, to trust in their own strength, to trust in their own story."

He turns the page and looks up. No pretense of reading this time. "But that is not all the story is meant to tell. The hero becomes what they're meant to be, but there is still a matter of the villain. And this little bird still needed to defeat the monster lurking in the forest."

I furrow my brow, confused at the sudden change in mood as the atmosphere darkens in the room. The drapes flutter, the roof creaks, the wind howls. The air in the room cools, and I shiver, goosebumps crawling up my arms.

"The hero's journey can only be complete when they become who they're meant to be and defeat the darkness within and without. The little bird had grown, but so had their doubt."

He lifts up the book from his lap, still lying flat. "And who are they meant to face?"

He turns the book slowly, and when the page faces me, I see—

I wake up.

I remember.

I feel my chest constricting, my airflow disrupted, but I close my eyes and focus on breathing in my diaphragm. *Breathe.*

After a few minutes, I start to process the dream. And the dream before that, and the dream before that. I'm suddenly aware of the breadth of what I've experienced with my head on the pillow of my small, stuffy bedroom, and the enormity hits me like a bull. The book, the story, little bird. And Uncle Jeremy.

My skin itches with the longing, a quiet but forceful presence that digs into my chest. Across the room, in a place of pride, I see the last wood sculpture Uncle Jeremy ever gave me, the likeness of a Trickster in flight suspended with a single leg holding it up on its wooden base. It had taken him many tries to get the balance right, he had said, and I wonder at my own struggle to balance my pride and vulnerability. I wonder if I explain all this to the bird, if Uncle Jeremy will hear it, and the thought both comforts me and fills my lungs with a caustic yearning.

I try to remember whether the bird had been in my dream, but it's all a blurry mess pieced together from different memories.

I lay back down and stare up at the black vinyl cutouts of swallows we'd carefully stuck onto my ceiling. He's been trying to tell me something, to show me something, but it's muddy in my mind. Every time I try to catch it, it flits away like a butterfly from a net.

There had been something he wanted to show me in the book. A monster, he'd called it. The Reaper perhaps—the snake certainly boasted the danger of a monster to the unwitting. But the pieces still don't fit together. There are things missing, edges that don't quite line up in the picture. Hunches and maybes weren't enough for Sheriff June. For me, either.

I trace the outlines of the swallows with my eyes, their forked tails and sharp wingtips. There are about ten of them in flight, separate except two together that Uncle Jeremy had jokingly called 'the love birds.' It was a terrible joke, but I'd let him do it anyway.

I'm projecting their flight path and how they're certain to crash given the direction of their flight when a memory surfaces.

Their duet is a warning cry.

I'd brushed it off as a rhyme at the records office when I'd shown the back records to Jethro, but I swear the verse mentioned The Reaper and The Trickster. Was there a connection between the two?

I reach for my phone on the nightstand, blinking against the bright light emanating from it as I turn it on. I remember the papers we'd found from Turney, the scribbled chaotic ramblings of someone close to death. Before I'd given them to the sheriff, I'd taken a photo of each, certain it would come in handy later.

Browsing through the torn-off pages, I'm certain 'the birds' means The Trickster, but that's not what gives me pause. Throwing the covers off, I move to my desk, pull back the chair, and begin to write down a plan.

TWENTY-FIVE

BY THE TIME SHERIFF JUNE walks through the door of the records room, both Mrs. Delaney and Jethro are seated in the chairs in the sitting area, watching me with confusion and suspicion as I line up several of the back records and documents I printed off the computer and my phone. I came in like a whirlwind that morning, restless to feel the taste of closure on my tongue like cooling mint.

When the sheriff enters, she has several documents in a manila folder in the crook of her arm. In lieu of a greeting, I point to them. "Are those the autopsy records?"

She shakes her head, not in 'no' but in confusion. "Wren, I don't know why I agreed to bring them, but I sure as hell won't let you see 'em until you give me a reason you should be looking at confidential police records from an open case."

The reprimand calms my nerves, and I inhale slowly to bring my manic energy down. "I solved the case," I say, but in the back of my mind, I'm hoping I don't have it all wrong.

She raises an eyebrow at me but comes closer. She sets her metal coffee mug on the counter, and it fills me with relief to see her with it again. A caffeinated sheriff is a patient sheriff. That and I haven't missed the rings around her eyes or the unruliness of her hair in her ponytail as of late.

She sets the records on the counter and inches them towards me, but her tone reeks with suspicion. "Not that I don't trust you, Wren, but you can't blame me for doubting you. You thought you solved this murder before and hurt poor Leigh in the process. I told you to stay away from Turney and his family, from this case. Are you certain this is something you want to pursue? And what exactly did you get into to solve somethin' we've been at for weeks?"

The suspicion stings, but I also know it's not without warrant. "I promise you, we only looked up the snake that bit me, but it's all related. The pieces came together finally. Scout's honor."

She clenches her lips into a line but nods, and I take it as permission to open the folder. Inside are several images of Turney's body, and I swallow down bile at the wreckage of what must have been several animals picking at his corpse, along with several days worth of decomposition and bug larvae. Instead, I focus on the photos surrounding the wound on Turney's leg. I wince at the ragged cuts but force myself to look closer.

Then I see it.

"There," I say, pointing at an edge of the cut where I can see a barely there fragment that must have at some point been a circle, swollen and necrotized to a centralized point. It's cut straight through by a jagged laceration. If she didn't know to look for it, even the studious Pat wouldn't see it. "That's where the snake bit him."

The sheriff pulls off her hat and rubs at her forehead. "Wren, I went over this with the coroner. She said it's technically possible he got bit, but it still don't make sense. She couldn't find any bite wound."

I want to smack the table in my impatience, but instead, I swallow my pride. "Please, listen. It'll make sense, I promise."

She's silent for a moment, but at last, she nods her approval. Jethro helps Mrs. Delaney stand up and grab onto her rollator, and they walk towards the counter so they can see the feast I've laid out in the form of a story.

I take a breath, channeling every bit of the storyteller my Uncle Jeremy thought I was to explain this in a way that won't make them turn away. For them to give me the time, to listen.

To understand.

"You were right about Turney, Sheriff. Leigh and her grandpa were close, and though they had their problems with Leigh takin' care of him, they still loved each other dearly. When Turney found out he had cancer, he refused to put Leigh through it and wanted to let her get married thinkin' they would be okay."

"He should have said something," Jethro says, and when I

look over, the light shines off his eyes. "They could have done what they had to do together. It was wrong for him to keep that from her."

I hum at that, not sure about my own feelings. "Maybe, but he did it with love, so it's hard for me to judge. I might do the same if it were me."

He chuckles at that. "Damn right, you would." Our eyes meet in understanding, and I continue.

"He was still recoverin', but he decided to go on a hike. That's when he ran into his murderer. The Reaper. It was an accident; he'd been slow, and the snake was more aggressive than usual. He was still weak from his hip surgery. He tried to get back to town, but the venom went into effect."

I pull out the copy I made of the Eastern Dusky Blacktail slide from the library. I point to one paragraph in particular. "'When exposed to the venom for too long, it causes disorientation, hallucinations.' Turney walked in circles, started writing nonsense. Including this: 'Gotta get it out.'"

I point to the photo I'd taken of Turney's notes, the script nearly illegible. "In his delirium, he decided to get *it* out himself. 'It' meant the venom. The wounds were self-inflicted."

Sheriff June's eyes widen, and she immediately grabs for the photo from the autopsy. Her eyes move in search, but eventually, they settle where I'd pointed—where the edge of the snakebite was nearly hidden by a rough knife wound. "Damn," she says and rubs at her cheek with her hand.

"I don't know if he got a blood clot from the knife wound first or if the venom caused the heart attack, but that's what killed him. It was The Reaper."

I carefully pile up the records I've already explained and slide over the records from the back shelves.

"There's more. This used to happen a lot."

Mrs. Delaney gasps at that. "You're right, child! The story I told you."

I grin at her. "Exactly. Here are logs of the deaths from The Reaper, though they never explain it was a snake. It just says, 'The Reaper,' because they just assumed we would know. They didn't think it'd be lost to time. And the final piece of the puzzle: the connection between the Reaper and the Trickster."

I open the book to where I slipped in a sheet of paper so I wouldn't lose my spot and read from the scrawling script. "'If Tricksters fly from sprig to bough, trilling notes of fear; their duet is a warning cry, the Reapers soon draw near. With eyes alert and gaze aimed down, make haste as you depart. If Reaper's fangs can find your flesh, the bite will stop your heart.'"

"The birds," Jethro says. "Before the snakes attacked, they made that weird call like they were talking with each other. You said you hadn't heard it before."

I nod at him in triumph, grinning. "Exactly. Because I'd never seen one of the snakes before. They knew, even if we've forgotten."

Sheriff June let's out a long sigh and pulls together all the loose records. "We wouldn't have known. Standard toxicology reports wouldn't have caught it if we ran one, and we only run tests for venom if we think there's a bite. They're so expensive, and we have such a small budget to begin with. We can't even

run 'em here; it'd have to be sent to a bigger city." She lets out
a rushed breath. "Figures it'd be red tape that kept us from
solvin' this sooner.

"You get me a copy of those logs as soon as ya can, Mrs.
Delaney. I need to show this to Pat. We'll need to validate some
of it, run a toxicology report on one of the remaining tissue
samples, but it all fits, don't it?" She's frowning, eyes far away
as if lost in thought.

When everything is together, she looks up at me with a
curious look. "How'd you get all this together, Wren?"

My smile fades, and I try not to let my sorrow through.
"Just needed to muddle over it, I guess."

"Hmph," is her answer. Gathering the papers up in her
arms, she nods at each of us and heads back to her office.

"Well, I've had enough excitement for the day," Mrs.
Delaney says. "But I'll get those papers ready for the sheriff.
How about you and Jethro take it easy? None of this is goin'
anywhere, the filing can wait." She grins, exposing her missing
teeth again, and it's contagious.

"Sounds good to me," Jethro says, but he seems less
delighted and more solemn. "You okay, Wren?"

The thought that he's worried about me fills me with
warmth, but the reminder of how I'd figured out the case cools
it quickly.

"I'm a little tired is all."

I feel the excitement from the moment drained from me.
I've been trying so long, so desperately to find out what had
happened to Turney, I'd not fully grasped what would happen

when we finally figured it out.

"I need to tell the rest of the Citizens," I say abruptly, gnawing at my bottom lip. "And Leigh. They deserve to know."

Jethro touches my arm gently, and when I don't pull away, he pulls me into a side hug and squeezes me once for comfort. "How about for now, you let the Sheriff do what she needs to do, and you take time for yourself? You've done more than your fair share."

I take in a calming breath, but it feels cold, and my lungs feel hollow no matter how much air I take in. All at once, I see Turney's face the last time I saw him, and I feel my throat constrict at the vision. Jethro rubs my arm—he must feel me tense—and for all I feel like the world is ending, maybe a new one is budding from the ashes.

TWENTY-SIX

"HEY, LITTLE BIRD."

I hear the words before I see the room. Before I feel the bedsheets, the mattress beneath me. Before I smell the linen and incense I'd lit before my head touched the pillow. I'm sitting up, and I'm the same age I was when I laid down in this same bed. And yet, I know I'm not really in my room.

I turn towards my right, and he's there, the same as before. The same plush chair. The same book. The same face, hair, clothes, scent, facial hair. Every little minutia is perfect, but I feel dull inside.

He smiles his crooked smile, his mustache uneven but I never had the heart to tell him so. He tilts his head in a way I've seen a thousand times, and I know that look. That look of pride.

"You did good, Wren," he says, and I don't miss that he uses my name instead of 'Little Bird.' The change catches in my throat.

"I'm proud of you," he continues, and the choking feeling grows. "I always knew that someday you would-"

"Stop," I say. "Stop. Please don't do this." The fear is like gnarled roots.

He tilts his head in question. "Do what, Wren?" I see in his eyes that he knows.

"Don't leave." My voice trembles into a whisper, the sound wet from the tears that fall from my eyes and stick to my lips. "Please don't leave me. Not for good. Stay. Please."

His expression is one of guilt. We both know how this dream is going to end—if it is even a dream at all.

"Little Bird. I was always meant to leave you someday. Better me than you. That's the way of things. I'm sorry it happened so soon. I want to be there for you, I do." He stops for a moment and inhales a shaky breath that whispers in the cold night air like a midnight wind. "I didn't want this to happen this way."

He holds out a hand, and I take it in my own. I feel his strength in that grip, remember the moments as a child that same hand held me in comfort or in joy as we traversed the unkind world together. My heart shatters like new ice.

"Everyone leaves, Wren. Our lives are not meant to be forever. Someday the people you love will leave, or you will leave them, but it will always end in heartbreak."

He squeezes my hand, and I'm drawn into his words like

a firefly. "But that's part of life, Wren. You gotta make the in-between worth the heartbreak. Nothing lasts except the memories you have behind you, and nothing is certain except for change."

I reach out, and he pulls me into his arms. I wonder that for all the hugs and comfort I've received over the last few days, his cold embrace warms my heart like nothing else.

He leans back and gently pushes me into the pillows.

"Now, one more story," he says, and he sits back in the chair to open the book. I pretend not to notice that it's the last few pages, but my muscles tense.

"There was a little bird who loved their uncle more than anythin' in the world. And why wouldn't they? They were the only family each other had. They breathed the same air, felt the same wind, drank the same water.

"One day, the little bird and their uncle decided to go into the forest to find the Trickster. He was a conniving bird, but they knew him well. They were determined to see him, and so they would.

"But after a while, the little bird's uncle began to feel unwell. He became pale and started to sweat. He—"

"No," I say, interrupting him. "Stop. Tell me a different story. Anythin', just not this one."

We meet each other's eyes. I feel wetness on my cheeks, burning in my throat as it closes away my air. But he looks back down to the book and continues.

"The little bird's uncle collapsed. The little bird was scared. They were too far in the woods to call for help, and their uncle was too big to carry. And so the little bird ran as fast as they could to the town."

"Please," I say. I don't know what I'm asking for, but he continues with his story undeterred.

"What the little bird doesn't know is that their uncle was still awake for a little while longer. He looked up at the leaves, yellow and green like lights above him between the blue skies. He saw their beauty, felt the wind on the cooling sweat on his brow. It was then he had the most wonderful thought."

He looks away from the book and back into my eyes. "His little bird was all grown up. And he couldn't be prouder of the Wren the little bird grew up to be."

He closes the book with a muffled thump and grasps it with both of his hands, eyes still focused on mine.

"I am so very proud of you, Wren. And I will love you always."

My body shudders with barely contained sobs. I feel an ache that will never be filled in my chest, and something clicks into place in my mind as if a universal truth has been revealed to me.

"Now, Wren, I need you to do one more thing for me," he says, and he holds the book out. I take it with shaky hands, and as I look down, I finally see the title.

"*The Fable of Wren*," I say between tears.

I look back up at him for what I know is the last time. He beams, and I burn every crooked tooth and cracked bit of skin into my memory.

"You'll keep writing it for me. The story isn't over, you

know." He holds out his hand, and I take it. His grip is like ice around my fingers, but I bear it to hold onto him one more moment.

"Only the author has changed."

TWENTY-SEVEN

WHEN I GET TO THE COMMUNITY CENTER, I'm barely
in the door before Sean is calling me over to his desk, waving
his hands as if his baritone doesn't already echo in the empty
room.

"Whaddaya need?" I ask, cautious. It felt like we had left
things on good ground, but I couldn't be sure with the mischievous expression on his face.

He leans forward on his folded hands, a sly, white-toothed
smile slapped across his face. "I have a proposition for ya,
Wren."

I scrunch up my nose before I can help it. "Sorry, I don't
date."

He sits back, frowning. "Ew. No. You're like a sibling. I

mean a *business* proposition for you."

His smile is back, this time proud, and he sets his shoulders back. "I found a private investigator that is willin' to take me on and help me get my license. He's a friend of the family, and he's retiring soon. He says I have most of the requirements; it's red tape left. This time next year, I can have my own business here in Spastoke. I'll be servin' the whole county!"

I feel excitement bubble up in my chest, surprising me at how much it means to me that he accomplished what he's been trying to do. *Is this what it's like to have a friend?* "That's wonderful, Sean! When do you start? Are you quitting here or staying on?"

His smile dims, and I know he's thinking about all the people he'll be leaving here. "I'm staying on a couple more months while the sheriff looks for a replacement. Then, yeah, I'll have to quit. So I guess you won't be seeing me around here as often after that."

The thought sobers the excitement a little, but I force my smile to stay on, still wanting to show my approval of his decision. "Still, it's not like you're leavin' town, so you'll still be around. We can still hang out whenever ya want."

He perks up at that, though he looks surprised too. "Yeah, I'd love that, Wren."

"So what's this proposition you have for me then?"

His Cheshire smile is back, and he claps his hands together in excitement. "Well, I want to hire ya."

My smile drops, my face blanking with my mind. "What?"

His grin broadens, and he sits back fully in his chair. For

once, I'm intimidated by his height. "I want to hire you as an assistant. When I'm full-time, that is. So this time next year, I want to hire you on. I heard how you solved the Turney case. I want you on my side."

I rub at my forehead, unsure if I'm hearing him correctly, not processing his words. "But why me? I don't understand. What's so special about me?"

He leans forward in his chair, a look on his face that says he thinks I've lost my mind.

"Why wouldn't I? You're tough as a pine knot, Wren. You don't let anyone intimidate you, so you'd be good at gettin' information. You're smart, though people underestimate that you are. You know the town and everyone in it. You'd be great at this!"

I lean forward against the desk, using my hands to hold myself up. I feel strangely faint. It's a foreign feeling, to feel fear at something like this, and I wonder why before I remember. *It's because I actually care what he thinks of me now. I don't want to let him down.*

I gulp down a pressure in my throat. "Can I have a chance to think about it?"

"Sure," he says, nodding. "Take your time. There's a year before I'd have to know anyway. Though don't make me wait that long!"

I snort. "I should, just for that."

He grabs a paper and reaches out to slap me with it, but I laugh and shy away from it.

A year, huh? What a year it's going to be.

—

Things are almost back to normal within the week, except for Jethro taking his place in our little records office semi-permanently. I perch on the edge of the counter, mindful of the door. When Mrs. Delaney comes in, she'll have my hide if she catches me.

After we made our discovery, Sheriff June put a flier out around town and made an announcement over the radio about the danger. The case is closed, but things still feel unfinished. I can't explain the sharp edges in my chest, the part of me that feels like the next bad thing is around the corner. I wonder if I ever will feel normal again.

"How about this?" Jethro says. He points to the screen, where he's setting up different check boxes and text input areas to put new records into the computer system. "We can include a section for remarks and mention in the text above to put all remarks in the same place."

I shrug, still not entirely on board with the computer system. While I can now see the need to keep records all in one place, my heart isn't in it.

He looks up at me and bumps my shoulder with his fist. Our mutual way of checking in on the other, an unspoken gesture that was hard-won. "What's wrong?"

I shrug and hop down off the counter. I wince as my legs quake on landing, and my knee twists at an awkward angle. He's up off his chair in an instant, and the chair squeals against the floor at the brash treatment.

"Are you okay?" He holds my forearm, but I brush him away.

"I'm fine," I say, embarrassed. "Not fully recovered and got a reminder of it is all." I lean back against the counter and lift my leg up minutely so I can roll it a little bit at the knee to stretch it out.

He pulls back the chair for me to sit, but I wave him off. "Sit back down. I'm tired of sittin' or lyin' down. Just let me stand a bit."

He does, and I'm thankful he takes what I say at face value. He trusts me to let him know if I need something. It's nice to have that again.

I know he'll leave someday because that's what people do. Either you leave, or you're the one left behind. I'm learning to be okay with that. For now, I'm glad for the companionship.

"I was thinkin'," I say, and the next words are rushed as I'm afraid I'll take them back. "We should look into digitizing the records. Especially the oldest books."

I sneak a glance at him, and his eyebrows are raised near to his hair, mouth slack.

I slap his shoulder. "Oh, come off it! Don't act so surprised!"

He closes his jaw with a click of his teeth, then grins widely. There's a transformation in his expression from sullen to excitement, like sunshine rolling in after a thunderstorm. I'm afraid he's gearing up for a big explanation of all that can be done, should be done, might be done, so I stop him before he can start.

"And from here on out, we can put all new records directly

into the computer. Except for the Citizen log. That stays mine."

He nods as if he expected that. "Wouldn't have it any other way," he says, and I let out a breath I'd been holding.

He stands up from the chair, approaches the shelf that holds the Citizens record book, and picks it up gingerly. He sets it on the counter and traces the edges reverently. "Can we scan it once in a while, though? For posterity."

I slide the book towards me and leaf through the pages and stop at the one with the latest entries. "I'll allow it," I say.

I grab a ballpoint pen from Mrs. Delaney's mug of stationary, and hand it to Jethro. "But you're forgetting somethin', ain't ya?"

The skin creases around his eyes as he smiles, and something catches in my throat. "I'd be honored," he says, and takes the pen from me.

In clean, crisp writing, he writes down his name, the time, and date of where we'd spotted the Trickster.

When he's done, he recaps the pen and sets it to the side. He looks at the record for a while and doesn't say a word, face unreadable. After a few moments more, he looks up at me. And there it is, the awe I'd been looking for that day we found the Trickster.

"You know, I may understand what all the fuss is about after all."

I give him my own wide smile, as full of hope as the new day dawning.

Everyone leaves someday.

Now has to be enough.

—

I sit cross-legged in front of Uncle Jeremy's gravestone, fingers running through the grass at my sides. The grass and moss have grown over the headstone, not yet encroaching on the text but close.

My chest tightens with guilt. I'm the sole caretaker of my uncle's legacy, and I've screwed it up. I claw back the greenery with my bare hands, my nails digging out the strands of grass, and I pick off pieces of moss over the stone. When that's done, I use my palm to wipe off the debris and dirt. It's not perfect but better.

I'm not sure how to begin or why I'm here. Three months past the day, and I still feel so raw, cracked. I wonder if the sharp edges around my grief will ever be burnished down or if it will always be so hard. When I reach inside myself to touch the loss, it feels as overgrown as the grass on his grave.

It feels like too much, like I can never get through all the pain and hurt. Like I've been asked to move a mountain, rock by rock.

It's time to try.

"I met someone," I say and wince at how it sounds. "Not that kind of met. Just a friend. Least I think so. Who knows? But I'm not lookin' for anything like that. Not now. Maybe never."

I look up at the sky- blue and cloudless. I scrape my fingers through the grass and dirt next to me. "He's an outsider. Or he was. You'd get a kick out of him. The guy does not shut up. You'd laugh yer ass off, but he's a good guy. You'd like him."

In chiseled relief on the stained stone, I see his name and the inscription I'd agreed on. 'Jeremy Nolan, Beloved Son, Brother, and Uncle. Forever Loved, Forever Missed'. My eyes scan the words several times before I feel the telltale pinpricks at the corners of my eyes.

My first instinct is to bury the feeling, to run away. It hurts in a way that feels dangerous to let myself feel. But I know now. If I don't let it through, that doesn't mean it goes away. It burns like smoking embers until it catches fire.

"I'm so sorry." The words sound wet to my ears. Muffled. "I'm so sorry, Uncle Jeremy. I couldn't save you. I'd do anythin' to have you here right now, but I couldn't save you. I miss you so goddamn much."

The tears fall proper now, and I wipe at my face with my forearm. It comes away wet, mixes with the dirt from my attempts at cleaning his grave into muddy streaks. I let out a short laugh and imagine what my face must look like. What Uncle Jeremy would have said.

"I'm a right mess." I pause to inhale, and my breath comes in sniffles. "I've messed up. I'm so lonely all the goddamn time, and I can't let myself feel it. I've been so angry, Uncle Jeremy. Everyone, everything makes me so goddamn pissed."

The panic builds like a storm cloud in my chest, but I remember to breathe. I inhale deeply, exhale longer. My eyes close. I imagine the stream on a crisp day, leaves passing downstream. Comforting. When I open my eyes, I'm calmer, and the panic eases. Not gone but managed.

"I love you, Uncle Jeremy. I know I didn't say it enough. I love you, and I miss you." I uncross my legs and turn at an angle so I can still see his grave but can stretch out the numbness. I know why I'm here. And though I'm afraid, I stay. Nothing feels solved, dissipated, easier. But for the first time, I don't turn away.

"I have so much to tell ya. It all started when that guy, Jethro, barged in when I was working at the records office with Mrs. Delaney..."

—

A niggling feeling makes me stop at Turney's grave once I think Uncle Jeremy has had his fill of my blathering. I'm unsurprised that Leigh is situated on her knees in front of the newly dug mound, thin sprigs of bright green grass forming over the disturbed ground. She wears a light sundress with small lavender flowers on a pale-yellow background. The back is already covered in dirt and grass stains that can't be washed out, but I can understand her lack of forethought. I'd done worse in my own early grief.

I purposely make noise and let myself step on the odd twig and fallen leaf as I approach her. She looks over her shoulder at me and looks equally unsurprised to see me. She doesn't stop the conversation with her grandfather, and I don't push her to rush.

I look around this area of the cemetery as I wait. Snippets

of her voice carry on the wind toward me, but I don't try to discern any of the words. I've done enough snooping into this family's life.

When she's finished, she clears her throat and pats the ground next to me. Already covered in grass stains, I don't think twice before I sit cross-legged next to her.

We're both quiet at first. I listen to the trills of birds and the chorus of the wind as it sweeps through the archways and gravestones. It's calm, peaceful, even in all its sorrow.

"Sheriff June told me what happened," she breaks the silence. Her voice is monotone. "They'd had it wrong; it wasn't a murder. He'd been bitten, went delirious from the snake bite."

There's a finality in her voice with a familiar hint of regret and uncertainty I know from my own brushes with it. The same sense of loss I still wander.

"I should be glad to know what happened," she continues when I say nothing. "But all I feel is lost. What am I supposed to do with this grief when there is nowhere to put it?"

I consider her words. I'd had myself to blame for Uncle Jeremy's death, but without the certainty that his death was my fault, I was left feeling I'd lost something for no reason at all. In that, we were the same.

"I wish I had an answer for you," I say, and I mean it. "For both of us. It's easier when there's someone to blame, ya know? When there's a meanin' and purpose, that something went wrong and that's why they're gone. But to have done everythin' right and they're gone anyway? It feels so wrong."

I pick at the grass next to me, pull up the dead, straw-colored bits, and throw them to the side. "It was easier when I thought Uncle Jeremy dying was my fault. That's crazy, innit? I thought as long as someone was to blame, things made sense. I fucked up, and Uncle Jeremy paid the price. But that isn't what happened, is it? Something bad happened and no one did anything to cause it. It happened. And the rest of us are left to pick up the pieces. Knowing that it can happen to any one of us. Or the ones we love."

I stop grooming the grass and lean back on my hands, elbows locked. I look up at the trees above us, shimmering green in the fading sunlight. When I turn towards her, her green eyes are locked onto mine.

"It's easier to blame someone. But it's not better. Easier and better aren't always the same thing."

She's quiet for a breath. "If there's no one to blame, how do I go on? How do I live with so much uncertainty? How are we supposed to go on doing everything like it's all normal? Like it's normal to expect the worst, that there's no rhyme or reason to nuthin' and we can't rely on anythin' in the end?"

I shrug. I have the beginnings of an answer, but it's my own, and I know it won't be enough. Other people's truths never are.

"We can rely on some things. I know that if something happens to me, Mrs. Delaney will still be how she is, trying to help me through it. I know Sheriff June would get to the bottom of it. I know Jet would worry his ass off and bring me food from the diner.

"I can't rely on the world, but I can rely on the people I know to be themselves. To be the people I fell in love with, in their own ways. Maybe that's all that counts."

She frowns a line thin as paper. "People change. People make mistakes. Things change who people are."

I shrug. "Maybe so. But not without reason. People change 'cause the world makes them. And maybe I don't like the thing they've changed into and we grow apart. It don't change who they was then, what they meant to me then. Even if they don't mean the same thing now.

"Look. You want guarantees. You want to believe you're safe, that if you do the right things, it will never change. But that won't happen. It's not what life is. I've learned that much at least from Uncle Jeremy. But what I've learned on my own is the only thing I can have faith in is my ability to survive as best I can. To face everything the way I know how. That's all anyone can really give you."

"And if that's not enough?"

"Suppose you'll always be chasing ghosts then."

She smiles, barely an upturn of lips, and I can feel the effort in that motion. She turns back toward Turney's gravestone. I look forward and past it. I feel like it's too private for me to look at it directly. The plot is toward the edge of the cemetery, overlooking a good half a mile of gravestones and markers sprawling down the hill scattered by occasional dirt pathways. There are ones that are bright and new, others dirty and covered in moss. They all represent someone's family, a friend. I wonder at the stories these stones could tell.

A lone red-winged blackbird sits on the edge of a flowering bush nearby, and I grin. At least they have a good view.

I drop my hands in my lap. "We've not talked much. Before. I always been a bit in my own head." I feel raw at the admission, but I press on, determined. "Well, my therapist—I go to one now, you see—says it'd be good to talk about 'em. About Uncle Jeremy, that is. You could tell me more about your grandpa too?"

She lets out a choked laugh at my stumbling and pats where my hand sits on my knee. "You mean like some sort of group therapy thing where we talk about our dead family?"

I flash a mischievous smirk at her. "Exactly that. We could meet at the diner. Jay makes the best meatloaf."

Her posture loosens as she pushes herself up onto her feet. She wipes her dress with a frown as I stand up too but gives up after a few swipes. She looks at me, head tilted, eyes searching. It's a moment before she finds whatever she was looking for and holds out her hand.

"Well, if Jay's meatloaf is involved, it's a deal."

I take her hand, squeeze it gently, and smile. A real smile.

—

When I run my fingers over its surface, the desk feels barren and cold, sleek and dusted to a sheen it never had when Uncle Jeremy was alive.

The boxes with his papers, books, and knickknacks sit open on the floor next to his bed, the first ones neatly packed and labeled in tidy script. Later on, the script had become desperate, the packing haphazard, papers bursting from the edges of boxes and falling to the floor. It has been too much too soon, but I'd needed to try.

I hadn't set foot in Uncle Jeremy's quarters or rec room on the second floor since he passed away. It had felt like if I kept that monument to him, I could ignore that he would never be returning. That he had only ever just stepped away and could be back at any moment. The shrine it had become gathered cobwebs and dust, but the feeling persisted.

It was in a moment of clarity that I tiptoed up the stairway to start going through his things, though at every step, I believed I'd hear his voice coming from his room. When it didn't come, I gathered my courage and the packing supplies and started with what I thought would be the least personal area of his room: the desk.

It has been a fool's errand, for all I've been brave to try. Each paper is a landmine, every letter a noose. The longer I push, the deeper the cuts. Finally, I wave the white flag and settle down with a piece of pine and a knife on his tattered wooden chair, the orange light of the setting sun draping along the desk and floor through the westward window above the desk. For all the act of removing Uncle Jeremy from the room feels wrong, simply being in his space feels comforting.

I whittle, and with each chip of wood removed, I

remember. Summers running through the sprinkler in the yard; picking raspberries along the road; dressing up as a pumpkin for trick or treating. My eyes water, and I pause in my carving until it passes. A part of me knows that this is where I need to be.

The body takes shape first, a large teardrop with a circle for the head on the larger end. I'm not trying for anything fancy. I barely know what I'm making myself, but my hands seem to. I remember when Uncle Jeremy taught me how to whittle, then carve, though I've never taken to carving as well as whittling with a knife. I remember my first project, lopsided and squashed; it wouldn't sit straight on the table, so we had to glue it on a stand. I smile at the memory even as a tear leaks through.

I whittle for hours until the sun has set deep enough into the landscape that it's too dark to see by, then I turn on the lamp next to his bedside and whittle more. It's near midnight when I sneak down to my room, quietly though I'm the only one there, then return to Uncle Jeremy's room with my find.

I fetch a hand broom and dustpan and sweep up the saw dust and chippings to deposit in the trash can, not wanting to risk splinters should I ever come up with bare feet. I turn off the lamp but pause before I exit the room.

On the table, the wren I carved and the Trickster Uncle Jeremy had carved for me sit on the empty desk, highlighted in the moonlight from the window. Their forms cast a shadow that merges into one, the manifestation of a memory that will never be forgotten. If the only thing that lasts are our memories, I'll carry him with me.

He'll always be part of my story.

the end

And there, in the wreckage, at the edge of it all,
caked in mud and ash, twisting in the whirls of wind,
withered at its edges as its roots cling to untethered soil,

a sprout grows beside crumbled concrete.

Thin, bright yellow leaves unfurl from its tip,
carefully greeting the unkempt landscape with cautious joy.
Quiet, unburdened by all that had come before,
but rooted in soil nourished from years of love
and companionship.

I sit with my knees crossed beside it and watch it grow.

I cannot bring myself to cup my hands above it,
to protect it from the harsh environment where it was
burdened with life.
I cannot give myself hope in a place so intangible
and impermanent,
the fall would shatter my cracked heart beyond repair.

But maybe,
If I sit at the edge of this wreckage—
With my ghosts at my side—
Holding hands with my pain—
Lean my head on the shoulder of my anxieties and what ifs—
Whisper fond and fragile memories to my grief—
Never walk away from yesterday—
My eyes to the budding flowers my sprout has become,
instead of the remnants of my past—

I can grow around it all.

HELLO READER

Thank you for reading *The Fable of Wren*.
It's readers like you that motivate me to keep creating.
Want to keep up to date with all the latest, get inside my head,
and find out what I'm reading?
Join the Sparks Newsletter at RueSparks.com/Links

Please Review This Book

If you enjoyed *The Fable of Wren*, please consider leaving
a review on Goodreads. Reviews help other readers find my books,
and lets me know you're listening.

Where to Find Me

On my website you'll find a bibliography of all my current works,
and news on new releases. You can also connect with me on Twitter
@sparks_writes, Instagram @rue.sparks, or send me an email.
Learn More at RueSparks.com!

A THANK YOU

To my mother and my little sister Caity for being there for me when I wasn't for myself. To Cam and Carol for being the voice of reason when my head was in the clouds. To Melissa for being my ever-present support, and my earliest reader when this was nothing more than a short story.

To Lou: without you, there wouldn't be a book. You inspired me to let this book blossom into what it became despite all the challenges. Even when I wanted to give up on it you had faith in it and me.

Thank you to Charlie for all the technical and editorial support through the whole process to make the manuscript shine. To Lily and Cheryl for being the ones who pushed me when all I wanted to do was curl into a blanket burrito and hide from the world. Thank you to everyone who beta'd, proofread, and encouraged me on this journey: Charlotte, Dreena, Em, Kerry, Kevin, Rita, Rosa, Vince, and countless others.

Thank you to everyone else in the Twitter #WritingCommunity who came together to make this book possible.

And to you, who read this book because there was a part of you that desperately wanted to feel like you weren't alone—thank you for your bravery and stubbornness in the face of so much pain.

Always remember: Grief is love. Grief is love.

THE DRAGON WARDEN

A queer, genre-bending, fantasy, steampunk, and speculative fiction whirlwind of a web serial.

Achilles has always liked drakes more than humans. These large, but flightless cousins to dragons—or more specifically, their knack at training them—was Achilles' ticket to a comfortable life in the world's center of commerce and industry: the city of Abylon.

Comfort has a cost, one that Achilles isn't willing to accept. Several years after abandoning their life and love at Abylon, Achilles sets out to make things right, with the help of their childhood friend and a crew of misfits from the cloud city of Aerie. But the rising tide of an empire bent on expanding their reign and the age-old mystery of the Old Ones complicates their seemingly simple quest.

Who knew rescuing dragons would be so difficult?

RUE SPARKS
WRITER | ARTIST

A widow, disabled, and a member of the queer community, Rue Sparks traverses the equally harsh and cathartic landscape where trauma and healing align to create stories that burrow into the hearts and minds of their readers.

In addition to *The Fable of Wren,* Sparks has authored the novella *Daylight Chasers,* the short story collection *The Stars Will Guide Us Back,* and writes the web serial *The Dragon Warden.* They live in Noblesville, Indiana in the USA with their sweet senior support dog and still draw and paint when they're physically able.

Made in the USA
Coppell, TX
16 June 2023

18186894R00177